KILLER INSTICT

A THOMAS SHEPHERD MYSTERY

DAN PADAVONA

GET A FREE BOOK!

I'm a pretty nice guy once you look past the grisly images in my head. Most of all, I love connecting with awesome readers like you.

Join my VIP Reader Group and get a FREE serial killer thriller for your Kindle.

Get My Free Book

www.danpadavona.com/thriller-readers-vip-group/

1

The clock told Officer Shawn Barrett that it was five minutes until quitting time. Trix was roasting a turkey with the kids and would have it on the table by six o'clock. The trouble was Barrett didn't figure he'd get out on time. Across from his desk, a teenager dripping with gang tattoos slumped in a chair and chewed a fingernail. A filthy habit.

"Tell me why I should believe you," Barrett said, folding his arms over his chest.

"Because if you don't do something to stop them, the 315 Royals will have half the city on drugs by New Year's. They're planning something big, bro. Don't know what it is exactly, but these won't be smalltime ops."

"And you know this how?"

"I have my sources," the teenager said, looking away.

"This is about the turf war. You want the Harmon PD to break up the Royals so the Kings can take over the city."

"It ain't like that. The Kings don't exist anymore. They haven't since Rev went to prison and LeVar left."

LeVar Hopkins, the most notorious gangster the city streets

had ever known, had become a sheriff's deputy for the county. Barrett would love to hear the story of how that happened. Was it true LeVar had enrolled at the community college and committed to Kane Grove University's criminal justice program? That sounded crazier than Red Sox fans cheering for the Yankees.

"Still, you ran with the Kings for how long? Three, four years?"

"Five," the boy said, lifting his chin.

Too many misled teenagers wore gang life as a badge of honor.

"All right, five," said Barrett. "That tells me you have loyalty to the Kings."

"How can I have loyalty to something that doesn't exist?"

"Then I'll put it another way. The Kings are yesterday's news, but the war against the Royals will never die. Admit it. This is about putting it to the Royals, not saving the community. You know how long I tried to make things right in Harmon? That ghetto you come from is nothing but drugs and people who make excuses for themselves. The Royals are the symptom, not the cause."

The kid leaned forward. "You don't know about me or my community, cop. You ain't got the right to speak on it. All my life, I been survivin' without you. We all have. Now I come to you for help, and all you see is a gangster who ain't worth the time."

Before Barrett could respond, the teenager stood and knocked his chair over. Chief Pauley rose, but Barrett held up a hand and set the chair upright.

"Thanks for nothing," the teenager said. "Not that I expected anything from the police."

After the former gangster left, Pauley emerged from his office.

"Want to tell me what that was about?" the chief asked.

Barrett sighed.

"That was a kid from the Harmon Kings trying to convince me the 315 Royals are destroying the city."

"Talk about the pot calling the kettle black. I thought the Kings dissolved."

"So did I, but the war will never end. He claims something big is about to happen in the drug trade, and the Royals are behind it."

"Do you believe him?"

"I put nothing past the Royals," Barrett said. "The prostitution ring took a hit after the sheriff's department arrested Troy Dean for kidnapping that college girl."

"Cut off one head and another grows back."

"I'll check with my informants and snoop around. If there's anything to the story, I'll find out."

"Let me know if we need to form a joint task force with Sheriff Shepherd."

"Will do." Barrett grabbed his keys. "I need to fly. Trix made turkey for dinner."

"That's a reason to speed on the way home, officer," Chief Pauley said. "Nobody cooks like Trix."

"Come over this week. How's Thursday? We'd love to have you join us."

"No can do Thursday, but I'll take a rain check for next week."

"Perfect."

"All right." Pauley slapped Barrett's shoulder. "Drive safely. Thanksgiving is almost here, and traffic is insane."

Barrett waved to a fellow officer on the way out and drove home. As the chief had warned, traffic was bumper to bumper in the city. He didn't even consider jumping on the interstate. Unbuttoning his collar, he counted the months until retirement. Forty-eight to go. He wondered how many years shift work had taken off his life. Wouldn't it be ironic if he survived street patrols in gang territory and died because of inconsistent sleep patterns? The doctor kept warning him to take an early retirement or transfer into a nine-to-five position. Easier said than done. Those jobs attracted dozens of bids from officers who wanted to escape the grind.

At the first opportunity, he turned off the thoroughfare and headed down a maze of side streets. During two decades working for the Harmon PD, he'd discovered the perfect alternate route when traffic clogged the city and interstate. He often joked with the other officers that he should sell the directions and become a millionaire.

After Barrett traversed three neighborhoods, he located CR 13, which would take him within a mile of his house. He'd need to navigate another maze when he reached town, but it was better than waiting in traffic for hours.

Flurries drifted down from the black November sky. He despised the early sunsets and couldn't wait for the days to lengthen. Even at six o'clock, driving in the dark tired him out.

He was almost home when he spotted the blinking hazard lights of a stranded motorist. Trix would never let him hear the end of it if he missed dinner, but one could die from exposure if left in the cold for too long.

Pulling onto the shoulder behind the vehicle, Barrett left his engine running. The chill struck him like a wall, and he yanked the hood of his sweatshirt over his head and shivered.

"What happened?" he called.

The wind grabbed his voice and tossed it over the hills. In the dark, the red blinking lights looked like a devil opening its eyes.

"You all right?"

Barrett rounded the vehicle. The hood was open, the car

running, but no one was checking the engine or in the driver's seat.

He looked behind him. The gray strip of roadway faded into the night.

"Are you injured or lost? Call out and I'll find you."

The car looked all right, and the motor seemed to run fine. So where was the driver?

The footstep behind Barrett gave him no warning. Something thudded against the back of his head, and he pitched forward and collapsed against the car.

Two hands grabbed him under the shoulders and dragged him toward the trunk.

At 6:35 P.M., Trix Barrett rolled her eyes and called the kids to the dinner table. Shawn should have arrived by now, and it bothered her that he hadn't sent a message. Obviously something had come up at work or he'd run into a traffic jam in the city. A phone call would have been nice.

"Where's Dad?" Jolene asked, kissing her mother on the cheek.

"My guess is he's stuck in traffic."

Bobby sprinted from his room—he'd complained for the last hour about how hungry he was—and helped Trix carry the food into the dining room.

As the two teenagers forked turkey, mashed potatoes, and broccoli into their mouths, she kept staring at the clock—7 p.m., then 7:30.

By the time Bobby and Jolene retreated to their bedrooms to finish their homework, Trix started to worry. A text to Shawn's phone went unanswered, and a call dropped her into his voicemail.

That's it. She needed to call the department.

The dispatcher recognized her voice and put her through to Chief Pauley.

"No, Trix. Shawn isn't here. He mentioned something about roast turkey and blew out of the office."

"Say, Carl, what time did he leave?"

"Over an hour ago. I wouldn't worry too much. I'm looking out my window, and traffic hasn't budged."

"Thanks, Carl. If you hear from Shawn, will you tell him to call his wife? His dinner is in the fridge."

The chief chuckled. "I will, Trix. Look forward to seeing you soon."

She set down the phone and cupped her elbows with her hands. The flurries outside the window turned into a squall. She couldn't see across the street, and a fresh inch of powder covered the walkway.

"Where are you?" she asked the night.

But Shawn Barrett never came home.

2

H is hands curled into fists, the fingernails etching sickles into his palms. This was his least favorite place.

The dentist's office.

Sheriff Thomas Shepherd forced himself to lay his hands flat on his knees, which bounced as though he rode a runaway horse. The receptionist behind the desk frowned at him and went back to work.

The stench of acrylic always set him off, and even if he ignored his nose, he always cringed at the whirl and grind of a drill excavating a decayed tooth. He lowered his head and scratched behind his neck. On the other side of the waiting room, a woman with crossed legs read a magazine. The girl next to her used a crayon to scrawl in a coloring book.

That was a great idea. The magazine, not the coloring book. He needed something to take his mind off the appointment.

Thomas sorted through the reading material and settled on *The Bluewater Tribune*, Wolf Lake's local newspaper. He didn't make it past the third page before his eyes settled on the story for which a reporter had interviewed him last week. After avoiding the newspaper for seven days, he thought he'd missed the article. Now it stared back at him in black and white.

Like a rubbernecker driving past an accident, he couldn't look away.

"To what do you attribute your department's success?" the reporter asked. "Investigating dangerous criminals must be a challenge for a sheriff with Asperger's syndrome."

When would they stop asking that question? He wasn't the only law enforcement officer on the planet who'd succeeded despite Asperger's, and he certainly wasn't the only success story outside of police work. After a decade with the LAPD, including several years as a detective, Thomas should have moved past this narrative. But it never stopped.

Which brought him back to the dentist appointment. He'd canceled twice before, and if he did it again they might tell him to find another practice. The high-pitched whine of the electric brush frayed his nerves and made him want to scream, and holding his mouth open for minutes at a time while someone picked at his teeth and gums with a sharp piece of steel was torture. To Thomas, there was nothing worse than a dentist appointment, not even the flashing lights of a cruiser and the shrill of a siren as he raced after a murderer.

The little girl recognized him from the picture in the newspaper. Her mouth fell open in awe, and she pointed across the room until her mother told her it was impolite. But now the mother was looking at him too, as if he were a carnival oddity on display.

He checked his watch. Twenty minutes past his appointment time. Deputies Aguilar and Lambert would wonder why he was late. Maybe the dentist had forgotten about him. Maybe he could leave and—

"Thomas?" a short woman with a surgical mask over her face asked.

He glanced around, hoping there was another Thomas in the room. There wasn't.

With reluctance, he stood and stretched his legs. Her eyes smiled over the mask.

"I'm ready for you. Follow me to room seven."

Room seven. Was seven a lucky number or an unlucky number? He couldn't recall. As his mind was wont to do under stress, it fixated on numbers and probabilities. There were 36 permutations if you rolled two dice, and 21 combinations resulted in the number seven. Twenty-one divided by 36 yielded 58.3 percent, so he shouldn't have been surprised his room turned out to be seven. Except that made no sense because nobody had rolled two dice and . . .

As he walked behind the woman, he couldn't help but look into the examination rooms. A man lay on a reclined chair; his foot jerked as the hygienist scraped away plaque. The many rooms reminded Thomas of medieval torture chambers.

No, that wasn't fair. *Dentists are wonderful people who provide an important function. Tooth and gum health are necessities.*

In room seven, whether it was lucky or unlucky, the hygienist invited him to set his belongings on the corner table. He did so, then climbed onto the chair, which she reclined with a humming motor. Now he stared up at a halogen globe on an arm that reminded him of the aliens in *War of the Worlds*.

A painted ivy pattern ran along the center of each wall. The ceiling was sky-blue. This wasn't so bad. As usual, worrying about the event was worse than the event itself.

Then she brought out the scraper.

He held his mouth open until his jaw hurt. She went after each tooth and chipped the plaque away. There were a few sensitive spots that made him wish she would hurry, but otherwise he coped.

"So what are you doing for the holidays?"

A silly question since he couldn't answer with his mouth open and a sharp piece of steel poking his gums. He did his best.

"Cooking a turkey with Chelsey and my neighbors."

That's what he said. It sounded more like *rooking a rurgee wiff Elsie an eye errors*, but the woman understood. Dental hygienists were well-versed in these odd languages.

"That sounds like fun. We're flying to Missouri to spend Thanksgiving with my father and his new wife."

"Oh, *shounds rike run.*"

"Except for the flying part. Every time I fly, the airline loses my bags."

"*Rye runner rand.*"

"I bet you do. Do you travel much for work? I suppose not, being a county sheriff and all."

"*Rum rhymes,*" he said.

She deftly interpreted it as sometimes.

"Yeah, it's never a good time. Flying, that is. Seeing family is great, though. How often do you floss?"

The question caught him off guard.

"*Roast rays.*"

"Most days? That's not good enough. Every day, Sheriff. Without fail. You have a lot of plaque built up from last time. Well, the last time we made it through a full appointment. You doing all right today?"

"*Yesh.*"

He wasn't. The scraping filled his head and reminded him of that poor girl buried alive and clawing at the casket. McKenzie Ossman. He wondered how she was getting along with her aunt and uncle. McKenzie had lost her parents and survived a kidnapping. All he needed to do was make it through his appointment.

"Hmm." It was never a positive sign when the hygienist

studied a tooth and muttered *hmm*. "I want the dentist to look at the shadow on your bicuspid. Does it ache?"

"*Roh.*"

"Hmm." There it was again. "I'll be right back with the dentist."

Thomas squirmed in the chair. After a minute, a tall woman with gray hair followed the hygienist into the examination room.

"Sheriff Shepherd," the dentist said. "Rena tells me you're having issues with a bicuspid."

"It feels fine to me."

"I'll give it a look. Open wide and turn your head. That's it."

His worst fears were realized. The dentist found a cavity. Within minutes, a needle numbed his gums and teeth. When the dentist leaned over his head with the drill, he squeezed the armrests. She glanced in concern at the hygienist, who got him talking to take his mind off the procedure.

"I read the article about you in the newspaper," said the hygienist.

Not the article again.

"It's amazing what you've accomplished. Since returning to Wolf Lake, that is. I didn't mean to imply—"

"It's all right. I understand what you meant."

"Wow. That was really something when you caught that serial killer. What was his name? Jeremy Hyde? How did you find him?"

"Actually, he found me," Thomas said.

"Try to remain still," the doctor said, placing a comforting hand on his shoulder.

But once the drill shrieked in his ear, he shot off the chair as if electrocuted.

"Mr. Shepherd, what's wrong?" the dentist asked.

He gathered his belongings.

"I can't do this."

"We have to take care of that cavity."

"Another time. I have an important meeting."

The dentist threw up her hands in exasperation. Thomas rushed out the door with the hygienist behind him.

"Are you sure you're all right, Sheriff Shepherd?" she asked as he unlocked his truck.

"I am now."

"Really, I wish you'd take a moment and breathe. We can try again."

"Not today."

She leaned through his open window.

"How is it you're not afraid of murderers but you run from dentists?"

3
—————

LeVar Hopkins swiped the dreadlocks off his shoulders and watched a lone boat cut through Wolf Lake. This close to the holidays, it was too cold for recreation, but a few brave souls ventured out and had the lake to themselves. This was the life. If he opened the door, he was only two dozen steps from the shore. And yes, he'd counted. Thomas allowed him to live for free in the guest house behind the A-frame.

Beside him, Scout Mourning set hands on hips and studied the front room. The teenager was grounded because of an ill-fated excursion into an abandoned house on Halloween night, but her mother Naomi allowed the girl to spend time with LeVar, Thomas, Chelsey, and any of the private investigators at Wolf Lake Consulting, provided they supervised her.

"I think if we move the couch over here," the girl said, "and slide the computer into the corner, we'll have enough room for two study spaces."

"Your mom is okay with you studying at my place?"

"For sure. She considers you my big brother and knows you'll keep me on the straight and narrow. Not that I'm a flight risk."

"Only when ghost hunting is involved."

"Funny. I learned my lesson."

LeVar surveyed the room.

"*Aight*, we can study together at the card table. Trouble is, where will everyone sit during private investigation meetings?"

"On the couch," she said.

"But there's never enough room on the couch and we have to set up chairs."

"And?"

"If the couch is next to the window, and the table is over here, the chairs will have to face in the opposite direction."

"I see your point." Scout muttered under her breath, then snapped her fingers. "New plan. Drag the computer where the couch used to be, then we can pull the table closer to the window."

"Won't work. The table will block people from entering the room. Unless you want to watch Darren trip and spill a pizza on my sister's head."

"I would very much like to watch that happen, but you're right." She glanced from one corner to the next, her lips working silently as she worked through the puzzle in her mind. "Let's try this."

With Scout's help, he dragged the couch against the far wall, placed the computer beside the window, and unfolded the card table in the center of the room.

"It's perfect," she said, smiling.

"Uh, it's exactly the same as it was all along."

The grin melted off her face. "Oh, yeah. I guess it is. Well, there's no point in fixing what isn't broken."

LeVar rolled his eyes.

"Good, because I enjoy having a lake view while I work on the computer. What if you bring your laptop? Where will that go?"

"If the card table doesn't work out, Mom will let me have her old nightstand in the basement. Set a folding chair next to it and presto, instant workstation."

"Make sure the nightstand is the correct height," he said. "You don't want to hurt your neck."

"I'm not a senior citizen like you, LeVar."

"Laugh all you want. Teenagers suffer from more back and neck problems than ever before. I learned that at school. Pay attention to your posture." He couldn't help but smile. "This will be amazing. Once I start classes next fall at Kane Grove, I'll have the perfect study place, and I'll only need to shift the table and couch for meetings."

"And you'll have me to bounce ideas off."

He couldn't be happier to work with Scout. Despite the age difference, she was the best friend he'd ever had, though he often worried their relationship would develop into something else. At sixteen, she was too young for a boy who would turn twenty next month. What would people say? Worse yet, if they broke up, it might ruin their friendship forever.

Scout, Naomi, Thomas, and Chelsey were more than friends; they were family. All four lived within steps of his home. Plus, he had these wonderful views to look forward to every day. In truth, the wind and cold off the lake got rough during the winter and made him long for a southern vacation, but the guesthouse was nirvana during the summer.

A motor drew his attention. In the A-frame's driveway, Thomas stopped his truck. The sheriff had scheduled his workday to begin after the dentist appointment. Why was he home already? Scout gave LeVar a concerned look.

They met Thomas in front of the house as he unlocked the door.

"How'd it go, Shep Dawg," LeVar asked.

"Uh, it could have gone better," said Thomas.

"You didn't bail on another dentist appointment, did you?"

"Not until the important part."

"Dude."

Jack leaped on the sheriff when the door opened. Thomas patted the dog's head. On the couch, Chelsey's cat, Tigger, mewled.

"I need to change my shirt," Thomas said.

"What's wrong with your shirt, dawg?"

"I kinda sweated through it."

"Thomas, I'm happy to go to your next appointment," Scout said.

"In my place?" Thomas asked with a hopeful gleam. "I doubt they'll believe you're me."

Scout giggled at the joke. "I can talk to you while the dentist works."

LeVar elbowed Thomas. "And you know she can yap with the best of them."

Scout widened her eyes. "Unlike you?"

"I'll think about it, Scout," Thomas said. "I'm in no rush to go back, and they're not eager to see me. Sorry to be short, guys, but I need to change and head to work."

"Shep," said LeVar, "we're about to jog to the state park. Want us to take Jack and get him some exercise?"

"That would save Chelsey and me time. I appreciate it."

"You got it." LeVar set his hands on his knees and smiled at the dog. "Want to go for a run, Jackie boy?"

The dog burst out of his fur and sprinted laps around the living room as Tigger eyed Jack with disgust.

Scout returned to the guest house in running shorts, sneakers, and a sweatshirt. While Jack wagged his tail with impatience, LeVar checked himself in the mirror.

"You're working out, not auditioning for the cover of *Men's Health*," she said.

"Always gotta look my best. You know how I roll."

Though Jack didn't contain his enthusiasm until they left, he proved to be as good a runner as he was a walker. He didn't tug LeVar up the trail. Rather, the dog kept a perfect pace and forced Scout and LeVar to challenge themselves.

Cold nipped at LeVar's nose, making him wish he'd worn something warmer, but halfway up the hill sweat rolled down his forehead. As he jogged, he studied Scout from the corner of his eye. Several months had passed since the spinal surgery that restored her ability to walk. He didn't want the girl to overexert herself. She grew stronger every time they ran, and sometimes he found it difficult to keep up with her, but the memory of the girl in a wheelchair stood front and center in his mind.

Scout raised her wrist and read her fitness watch. "We're setting a record pace. This is great."

"Not too fast. The doctor told you to take it easy."

"Yeah, over the summer. It will be December before you know it."

"Scout," he said, raising his voice.

"I hear you."

She slowed enough that he stopped worrying. Naomi trusted him to care for her daughter. He wouldn't let the woman down.

The leaves had fallen off the trees and left a crunchy bed on the forest floor. Evergreens blocked the sunlight and left the woods dark and foreboding. His friend Darren was the park ranger here, but the forest could be unsettling.

For the first time since they'd left the guest house, LeVar felt a trickle of unease. He glanced around the forest, searching for an animal. During the cold months, bears wandered into these woods in search of food. Something was out there.

"You sense that?" he asked.

She stared at him. "Sense what?"

If a predator was nearby, wouldn't Jack alert them?

"It's nothing. Never mind."

But as they ran toward the cabins, leaves crackled under a foot.

———————

4

A buzzing beside his head brought Officer Shawn Barrett awake and slapping at the air. He blinked as if he were trapped inside a dream. Bright, depthless light shone like a hazy sky, but a sheet of plastic, not clouds, served as his sky. He rubbed his eyes and studied the plastic sheeting around him. A greenhouse?

As soon as the officer moved, the pain made him wince and roll onto his side. He touched the back of his head, expecting to find blood.

No blood, but an egg-sized lump. Had someone attacked him? Where was this place?

His head spun as he forced himself into a sitting position. He continued to hold the back of his head, but his brain wouldn't function. What day was it? Was he at work?

Out of the farthest reaches of his mind, he retrieved a memory: driving home from the police station and taking an alternate route because of traffic. Nothing since.

The possibility that he'd crashed and was in a hospital made him wonder if anyone had contacted Trix. But if he was under a doctor's care, why did he have a sweatshirt over his work clothes?

The buzzing came again, and Barrett blindly swatted a hand above his head. On the ceiling, crawling toward the opaque light, was a wasp the size of his pinkie finger. All forms of flying, stinging insects terrified him. Four years ago, while on vacation in Ocean City with Trix, a bumblebee had stung him on the shin. He'd thought nothing about it—bees and hornets had attacked him many times throughout his life—until his eyes puffed up. Trix rushed him to a nearby hospital. He arrived just in time. His throat was closing up, and he wheezed when he breathed. A shot and an IV saved his life. The physician told him he'd developed an allergy to bee stings and would need to carry an EpiPen. But that was during the summer, when bees, hornets, and wasps were everywhere. It was almost December. Why was a wasp crawling around in this enclosure?

A closed door stood behind the plastic. There wasn't much he could discern about the room. It didn't look like any lab he'd encountered inside a medical facility. One window let in pale light. He noticed a wood table holding a drill and three planks. A sweet scent he couldn't place pervaded the room.

Had he been abducted? By whom?

In his mind, he sorted through the enemies who would want to hurt him. He'd angered many people during his career. That was a hazard of the business, especially when you patrolled gang territory. Troy Dean, the former leader of the 315 Royals, had wanted him dead, but Dean was behind bars. That wouldn't stop the gangster from ordering a hit on someone. The Harmon Kings had lost power and scattered like roaches escaping the light, but their members were still around, and they hated cops. He thought about the drug rings he'd busted, the white-collar criminals he'd handcuffed and led out of the city's skyscrapers. So many people wanted a piece of him.

His thoughts returned to the tattooed teenager, the former member of the Kings. The kid had left the station in a furious state. Angry enough to knock a police officer over the head and imprison him?

The plastic sheeting wouldn't hold anyone. A determined child could rip the walls apart.

Fighting a dizzy spell, he pushed himself to his feet and wobbled. As he touched the wall, a door opened beyond his enclosure, and a man entered wearing what appeared to be a white protective suit. A horrific thought stabbed the police officer's brain: He'd contracted a deadly virus, and the man beyond the plastic sheeting required a suit to protect himself.

So why was this doctor holding an automatic weapon?

"I figured you'd wake up around now," the man said.

His deep voice sounded hollow inside the suit, too muffled to be recognizable.

"Who are you?" Barrett asked.

"Someone you don't want to piss off. Step away from the wall, Officer Barrett."

"You know my name?"

"Do as I say." The man aimed the gun at his chest. Barrett complied. "Very good. Have a seat in the center of the enclosure and relax. It will go better for you if you do."

Barrett moved into the center, but he refused to sit. Following the man's orders might be a death sentence. If he stayed on his feet, he stood a chance of fighting back. But how would he combat a kidnapper holding an automatic weapon? He didn't even have his service revolver.

"Why am I in here?"

"Because it's safer for me if you are."

"Am I sick or something? If you're a doctor, you're obligated to tell me what my ailment is."

The man chuckled. "This is a Hotchkiss machine gun. It says

I don't have to tell you anything. But you're not sick, Officer Barrett. No deadly strain of flu."

"Dammit, then tell me why I'm here. What's with the machine gun and the plastic sheeting? If you're a cop, read me my rights. If you're a doctor, tell me why I'm trapped in this enclosure."

"Your demands amuse me," the man said.

At that moment, the wasp flew from the ceiling and landed on Barrett's arm. The insect was an ugly thing—mutant-sized and brandishing a stinger half as long as its body. He cried out and swatted the wasp. Brushing the dead insect off his forearm, he examined his skin.

Please tell me the wasp didn't sting me.

He hadn't felt pain, but even a tiny nick could cause his tongue to swell and his breathing passages to constrict. Beyond the plastic, the man leaned his head back and laughed.

"Very good. You're quick, but then I figured you would be. Must be nerve-racking to go through life afraid of stinging insects. Didn't your mother tell you that a wasp is more afraid of you than you are of it?" He tutted. "Pick on something your own size."

The officer straightened his shoulders. "Like you?"

"You don't want a piece of me."

"I don't? Put down the weapon and find out."

More laughter. "You think you can goad me into a fight? You're an idiot. Always have been."

Barrett ignored the man's warning and left the center of the enclosure, walking to the wall.

"You can't keep me in here."

"Says who?"

"Tell me what this is about."

"You should already know what this is about, Officer Barrett."

The man centered the gun on his head.

"So you're just gonna shoot me in cold blood? You're a coward."

"A coward? That's funny coming from a bully who picks on tiny insects. I bet you wouldn't act so brave if he'd come at you with a few of his friends."

The officer didn't have time to ask what the man meant. The kidnapper pointed at a white box dangling from the top of the enclosure. Barrett hadn't seen it until now. It blended with the white ceiling.

With a chuckle, the unknown man removed a remote-control device from his pocket and aimed it at the ceiling. The box fell.

Barrett leaped back. The box shattered upon impact. Hundreds of angry wasps swarmed out.

The officer swatted at the insects, but there were too many. In seconds, he sustained dozens of stings. More wasps attacked, an unstoppable army.

He screamed and thrashed, feeling a hundred venom-laced needles pierce his skin. The wasps were in his hair, his shirt, his ears. One landed on his eye and dug its stinger straight through the mucous layer and into his cornea. He couldn't suck oxygen into his lungs. They swarmed inside his mouth and stabbed his tongue, congealing like a writhing paste on the roof of his mouth.

Torturous agony gave way to immutable sleep. The wasps wouldn't allow him to breathe his last breath.

5

L eVar returned from class at the community college and set his book bag on the couch. He was hungry enough to eat an entire submarine sandwich, but his sister Raven had warned him about overindulging before the holidays.

"One of these days," he remembered her saying, "that metabolism of yours will crater, and you'll blow up like the Stay-Puft Marshmallow Man. Is that what you want, LeVar? You want Bill Murray zapping you with a proton pack because you're too fat to walk through the village without crushing innocent shoppers?"

He settled on a bowl of Greek yogurt and frozen berries. After swallowing the last spoonful, he turned the bowl upside down and shook it.

"That's all there is?"

He could go for a pepperoni pizza. Too bad the only ice cream stand open year round was on the other side of the village.

Trying not to think about how hungry he was, he pawed through the closet and found a roll of weatherstripping he'd purchased at the home improvement store. This was his second winter in the guesthouse, and the first had taught him that the windows couldn't stop a frigid January breeze. Next spring he'd help Thomas replace the windows with energy-efficient versions. For now, he wanted to ensure the wind didn't cause goosebumps to form over his skin once the calendar changed to December.

As he worked on the windows, he caught sight of his mother's car in Naomi Mourning's driveway. In celebration of their record quarterly earnings, everyone at Shepherd Systems had the day off. Naomi ran daily operations, and LeVar's mother Serena oversaw the sales team. With Scout at school, the two women were baking up a storm in the Mournings' kitchen. They'd promised The Broken Yolk cafe enough dessert items to get them through the week, and the mothers wanted to surprise Mora Canterbury at the Harmon soup kitchen with pies for her guests.

LeVar spotted his mother through the sliding glass door leading to the kitchen. She waved, and he set the weatherstripping aside and crossed the yard. Maybe they would give him samples. He was an expert taste tester; if that was a major, he'd change his curriculum. The stroll chilled him to the bone. Though the wind was light in the village, it roared off the lake, seeking fresh victims to encase in ice. He wanted to chip frost off his skin when he opened the door.

"Oh, that's nice," he said, stepping inside.

"The apple pie?" Serena asked.

"I meant the heat, but the pie too. Wow. It's cold enough for a blizzard."

"How was class?" Naomi asked, washing her hands in the sink. She wore an apron over her shirt and blue jeans.

"Slow today. Lots of theory and not enough practice."

"Boy," his mother said, "you better not ask for handouts. These desserts are for the cafe and the soup kitchen. Besides,

Raven warned me about you. Did you really eat a Sicilian pizza by yourself?"

"Well," he said, shifting his shoulders. "Not by myself. Darren ate a slice."

She waved a spatula at him. "All that cheese will bind you up like quick-dry cement in a copper pipe. You been regular, LeVar?"

"Ma!"

Naomi snickered.

"Ain't no shame in admitting you're constipated," Mom said. "What you need is roughage. Oatmeal, whole grains, a salad. When's the last time you ate something green?"

"Does cake frosting count?"

Mom looked at the ceiling and shook her head.

"I don't know what I'm gonna do with you. Now answer me. When's the last time you pooped?"

"Why are we discussing this?"

"Reach into my purse. I bought a fiber bar you ought to try."

LeVar screwed up his lips. "No way. I ain't eating a fiber bar."

"It'll do you some good. Keeps things flowing."

"That's disgusting," he said.

"You obey my words and eat a salad with dinner this afternoon. Hear me, child?"

"I eat salads. You don't have to tell me to eat nutritious food. Look at these." He flexed his biceps. "You know what these guns are saying? They're saying, 'give me muscle-building food, LeVar, and a lot of it. We gotta put a headlock on crime.'"

Mom glanced at Naomi. "See what I have to deal with?"

"I thought you were weatherstripping the guesthouse," said Naomi.

LeVar sat. He set an ankle on his knee and leaned back in a chair. "I'm working on it, but I wanted to see if you needed any help."

"Aren't you a charitable soul," Mom said. "You're here to steal samples. I raised you, boy, and I know your tricks."

"I want to ensure those folks at the soup kitchen receive the best. I'm all about quality control."

"Uh-huh."

LeVar turned to Naomi. "How are Scout's grades? She's not struggling after the Halloween incident, is she?"

"Scout is keeping her grades up," Naomi said, flattening dough with a rolling pin. "She'd better. To say she's on thin ice would be an understatement."

"She was terrific in helping me redesign my front room yesterday."

"Oh yeah? What did you settle on?"

LeVar coughed into his hand.

"We put it back the way it was. Don't mess with success."

"Scout's a smart kid with a good head on her shoulders, but it's important she learns right from wrong. Breaking into an abandoned house. What was she thinking?"

"And she didn't even catch Alec Samson's ghost."

"True. All she caught was the worst cold she's had in years. Liz came down with the same thing. That's what you get when you stay up late and inhale mold. At least the girls learned a lesson."

"I take it Liz is still grounded too?"

"Mrs. Yarwood refuses to let her daughter out of her sight."

"That girl has an eye for you," Mom said, pointing a finger at LeVar.

He swallowed down the wrong pipe. "Ma, Liz is a baby."

"That don't stop her from looking. You be careful around that one, you hear? No funny business."

LeVar stood. "That's my cue to leave."

Naomi clamped her lips shut to keep from laughing. "Want

me to send Scout over to study after school, or do you need time to yourself?"

"She's always welcome. I'll teach her to weatherproof a house."

As he walked toward the sliding glass door, he glimpsed a shape behind the trees. The same feeling he'd experienced running with Scout and Jack returned to him.

"There's someone in the backyard," he said, pointing at the tree line.

Mom dried her hands on a towel and joined Naomi beside the door. "Where?"

"Behind the trees and along the shore."

"You're seeing things, boy. There's nothing out there but wind and waves."

"Are you questioning a sheriff's deputy?"

"All right, Deputy Hopkins. Show me this mysterious intruder."

Was that a smart idea? If someone was outside, he'd put Naomi and his mother at risk by letting them follow him to the yard.

"Why don't you stay inside and let me check things out?"

"So you can claim you chased the bad guy away?" Mom glanced knowingly at Naomi and grinned. "He thinks if he acts the hero, we'll give him dessert."

"Suit yourself, but it's cold outside."

All three rubbed their arms as they crossed the backyard. Frost clung to the trees, and the shadows held islands of snow. Beyond the thicket, waves crashed against the shore, driven by a polar wind.

"All right," Mom said, setting hands on hips. "Where's this mysterious trespasser?" LeVar glanced around. He swore someone had hidden along the shore. "Watch this. If we didn't accompany him, LeVar would run back and say he'd chased away the intruder."

"There was someone, I swear."

"Maybe it was a kayaker or a canoeist," Naomi said.

"In this cold?"

"Whoever it was, they're gone now. Come on, Serena. The show is over."

He opened his mouth to argue as they walked back to the house. Ice crystals formed on his pant legs, and the spray dampened his clothes, adding to the chill. Naomi and Mom were right. No sense freezing to death out here.

But as he turned around, he spotted a sneaker print in the mud, much too large to belong to Naomi or Scout. He crouched and snapped a picture with his phone.

Nike Air treads. Canoeists didn't wear expensive sneakers when they ventured out on the lake.

But where was the trespasser now?

6

R aven Hopkins tossed her car keys inside her desk at Wolf Lake Consulting and joined Chelsey in the kitchen. The converted home featured a dinner table and a fully stocked refrigerator. The investigators usually ate at their desks when pressed for time. At ten o'clock, Chelsey dumped spinach and frozen fruit into a blender and started the motor.

"Making smoothies?" Raven asked.

Chelsey jumped, not hearing Raven approach.

"You scared the heck out of me. I thought you weren't coming in until eleven."

"Doctor's appointment ended earlier than expected."

"I hope you didn't run away like Thomas at the dentist."

Raven quirked her lips into a smile. "No, I was a good girl."

"That's nice to know."

"So Thomas pulled another disappearing act at the dentist?"

"Yeah," Chelsey said, blowing the hair off her forehead. "The noises bother him, and it doesn't help when the dentist brings out the drill."

"Can't Thomas's doctor do anything to help?"

"Medications for Asperger's? None exist. And he won't take anti-anxiety meds, even if it's just for dentist appointments. Can't say I blame him. The few times I took anti-anxiety pills, I was too tired to function and they upset my stomach."

"Can the dentist put you under?"

"Sure, but only in extreme cases, and there are risks with sedation. I don't want that for Thomas, and he doesn't want it for himself. I'm not sure what the solution is."

The blender stopped, and Chelsey added protein, ginger, and two teaspoons of organic cacao powder. Both Raven and Chelsey swore by the positive vibes cacao lent them, but they couldn't convince LeVar to partake.

"Ain't natural adding chocolate to fruit," Raven heard him say in her head.

Of course that didn't stop LeVar from eating chocolate-covered strawberries. On Valentine's Day, her boyfriend Darren had brought her a box and LeVar consumed half before Raven ate one.

"What did the doctor say about your concussion?" Chelsey asked.

She waved away her friend's concern. "He cleared me for field duty."

"Didn't he tell you to take it easy? You've had a rough few months."

Raven's problems had started when a prowler hit her in the head during a stakeout. She rapped her knuckles against her skull.

"That's one advantage of being hardheaded."

"You're not pulling my leg, are you?"

"What do you want, a note from the doctor that says I'm free to chase criminals and play kickball in gym class?"

Chelsey laughed. "Don't sass me. I'm looking out for my

friend." Chelsey poured a glass. "Here you go. Energy for the rest of the day."

"I could use some. Darren snored all night. It got so bad that I curled up on the couch. Problem is, you can't escape all that racket when you live in a ranger's cabin. We need dividing walls."

"Does he always snore?"

"Only when his allergies act up. It's the dead leaves. Leaf mold plays havoc with his sinuses."

"My father gets it so bad that he wears a mask while he rakes," Chelsey said.

She snorted. "Fat chance Darren will wear a mask in the woods. He's too macho to admit he has a problem. Every day he hikes the trails and checks the cabins, but we've only had one guest in the last two weeks, and that guy is a Grade-A loudmouth."

"Sorry."

"Be happy you don't have to deal with him. From the second he checked in, it's been one complaint after another. You'd think he'd rented a five-star resort, not a state park cabin in the woods. And the way he treats his wife, always barking like a rabid dog. I'd like to—"

"Please don't punch his lights out. I kinda value your abilities and need you at the office."

"Your husband loves me and will let me out of the clink," said Raven.

"For you, he probably would."

The door opened down the hallway.

"Did you schedule a client appointment this morning?"

"No," Chelsey said, crinkling her brow. "Is it LeVar?"

"Is anyone here?" a woman called.

"Looks like we have a customer."

A woman with short, curly white hair waited in the entry-way. She gave a start when Chelsey and Raven appeared.

"Chelsey Byrd?" the woman asked.

"Yes, and this is my partner Raven Hopkins. May I help you?" Her eyes glistened. "I hope so."

"Come inside and warm up. Raven, can you—"

"I'm one step ahead of you," Raven said. "Coffee, tea, or hot chocolate, ma'am?"

"That's okay," said the woman. "I don't want to put you out."

"We insist," said Chelsey. "You look like you could use something warm. It's freezing outside."

"Hot chocolate, I guess. Thank you."

Raven hustled into the kitchen and heated water in a kettle. When the drink was ready, she carried the mug into the office, where the prospective client sat at Chelsey's desk.

"And you talked with the police?" Chelsey asked. She turned to Raven. "Her husband is Shawn Barrett with the Harmon Police Department. He went missing two nights ago."

Raven slid into a chair beside Chelsey. She knew of Shawn Barrett but hadn't met the man. Law enforcement was a tightknit community. She wondered if Darren was close to Barrett. Likely not, as he would have mentioned the missing officer.

"They're on the case," Mrs. Barrett said. "Everyone at the department loves Shawn, so of course they're worried sick, but they should have found him by now. That's why I came to you. Wolf Lake Consulting is the top private investigation firm in the region. If anyone can find Shawn, it's you. But I fear that . . ."

Mrs. Barrett trailed off and sobbed.

"Here you are, Mrs. Barrett," Raven said, handing the woman a box of tissues.

"Call me Trix, please. I haven't been Mrs. Barrett since I stopped teaching. Shawn is so close to retirement. For decades, I worried something terrible would happen to him. He patrols the worst sections of Harmon."

"Is there anyone your husband arrested who might want revenge?"

Trix groaned. "The entire 315 Royals organization. He made enemies with the Harmon Kings too. Thank goodness they're gone for good."

Raven hoped Trix wouldn't say something crude about LeVar. Had the woman made the connection after Chelsey introduced her as Raven Hopkins?

"Did the Royals threaten your husband?"

"They threaten every officer who cruises through their neighborhoods. You'd think they would run from patrol cars, but they're above the law." Trix glanced at the ceiling in thought. "One man harassed Shawn for months after a DUI arrest."

Chelsey took out a notepad. "Name?"

"Wilson Manfredini. Shawn caught him on I-81, weaving from one lane to the other. The maniac could have killed someone. Because of the arrest, Manfredini lost his job. Boy, did he hate Shawn. Every night Manfredini called and blamed my husband for destroying his life."

"Manfredini." Chelsey scribbled the name. "Don't know the man, but I'm happy to look into him. Did he threaten your husband?"

"Shawn claimed he didn't, but I'm not so sure. Those phone calls upset my husband so much."

Raven and Chelsey recorded Trix Barrett's information until the woman had nothing else to offer. They agreed to take the case. Anytime an officer of the law disappeared, the private investigation community supported the police.

"I'll phone Thomas," Chelsey said after Trix left.

The sheriff's voice came over the speaker.

"Hey, Chelsey. How's your morning?"

"Doing well. You're on speaker phone with Raven."

"That's so you two don't make any mushy comments," Raven said. "Thomas, what do you know about Officer Shawn Barrett's disappearance?"

"Ah," he said. "Harmon PD. We're supporting them in any way we can, but nobody has seen Barrett since the night before last."

"According to his wife," said Chelsey, "he took the back roads home to avoid traffic and never arrived."

"You got the story correct. When did you talk to Trix Barrett?"

"Just now. She hired us to find her husband."

"Looks like we're working together. I don't know, though. This case leaves me with a sick feeling."

"Any chance Barrett left his wife?"

"And threw away his job? Doubtful."

"Think Barrett is still alive?" asked Raven.

"I would never admit it to his wife or his fellow officers, but no. Officer Barrett could defend himself. Someone should have heard from him by now."

"How do you want to handle this?" asked Chelsey.

"Let's create a digital document and share evidence. Once someone finds a clue, we'll all know."

"Sounds good."

"The generous owner of Shepherd Systems supplied our department with new laptops, so I can work remotely." Thomas owned Shepherd Systems. "Might be more effective if I work on location with you guys."

"That's fine with me. We have an open desk."

"It sure would be nice if that benevolent dude at Shepherd Systems bought new laptops for Wolf Lake Consulting," said Raven.

Thomas laughed. "Your computers are light years ahead of

ours." Deputy Aguilar spoke in the background. "I need to run. Stay in touch, and let's hope my worries about Barrett are unfounded."

Chelsey hung up the phone. "Having Thomas in the office will make collaboration easier."

"Not to mention you can bat your eyelashes at each other."

"We already do that on Zoom."

"Thanks for the image. I won't be able to unsee that for the rest of the day."

"Hey, when you go back to the cabin for lunch, will you ask Darren about Officer Barrett?"

"Definitely. Darren knows most every officer at the Harmon PD. Chances are he worked with Barrett."

Raven pursed her lips in thought. During his gang days, LeVar had told her about corrupt officers in Harmon, cops who took money under the table to look the other way. Once a gang placed an officer on the payroll, they expected the police to leave them alone. And if the officer knew too much, he disappeared.

Was Shawn Barrett a corrupt cop?

7

R aven stomped the snow off her boots outside the ranger's cabin. The scent of smoke from the wood-stove hung over the state park, making her long for the cozy interior. Maybe Chelsey would let her telework from the cabin someday.

"Darren?" she called in the doorway.

"Back here." Darren stood up behind the dinner table. "I was rearranging the cupboards. Now everything fits."

"You're quite the happy homemaker this afternoon."

"Better than working outside. Every time Mr. Rose spots me, he has another complaint about the cabin. Too hot, too cold. He's worse than the three bears." Darren kissed Raven's cheek. "How was your doctor's appointment?"

"I'm back to a hundred percent. As if you didn't know."

Darren purred. "Yeah, last night was pretty steamy." He brushed the frozen powder off her shoulder. "I take it the weather changed?"

"Started snowing an hour ago. There's a fresh inch on the ground."

"That's good for the ski industry. They started complaining before Halloween—all this cold but no snow."

Raven pried off her boots. Two pairs of socks kept her feet warm this time of year, but the cabin felt like a hothouse compared to the outside.

"Darren, do you know a police officer named Shawn Barrett?"

"Harmon PD, right? We worked a joint investigation several years ago, before I left Syracuse. Why do you ask?"

"He went missing the night before last."

"Huh. I should have heard, but I've been out of the loop for a few days."

"Were you friends?" asked Raven.

"Can't say we were. Acquaintances. That's the best description. I usually keep my ear close to the law enforcement community. Do the police have any ideas?"

"The Nightshade County Sheriff's Department is assisting Harmon PD, and Barrett's wife stopped by the office and hired our team."

"Then I guess I'm on the case."

"If you're free to help, sure."

"As long as Mr. Rose doesn't run me ragged," Darren said.

"Is he still causing problems?"

"This morning he said the windows were too drafty. It's a cabin. What does he expect? Besides, the bed is clear on the other side of the room, so it's not like he can feel the draft unless he stands next to the window. Which I'm certain he does. Anything to make my job miserable."

"What did you do?"

"Not much I can do. They're old windows, circa-1980. I applied plastic over the pane, but now he's upset because the view is blurry." Darren opened the cupboard. "I was about to mix some hot chocolate. Care for a mug?"

"Can't now. I have forty minutes to eat and drive back to Wolf Lake Consulting. Guess what? Thomas will work remotely for the next few days, probably so he can hang out with Chelsey."

"What about his deputies?"

"They'll stop in. We're all looking into the Barrett disappearance." Raven untied a loaf of bread and pulled turkey and condiments from the refrigerator. "In many ways I don't blame Thomas for working with us. The Nightshade County Sheriff's Department outgrew its building long ago, and the ancient wiring causes havoc with their computers."

Darren eyed Raven over the rim of his mug. "They need a new headquarters. Wouldn't it be something if the sheriff's department worked out of Wolf Lake Consulting?"

"Can't happen. The house isn't big enough to hold their department and ours, plus the private sector would scream that they were giving us preferential treatment."

"True," he said. "But it would be easier than driving across town to collaborate."

"That's what Zoom and Google are for."

"It's not the same."

As Raven bit into her sandwich, the door opened and LeVar walked inside, tracking snow across the floor.

"Sneakers on the rug, LeVar," Raven said.

"Oh, whoops." LeVar took off his sneakers and blew into his hands. "It's cold out there. You'd think it was January, not the week before Thanksgiving."

"How are the roads?"

"A mess. The village hasn't plowed the hill, but I think the snow took everyone by surprise. Last I checked, the forecast said an inch of snow by evening. There's already twice that out there, and it's snowing to beat the band."

"Can't trust those forecasters."

"Sure you can," he said. "It's a thankless job. Did you know a two-degree temperature change can mean the difference between a half inch of rain and five inches of snow? Think you're good enough to forecast temperatures within two degrees?"

"How did you learn so much about the weather?"

"Had to take an elective this semester, so I chose atmospheric science. Guess who has an A-average?"

"All right, Al Roker. Why are you dripping melted snow on our floor?"

LeVar shook the ice out of his dreadlocks. "Needed to get away from the house for a bit. Mom and Naomi keep making fun of me because I claimed someone was hiding in the backyard."

"And was anybody outside when you checked?" Darren asked, grinning.

"No, but I found a sneaker print. Nike Airs."

Raven set her plate on the counter. "Did I mention my brother is an expert at identifying sneaker treads? Where did this stranger run off to?"

"Well, it's too cold to jump in the lake, but when someones sees me coming, diving into icy waters seems like a smart idea. Maybe that should be the next investigation we undertake."

"Tempting, but the Scooby Doo club already has a mystery on its plate. Officer Shawn Barrett with the Harmon PD vanished two nights ago, and we're on the case."

"Officer Barrett? I met that dude."

"During your Harmon Kings days?"

"Thank goodness, no. I just want to put those memories behind me. Officer Barrett spoke in class last spring. Genuine guy. He discussed the 315 Royals and patrolling gang territory. He admitted to receiving death threats from the Royals."

Darren, who was leaning against the counter, drew himself

up. "Death threats? I wonder if the Royals have anything to do with the disappearance."

"Troy Dean is in prison."

"Yeah, but the gang is still operating. Any chance you know who's running the show?"

"Bro, how would I know? I waged war against the Royals; I didn't run with them."

"Sure, but you have friends in Harmon, don't you?"

LeVar looked away. "Not anymore. Nothing good comes out of that city. You escape, or Harmon kills you."

"It can't be that bad. The gangs don't control every inch of the city."

"Let's not talk about Harmon. I drive past on my way to the community college, and that's as close as I want to get."

Raven shared a look with Darren. She was happy for LeVar and his new life, and she loved closing her eyes at night without worrying about where he was or the company he was keeping, but it was important to remember one's roots.

"I'll help you with the investigation," LeVar said, "but I don't know what's happening with the Royals. It would be best if they vanished. That's the only way Harmon can turn itself around."

"You want nothing to do with the city," Raven said, "but will you still volunteer at the soup kitchen with us?"

"Yeah, I guess, but I'm searching for volunteer opportunities in Wolf Lake. The village has its own problems."

"But Scout works at the soup kitchen. The two of you are as thick as thieves."

"That's her punishment. I'm not the one who broke into an abandoned house to catch Alec Samson's ghost."

Weird. Until last week, LeVar had enjoyed working at the soup kitchen with Scout and the investigation team.

"Then I won't ask you again," Raven said. She buttoned her

coat. "I'd better fly if I want to make it to work before the lunch hour ends."

"Careful on the hill, sis. Schedule an appointment to put your snow tires on."

"Thanks, Dad."

"Just looking out for you. Meet you at the office later?"

"If you're free."

Raven tugged a winter hat over her head and stepped into her boots. When had LeVar become so responsible?

8

The clock read 1:37 when a yellow school bus stopped with squealing brakes outside the Mournings' house. LeVar watched Scout hop down and jog up the porch steps, her coat held together with one hand. The snow had stopped, but four heavy inches covered the roads, and schools had let out early.

Knowing it wouldn't be long before she knocked on the door, he cleared off the card table and made room for them to study. His gaze flicked to the yard outside his window and searched for fresh prints in the snow. Except for rabbit tracks, nothing had come through in the last two hours. Was he overreacting? Perhaps he'd seen nothing but the shadow of a tree in Scout's backyard.

Except trees didn't wear sneakers and leave tread marks in the mud.

He set up a space heater to dampen the chill from the drafty windows. The weatherstripping helped, but he couldn't keep the temperature above 66 degrees without supplemental heat. As expected, Scout knocked on the door five minutes later.

"It's open," he called from the front room.

"We had an early dismissal," she said as she draped her coat over a hanger.

"I figured. Come on in."

She padded into the front room wearing a gray sweatshirt, blue jeans, and white socks.

"Your mother said you're a ghost hunter like Liz and me."

"A ghost hunter? Oh, the intruder. Ma is quite the comedian."

"Are you sure someone was behind my house? I checked the camera and didn't see anyone."

"You wouldn't," he said. "The guy was standing beside the shore with the trees in the way. How was school?"

"Blessedly short."

"Is that Dawson boy still bothering you?"

"Not as much. Once in a while, I catch him looking at me. I can't help it if he's lovestruck."

LeVar laughed. "If he causes a problem for you, let me know."

"All I have to do is tell him my best friend was the enforcer for the Harmon Kings. That will scare him off."

He turned away and pulled two books from his knapsack.

"Did I say something?" she asked.

"Nah, it just makes me queasy that people are still afraid of the old LeVar Hopkins."

"Can't blame you. Not that I knew you back in the day, but you're a changed person. Heck, I've noticed a huge difference since summer."

"I'm working on myself. Gotta move away from who I was so I never make those mistakes again."

Scout dropped her bag beside the card table and opened a notebook.

"Hey, mind if I play some tunes while we work?"

"As long as the music doesn't distract you."

She used a Bluetooth connection to send music to LeVar's portable stereo. In seconds, a grungy, thunderous hip-hop beat kicked through the speaker. Loud and angry.

"What's this?" he asked, scrunching his forehead.

"The new release from Griselda," she said, staring at him as if he were from another planet. "You got me into them last year, remember?"

"I guess I did. Didn't realize they had new material. Kinda explicit, isn't it?"

"Want me to turn it down?"

"We could use better studying music."

"This is perfect studying music. It psyches me up."

"Not me," he said. Scrolling through his playlists, he connected his phone to the speaker and switched to jazz. "Better?"

"When did you get into jazz?"

"A couple of dudes at the community college turned me on to jazz. Smooth, isn't it?"

"I suppose."

"You don't like jazz?"

"It's awesome. Most forms of music are. But it sounds more like something my mother will listen to than—"

"Than a kid from Harmon would dig?"

"That's not what I meant," she said, blanching.

"Sorry. I didn't mean it to come out that way. People keep asking me about Harmon, like I have the inside scoop on what goes down in the city."

"I understand. You moved on."

"Damn straight. See, you get it."

"Of course I do. I support you, LeVar."

"I'm glad someone is intelligent enough to recognize," he said.

"Look up 'intelligent' in the dictionary. It shows my picture."

His shoulders bounced with laughter. "Speaking of intelligence, I'm checking out Kane Grove University tomorrow. Why don't you come with me?"

"I doubt Mom will allow me to go."

"Let me talk to her. I'll smooth things over."

"Cool. Is this a tour or something?"

"Not an official tour. More like a LeVar and Scout investigation trip. I can walk around with a tour group anytime, but if I want the unofficial story on Kane Grove—the real deal—I gotta snoop around on my own. You down?"

"If Mom agrees, then yes. This will be my first official-unofficial college tour."

"*Aight*, it's a date." Heat built in his cheeks, and he regretted his choice of words. "I mean—"

"No need to explain. We're on the same wavelength."

"Like brother and sister," he said.

"Better than brother and sister."

He worked a knot out of his neck. When would he learn to watch what he said? As Scout scribbled in her notebook, he pulled a tie out of his pocket and wrapped it around his hair.

"Yo, Scout."

"That's my name; don't wear it out."

"Take that nonsense back to the eighties. Be serious for a second."

She drew a pretend zipper across her lips and straightened her brow.

"That's better," he said. "What would you think if I cut off the dreads?"

She leaned over and coughed.

"Why would you do that?"

"Because of the looks I get when I'm on patrol. People don't take me seriously. Are dreadlocks proper for a deputy?"

"Did Thomas tell you to cut your hair?"

"No, he wouldn't—he don't like confrontation—but he probably thinks I should."

"Before you do anything rash, ask him."

"Why is cutting my hair rash?"

"The dreads are part of your identity, LeVar. You don't want to lose your strength like Samson."

"But it's not my identity. Who I am is in here."

He touched his heart and head.

"Agreed, but it's okay to be different. Don't conform." Scout set an elbow on the table and put her chin on her palm. "This break with your past—it won't affect your volunteer work at the soup kitchen, I hope."

"Shouldn't. Not that I enjoy going down to Harmon, but I want to help until I find a volunteer job close to home."

"It's okay to better your life, but you should take pride in where you came from."

LeVar loosened his collar and turned down the heater. "What are you, sixteen going on thirty-six?"

"Come on, LeVar. Harmon is a part of you. It taught you life lessons."

"It don't have to be a part of me. I severed those ties. Look at you. You're a different person. A wheelchair doesn't define you."

"I'd never go back to that," she said, "but living in a wheelchair helped me become who I am today."

"Explain."

"There is never a day when I take walking and running for granted. Going outside to sniff a flower in the spring, or make snow angels during the winter—those are things that bring me more joy than I can put into words. Most people go through life without realizing how fortunate they are. Me, I live every day to the fullest."

"Those are wise words."

"You bet they are. Never forget where you came from. You won't appreciate your new life if you do."

"I'm not sure that's true. Where's the benefit in acknowledging I ran with a gang? You went through a traumatic, life-changing event. I just made a regrettable decision." He opened a textbook. "We'd better get to work."

As LeVar concentrated on his studies, he sensed Scout staring at him. Why did everyone want him to treat his teenage years like they were his golden days?

9

W hen Thomas awoke the next morning, Chelsey was already at Wolf Lake Consulting. He'd worked until late, following up on leads with the Harmon PD, but nobody knew where Officer Barrett was.

He took care of the pets, then hopped into the shower. Besides spending time with Chelsey, working at WLC had its advantages. The private investigation firm sported a full kitchen with a stove and microwave. Instead of wasting time making breakfast at home, he could wait until he arrived and work while he cooked. If only the sheriff's department would build its head-quarters inside the converted home.

On his way to work, Deputy Lambert briefed him. No new evidence. It was as if the ground had swallowed Barrett. Deputy Aguilar needed to get her Rav4 serviced this morning before she joined everyone at the private investigation firm.

Thomas opened the door to the scent of eggs frying in a pan. His hunger never approached LeVar levels, but the scents reminded him he hadn't eaten since yesterday afternoon.

"Welcome, stranger," Chelsey said as he entered the kitchen. She flipped the eggs. "Sunny side down okay this morning?"

"Bring it on."

Beside Chelsey, Raven popped two slices of bread into the toaster. The blender ground through frozen fruit, protein powder, and oat milk. The blender at the sheriff's department was on its last legs. Another issue with working in the ancient facility.

While Thomas answered emails on his new laptop from Shepherd Systems, he stood watch over the blender and pan. When the food was ready, he sat at the table and ate while replying to messages. This was so much better than the cramped confines of his office. He could get used to this.

"Darren will stop by after ten," said Raven. "He has to take care of a few things at the park before he joins us."

"And Scout is on board once she gets out of school," Chelsey added, spooning leftover fruit onto their plates. "What about your brother?"

"He wants in as well. Apparently, he met Officer Barrett at a school function last spring."

"That's fine," said Thomas, "but I don't want to lean too heavily on LeVar. Between his classes, studies, and him working a weekend shift at the department, I don't want to take advantage of his time. He's already paying me half his salary to live at the guest house."

They agreed.

Chelsey pointed a fork at Raven. "How's your mother and Buck Benson doing? Are they still together?"

Raven snorted. "The lovebirds. Why they pretended to be friends for so long, I'll never understand. As if nobody could tell."

"It's wonderful that she's happy."

"Everything is perfect for Mom. She adores her therapist. The position at Shepherd Systems is a great fit for her, and she really likes volunteering every week at the soup kitchen. She wants to give back to Harmon."

"She's a righteous soul."

"Then there's my brother," Raven said, dropping a slice of bacon off her fork.

"What's wrong with LeVar?"

"He's second guessing the volunteer work. Harmon isn't good enough for him anymore."

"That doesn't sound like your brother."

"Have you spoken to him lately? He's all about what's best for LeVar. Nothing wrong with self-improvement, but it seems . . . selfish, like he'd be elated to volunteer at the Wolf Lake marina and support rich people who overpaid for their boats."

Chelsey frowned.

"I'm sure you're exaggerating."

"Maybe a little. I love LeVar, but he gets weird ideas in his head sometimes. Too impulsive."

"Unlike his sister?"

Thomas choked on his food. "Are the two of you like this every morning?"

"Pretty much," Raven said.

"Excellent. I'm moving in. Can I have a bedroom? This is pure entertainment."

"Suit yourself, but you'll have to work around Chelsey's dresser of extra-large sweatshirts. I suggest living out of a travel bag."

After breakfast, Thomas washed everyone's dishes and set them on the drying rack. He carried his laptop to the operations room, where Chelsey and Raven were hard at work.

"Pull up a seat, Sheriff," Raven said. "We're going over the notes from our interview with Trix Barrett."

"As I wrote you," Chelsey said, "Shawn Barrett ran into trouble with Wilson Manfredini."

Thomas stroked the stubble on his face. "The guy lost his job after a DUI arrest. I remember."

"Mrs. Barrett suspects Manfredini threatened her husband."

"And LeVar confirmed Officer Barrett received threats from the 315 Royals," Raven added.

"Furthermore, Chief Pauley mentioned a gangster who visited the office on the afternoon Barrett disappeared. The kid claimed he was a part of the Kings before they disbanded, but Pauley thinks he might be a Royal in disguise."

"Any clue what Barrett discussed with this kid?" Thomas asked.

"Something about the Royals moving narcotics through Harmon."

"Why would a member of the Royals admit that?"

"Could be a diversion to hide a larger operation. I don't know."

"We need the kid's name."

"Working on it. For now, I want to run surveillance on Wilson Manfredini."

Thomas shook his head. "Not if this guy has a violent streak. I'll send Aguilar with Lambert after she arrives."

The door opened, and Aguilar called from the hallway.

"Thomas? Chelsey?"

"We're back here," said Chelsey.

Deputy Aguilar, all five feet of her, strutted into the office with a glass container in hand.

"I made everyone homemade protein bars. No artificial ingredients or chemicals like the garbage grocery stores sell."

"You didn't have to do that."

"Sure I did. It's my way of saying thanks for letting us work here."

"How was your service appointment?" he asked.

"The service was actually for my Rav4, not for me."

"Here we go. I rue the day I taught you to be snarky."

Aguilar threw up her hands. "Did you know a simple oil and filter change is over $70? Ridiculous. I need a raise, Thomas."

"As soon as the county increases our budget by, oh, a few thousand percent."

"So next November?"

"If you say so."

The deputy grimaced at the surroundings. "I truly hate coming here."

"Whatever for?" Chelsey asked.

"It reminds me of how much space you have compared to us. We work in a tomb."

"It's not *that* bad," Thomas said.

"When you win the lottery, convert a sweet house in the village center into a sheriff's department." Aguilar rolled a chair over to them. "What are you working on?"

"Wilson Manfredini," Thomas said. "This is the guy Barrett had issues with."

"Mr. DUI?"

"That's him. Pick up Lambert at the station and speak to Manfredini."

"Thomas, I'll go alone. I don't need Lambert to keep me safe."

"Never said you did. I figure Lambert can defend Manfredini from you."

"Stop. I may be rough around the edges, but I'm not the Terminator."

"Find out if he had anything to do with Officer Barrett vanishing."

Aguilar grabbed her keys. "Right away." She pointed at the container. "Those protein bars are for everyone, not just LeVar."

"We'll eat them before my brother arrives," Raven said.

After Aguilar left, Chelsey turned to him. "How long do you intend to work remotely?"

"As long as I can before someone notices," he said. "Which is probably like a day or two. Aguilar made a valid point about our headquarters. It's nothing like this place."

"You're always welcome here."

She kissed his cheek.

"Oh, get a hotel room," said Raven.

"But we live together."

"True, but I won't stand for public displays of affection."

"What about you and Darren?"

Raven shifted her shoulders. "We don't display affection in public."

"You sure about that?"

Suddenly, Raven looked uncomfortable. "Okay. Perhaps we do once in a while, but that's because you make me work long hours and I never see him."

Chelsey smiled at Thomas. "It's always my fault. Get used to it."

He sipped from a mug of green tea. "Pull up Mandredini's background information. Let's dig up some dirt."

10

Wilson Manfredini lived in a single-story, blue-gray house with a chimney puffing smoke. Snow and ice covered the walkway and steps, and Aguilar grabbed Lambert to keep the taller officer from falling. He kept his hair short. By his appearance, one would assume he was still in the army.

Aguilar pressed the doorbell and waited. A car drove by with music thumping inside. After nobody answered, she tried again.

"Car is in the driveway," Lambert said, holding the rail so he didn't slip.

The door opened, and a middle-aged man with booze on his breath poked his head out the door.

"Yeah?"

"Wilson Manfredini?"

"What's it to you?"

"Nightshade County Sheriff's Department."

"I can see that. Yeah, I'm Manfredini. Why are you bothering me?"

"We need to talk to you about a missing person."

He squinted at them. "Nobody I know is missing."

"It's Officer Shawn Barrett with the Harmon PD," Lambert said.

"Maybe he took a long walk off a short pier. How the hell would I know where he is?"

"I understand you had trouble with Officer Barrett," said Aguilar.

Manfredini spat off the porch. A brownish mass landed in the snow.

"Trouble ain't the half of it. I lost my job because of that idiot."

"He arrested you for DUI. Is that correct?"

"What he did was railroad me. I caught a cold at work and took cough medicine. A few spoonfuls wouldn't have made me drunk, but he smelled it on my breath and jumped to conclusions."

"The Harmon police have eyewitness reports of you drinking at King's Tavern that evening," Lambert said.

"Lies. The police pay people to say things. It's all about kickbacks. My cousin is a retired cop, and he told me his department had a DUI quota. If he arrested the most people for driving under the influence, he got a bonus in his paycheck. That's why Barrett said I was drunk."

"The city doesn't pay its officers bonuses to arrest people," Aguilar said.

"Prove it!"

This was going nowhere. Aguilar chewed the inside of her cheek.

"When's the last time you spoke to Officer Shawn Barrett?"

"At the hearing. He perjured himself in front of the judge. If anyone deserved a night in jail, it was him."

"You didn't call him at home?"

"I may have, once or twice."

"What did you discuss?" she asked.

"None of your damn business." He tried to close the door, and she blocked it with her foot. "Persistent, ain't ya?"

"I'll bet the DUI charge made you angry," said Lambert, his teeth chattering.

"Of course it did. I lost my job."

"Did you threaten Officer Barrett?"

"Hell no."

"We spoke to a witness who says you did."

"Another liar. Tell me who it is, and I'll make sure they speak the truth from now on."

"Mr. Manfredini," Aguilar said, "where were you two nights ago between six and ten o'clock?"

He pursed his lips in thought. "Grocery shopping until seven. Then I watched the Rangers game."

"At the bar?"

"At home."

"Can anyone verify you were at the store or at home?"

"I live alone, so no."

"Credit card activity?"

"Paid cash at the store. Now get off my porch so I can go inside. It's cold out here."

"Which grocery store?"

"Bob's on McGraw Road. I'm not asking you again. Get off my porch."

The door closed. Aguilar wanted to jam her finger against the doorbell, but Lambert talked her out of it.

"What's your opinion of Manfredini?" she asked on the way back to the cruiser.

"He's a bit of a conspiracy theorist."

"And angry as hell."

"That doesn't mean he killed Officer Barrett."

"His temper is short enough that I believe he's capable of murder."

The interior of the cruiser was toasty. She started the engine.

"I'll call Thomas and give him the lowdown," Lambert said.

As the cruiser pulled away, Aguilar saw Manfredini watching through the window.

~

"THANKS FOR THE INFORMATION, LAMBERT," said Thomas. "Keep an eye on Manfredini. I want to know if he leaves the county."

"Will do, Sheriff."

Thomas hung up and set down the phone.

"Manfredini didn't confess to murdering Barrett?" Chelsey asked.

"Not exactly," he said.

"Our offer to monitor him stands."

"I appreciate it, but all we have to go on is Barrett arrested him, and Manfredini harassed the officer over the phone. According to Officer Barrett, the jerk never threatened him. He's just one suspect. The gangster at the police station is another. I'll speak to Chief Pauley and get the name. The kid had to check in at the front desk and the police have him on camera, so he won't be difficult to identify."

Chelsey touched his shoulder. "I'm thankful every day that you're a county sheriff and not a patrol officer in Harmon."

"And I'm glad Darren left the Syracuse PD and decided to become a ranger," Raven added. "I might not have met him otherwise, and the woods are safer than city streets."

"Unless a bear eats your face off," Thomas said.

"Fair point."

A crash outside brought Thomas out of his chair.

"That didn't sound good," Raven said, looking up from her computer.

Chelsey craned her head beside the window. "Ice and snow fell off the roof. I hope it isn't too heavy over the entryway."

Raven rushed to the window. "I parked near the building."

"You might want to move your Rogue before an icicle blasts through your windshield. I'm worried about the entryway. We can move our vehicles away from the house, but the snow over the entrance is a safety issue."

Thomas bundled into his coat. "I'll take care of it."

Before they could argue, he slipped a hat over his head and donned winter gloves. Outside, he located a shovel. A mass of snow teetered over the edge of the covered entryway. If it fell on somebody, Chelsey might get sued.

The women came outside to help. Raven grabbed everyone's keys and ensured the vehicles were far from the building, and Chelsey threw salt on the steps and used a push broom to clear snow off the roof.

Standing on tiptoe, Thomas scraped the snow with the shovel and let it topple off. Doing so left two huge mounds on either side of the entrance, but at least the area was safe.

"Better?" he asked.

"Much," she said, bouncing to stay warm. "When will it be summer again?"

Raven hurried across the lot, slipping and sliding on nature's ice rink. The phone rang inside, and Chelsey rushed ahead of the others. She picked up the call and pressed the receiver to her ear.

"Who did you say this is?" she asked. Thomas and Raven joined her. "Oh, Deputy Aguilar. I couldn't understand what you said with the shouting in the background. Hold on. Thomas is right here."

Chelsey handed him the phone as he brushed the snow out of his hair.

"Yeah, Aguilar?"

"A farmer found a dead body five miles outside of Wolf Lake," the deputy said.

Thomas held his breath. "Is it Barrett?"

"We don't know. Lambert and I are driving out there now. I'll give you the address."

Thomas snapped his fingers and pointed at Chelsey's notepad. She handed it to him, and he copied the location on the paper.

"Give me ten minutes. I'll meet you there."

"State police are on the way," Aguilar said. "Someone should notify Chief Pauley."

"I'll let you know if it's Officer Barrett," Thomas whispered to the others before returning to the call.

"We're coming too," Chelsey said, zipping her jacket.

"Can't we tell by comparing the deceased's face with Barrett's picture?" he asked his lead deputy.

"That's the issue. The farmer said the guy . . . doesn't look human. He's all puffed up."

"Puffed up?"

"I'm just repeating what he told me."

"Gotcha. See in you in ten."

Thomas ran to his truck. He prayed the dead man wasn't Officer Shawn Barrett.

11

T homas arrived at the scene with the WLC crew right behind. Aguilar and Lambert joined them. They walked together across a snow-covered field. Patches of dead weeds stuck out of the powder like skeletal arms, and ice crunched under their boots.

"The farmer's name is Zeph Wheeler," Aguilar said, speaking over the wind. "He's meeting us beside the body after he changes into a coat."

"How long has the victim been in the field?"

"Wheeler isn't sure. He spotted a dark form in the snow a half hour ago and walked outside to inspect what it was."

Another vehicle stopped along the road. Thomas glanced over his shoulder.

"That's Claire Brookins," he said.

"I'll help her carry the equipment," Lambert offered. "Her college interns are on break."

"Thanks, deputy."

A silo rose off the land, and beside it stood a weathered barn with open doors. About fifty paces in front of the barn, the silhouette of a corpse lay partially covered by snow. The man had lain there since before the squall hit Nightshade County.

"There he is," Aguilar said.

The sheriff caught the sharp scent of cow manure as they approached. He kept repeating in his head that it couldn't be Officer Barrett.

Chelsey hissed. "I see what the farmer meant."

Raven crouched for a closer look. "What the hell happened to this guy?"

Repulsed, Thomas took a breath. The dead man's face appeared alien, eyes swollen shut, discolored mounds growing from his scalp to his neck. Even his hair jutted out unnaturally.

"If that's an allergic reaction," Thomas said, "it's the worst I've ever encountered."

"He wasn't beaten," said Aguilar. "What would make someone react like this?"

Claire Brookins arrived with Lambert. Out of breath, the county's first female medical examiner huffed and puffed.

"I should have dressed warmer," Claire said, stomping her feet. Then she saw the victim's face. "Good God."

"Glad you're here," Thomas said. "I don't know where to begin. That's an allergic reaction, but I couldn't tell you what kind."

"Insect stings." Claire took her bag from Deputy Lambert and strapped a camera around her neck. As she snapped pictures, she spoke. "I heard of a man's arm puffing like this after he walked into a nest of black widows, but these are stings, not bites, and black widows aren't native to New York. If you ask me, those are hornet or wasp stings."

"Are you sure?" Lambert asked. "It's November, and the weather turned cold before Halloween. Where would this guy encounter this many stinging insects?"

"I can't identify the venom in his system until I get him back to the lab. By the way, I'll need help transporting the corpse."

"We got you covered there," said Thomas, "but I don't understand how this guy ran into a hive."

"Obviously he's been here since before the snow fell. His legs are an inch below the powder. Plus, I didn't see shoe prints leading to the body. I can't give you an answer about the stings. Makes no sense to me."

"My uncle got stung at a Christmas party," said Raven. "He climbed up to the attic for decorations. It was mild that Christmas, and the attic stayed warm enough to awaken the hornets that had nested there over the summer."

Zeph Wheeler, the farmer who owned the property, shuffled over to them. At the medical examiner's orders, he remained several steps away from the corpse. Wheeler had a grizzled face, lined and pockmarked by a lifetime of strenuous work in the elements. He wore a red-plaid parka and a winter hat.

After introductions, Thomas asked, "You've never seen this man before?"

"Never," the farmer growled. "I suppose it's possible he's a neighbor, but how can I tell?"

Aguilar and Lambert brushed the snow off the victim's upper body, revealing a hooded sweatshirt with "Clarkson" written across the front.

"Was Officer Barrett a Clarkson grad?" Aguilar asked.

Lambert pushed the sweatshirt up to the dead man's chest and frowned. "That's a Harmon PD uniform underneath."

"Dammit," Chelsey muttered.

"It's Barrett," Thomas said, reading the man's badge. A Harmon PD cruiser stopped behind the train of vehicles. "And that must be Chief Pauley. I'll give him the news when he arrives." He turned to Wheeler. "The victim wasn't far from the barn. Was there a wasp nest inside?"

"Barn is open and unheated," said Wheeler. "I get nests near the ceiling every summer, but the bugs aren't flying anymore."

"If it's all the same, we'll need to check out your barn."

"Suit yourself."

"What about inside the house?" Lambert asked. "I'm sure the interior is warm enough for insects to survive."

"Sure is, but why haven't I gotten stung? You're free to search my home, but this person never set foot inside."

A heavyset man with a gray mustache high-stepped through the snow. Chief Pauley was in full uniform.

"Sheriff Shepherd," Pauley said, touching the rim of his cap.

"I'm afraid I have unfortunate news," Thomas said.

The chief's face paled. "No. Tell me it's not Barrett."

"I'm sorry."

Pauley's eyes glistened. He drew himself up and said, "Show me."

"I should warn you. Officer Barrett doesn't look like himself."

"Don't care. Barrett and I go back twenty years. I can handle it."

Still, the chief flinched upon examining his officer's body.

"Claire says those are stings on his face and torso," Thomas said, answering Pauley's question before he asked. "Hornets or wasps."

"Some bees hit you without losing their stingers," Pauley said, looking nauseous. "But nobody gets swarmed after winter weather sets in. Not in New York. Officer Barrett was deathly allergic to bee stings. He carried an EpiPen everywhere."

"Someone placed the body in the field," said the medical examiner. "The elements haven't worked on Barrett for more than five or six hours."

"And I was inside all morning," Wheeler said, as if the others suspected him. "Whoever dumped him in my field, I didn't see."

It was one thing for Thomas to accuse the farmer of

murdering Barrett, but where had Wheeler found a nest of wasps? His body should be covered with stings as well.

While the medical examiner looked over Officer Barrett's body with the deputies, Thomas, the WLC team, and Chief Pauley investigated the barn. As Wheeler had said, the barn was as cold as a freezer. He spied the remnants of an abandoned nest in the far corner, but nothing buzzed in and out.

With the farmer leading the way, the team checked inside the house, concentrating on places wasps might congregate over the winter without Wheeler noticing—the attic, a storage room at the back of the basement, even closets in seldom-used rooms. No nests, no stinging insects.

"Like I told you, Sheriff," said the farmer, "if wasps set up shop in my house, I'd know about them."

Aguilar and Lambert took Wheeler's statement while Thomas, Chelsey, and Raven conferred with Chief Pauley.

"This is the strangest case I've ever encountered," the chief said. "I wish I could give you an explanation."

"The gangs inside Harmon," said Thomas. "They occupy heated buildings. Those could support wasps over the winter."

Pauley removed his cap and scratched the top of his head. "And the 315 Royals had a motive to get rid of Barrett. He arrested quite a few of their members."

"It's worth looking into."

"So what are we saying? The Royals abducted Officer Barrett on his way home, took him to Harmon, and wasps attacked him inside a building?"

"Makes no sense to me either," Thomas said. "Besides the gangs, can you think of anyone who would want to hurt Officer Barrett?"

"No way."

"What about Wilson Manfredini?"

Pauley sneered. "I forgot about that weasel. One DUI, and that guy caused a year's worth of problems for my department."

"You're aware he called Barrett at home?"

"Yeah, I am."

"Any chance he did this?"

"It's conceivable," the chief said. "He hated Officer Barrett."

12

In his black Chrysler Limited, LeVar cranked the heater as he waited outside Wolf Lake High School. It had taken little convincing for Naomi to let her daughter visit Kane Grove University. In the mother's words, Scout needed to see what taking care of herself was like.

He set his elbow on the armrest and fiddled with the radio. School buses lined up ahead of him, and students filed out of doorways, kids forming snowballs and tossing them at each other. He wondered what it would have been like growing up in the village and attending school here. Gangs weren't an issue in Wolf Lake.

A knock made him turn off the radio. A sixty-something man with white hair stared through the window. He wore a business suit; his tie pressed against the glass. A principal, LeVar thought, lowering the window.

"Yes?"

"Students and parents only."

"I'm picking up a student."

The principal glared at LeVar. "No gang members on high school grounds."

"What makes you think I'm in a gang?"

"I can tell by looking at you."

"What's that supposed to mean? Because I'm black?"

"Get out of here. If I catch you on school grounds again, I'll have you arrested. Drive before I call the cops."

"I *am* the cops."

Before LeVar produced his badge, Scout squeezed around the principal and slid into the car.

"Mourning," the man said, "I would have thought you smart enough not to hang around with riffraff. Does your mother know you're friends with this . . . person?"

Scout smiled. "You mean Deputy Hopkins? Why yes, my mother knows."

"*Deputy* Hopkins?" asked the principal, taken aback. "I don't believe it."

"Have a pleasant afternoon."

LeVar pulled away. Through the mirrors, he saw the man staring until they turned the corner.

"That was wonderful," he said. "Are all Wolf Lake High School principals racist?"

"Mr. Hurst is a jerk-wad. Don't let him get to you."

"He profiled me because I'm black and ran me off." LeVar slapped the steering wheel. "You know, I should go back and let him call the sheriff's department. I want to see the look on his face when Thomas shows up and tells the guy who I am."

"Easy, LeVar. You're letting him get the best of you."

"It's not right. If I cut my hair and removed the tats, would people treat me differently? To some, I'll always be a gangster because I can't change the way I look."

Scout pressed her lips together and watched the scenery stream past the window. He took a deep breath. It was time to move on. Kane Grove University awaited, and the four-year school would give him a fresh start.

She still wasn't talking. When they were five minutes away from the college, he turned to her.

"Sorry for losing it."

"I don't blame you. Nobody likes Principal Hurst. He prejudged you, and that's not fair."

"That's right," he said, sitting up a little straighter.

Having her on his side lightened his mood. He turned on the stereo and listened to an old-school hip-hop playlist. No explicit lyrics this time. As he drove, a fast-moving SUV with a tinted window caught his attention in the mirrors. It drifted in and out of traffic, as if the driver were in a hurry to get somewhere. He thought little of the SUV until it pulled behind a truck and paced them. Two minutes later, it was still there.

He parked in the visitors' lot and hopped out. Students carrying book bags walked toward the quad. He couldn't wait to join them next fall.

Scout climbed out of the car and took in the buildings, some of which had ivy growing up their brick facings.

"Whoa, this is terrific, LeVar. I understand why you chose Kane Grove."

"Come on. I can't wait to show you around."

They climbed a flight of concrete steps that deposited them a few hundred feet from the quad. During nice weather, students hung out on the grass and tossed Frisbees. It looked like a great place to study. Today everyone bundled up and shivered, hurrying to get to class.

"That's the Jamison Science Building," he said, pointing to the left. "And that glass structure belongs to the psychology department."

"This is great. How many times have you visited?"

"Officially? Just once. But I came on my own a few times, and Thomas and I came for an investigation."

"Oh, yeah. The football player. I forgot about him."

"Follow me. I'll introduce you to our new department chair."

Entering the building thawed his face, and he could finally feel his hands again. A uniformed officer with the Treman Mills PD walked past.

"Know that officer?" Scout asked.

"Nah, but the department brings in law enforcement to speak to classes. I should tell them about Agents Bell and Gardy. The school probably doesn't get too many FBI profilers."

Upstairs, LeVar led the way down a hallway that appeared dark after the brightness of the snow. His eyes were still adjusting when he knocked on a door.

A woman with long blond hair stood. Michelle Carpenter ran the department and had convinced LeVar to choose Kane Grove.

"Deputy Hopkins, taking another tour?"

"Not officially, Mrs. Carpenter. Just showing my friend around."

"Michelle Carpenter," the chairperson said, offering a hand.

"Scout Mourning."

"She's a future FBI profiler," LeVar said.

"Oh, is this the girl you told me about?" asked Carpenter. "The teenager who helped the sheriff's department catch that serial killer?"

"In the flesh."

Carpenter's face brightened. "Are you considering Kane Grove?"

"Maybe someday. I'm only a junior."

"Now's the time to tour schools. My advice? Start applying to schools this spring, then make a choice during the fall semester of your senior year. That way you can enjoy your final high school semester."

"Listen to her," he said. "Professor Carpenter won't lead you astray."

The chairperson handed Scout a packet. "Look these over when you get home. If you have questions, call me anytime."

Scout thanked her.

Outside, he pointed out the academic buildings and dorms. He'd memorized the names. Her head spun.

"That's the physics lab, and over there is the football stadium."

"I bet they have tailgating parties before games."

"Oh, yeah. Burgers, dogs, and a few beverages you're not allowed to drink for another five years. Or fifty."

"Got it."

She stumbled on a patch of ice and fell against him. He caught her and held on until she found her footing. Clearing his throat, he set her on her feet and averted his eyes.

"Now for the fun part," LeVar said, walking around a mound of snow. "I'll show you the student lounge. They sell extra-large sundaes."

"Now you're talking."

Despite the winter weather, he never said no to ice cream. The student lounge was packed when they arrived. Scents of pizza and grilled burgers drifted to his nose, tempting him to order dinner and dessert. He probably shouldn't. Raven was right about his metabolism. He wouldn't stay young forever.

They shared a table in the back of the lounge. A large wall-mounted television played sports highlights, and a couple of girls at the neighboring table read paperbacks and chatted over lattes. Outside the window, two dorms stood on the far side of the snow-covered lawn.

"Did you ever consider living on campus?" Scout asked, spooning strawberry sundae past her lips.

He dug into his chocolate and banana sundae. "Considered the option, but why waste the money? Am I right? Besides, I'd miss everyone."

"Including me?"

"Especially you."

They clinked their spoons.

"I can't wait to go to college in two years," she said. "This is so cool."

"Don't rush through high school. College will be here before you know it."

"Yeah, but being able to make my own decisions and choose what I want to do every day . . . I can't imagine what that is like."

"You won't be one of those irresponsible kids who parties herself into oblivion as soon as she breaks away from home, will you?"

She snorted. "As if. I love my mother, but it will be awesome to make my own choices. Heck, I could schedule all my classes in the afternoon and sleep all morning."

"Why would you sleep in?"

"So I can stay up late watching scary movies."

"Ah. There's more to life than horror flicks."

"You sure about that?" She gazed across the lounge. "I totally see myself eating meals in a student lounge, reading novels in some quiet nook inside the library, sunbathing with friends on a hot day. College sounds a lot more fun than high school. And I won't have jerks like Principal Hurst to deal with."

"Can you picture yourself at Kane Grove?"

"Definitely. I could get away from home and still be close enough to visit."

"Because you'll want your mother to do your laundry."

She gestured at him with her spoon.

"I'll have you know I do my laundry. And Mom's. That's one of my chores."

"How very responsible of you."

"I'm more than good looks and a sexy body."

He choked on his ice cream.

"Damn. Don't do that to me while I'm eating." He swallowed the last scoop. "What do you say? Ready to head back to Wolf Lake?"

"I don't want to leave. You sold me on college, LeVar."

"Can't stay here forever. Come on. Your mother will worry if I don't get you back before dinner. And you'd better eat. Don't tell her I bought you ice cream."

"Mum's the word."

They retraced their steps through the university. Salt melted snow and ice on the sidewalks and formed slushy puddles. Light faded from the sky as the calendar marched toward the winter solstice. Two boys passed and nodded. Were they saying hello to LeVar or interested in Scout? He pushed the thought from his head. She was growing up fast. Too fast.

The atmosphere inside the car was festive when they hit the highway. She couldn't stop talking about college, and he'd forgotten the prejudiced high school principal. Yes, he'd made the right decision by choosing Kane Grove. Next fall couldn't come soon enough.

He was almost at the Wolf Lake exit when he spotted an SUV with tinted windows a hundred yards behind them. The same one that had trailed him earlier? He wondered if Scout had noticed, but she was texting Liz about the college visit.

When he glanced in the mirror, the SUV was gone.

13

Inside his office atop the Jefferson Building, in the center of Harmon, Christopher Fieldman clicked the documents together on a cherry wood desk and filed them away. He shot an annoyed look at the welcome area. Mary was gone from her desk again, probably hiding in the bathroom and chatting with friends as she liked to do. He knew all her tricks. Perhaps he should dock her pay for every minute she spent away from her post.

Fieldman swept a hand across his slicked-back hair and arranged the pens. He left nothing out of place. Harmon wasn't exactly the Big Apple, but he took pride in conquering his city. At only thirty-one, he was worth more than all his closest competitors combined. He owned dozens of commercial properties, so many that he often forgot some until Mary reminded him.

Mary. Why hadn't he replaced her with someone who worked for a living?

Her legs. Yes, he had to admit that was the reason. If she took to dressing in Hillary Clinton's pantsuits, he'd replace her in a heartbeat.

The wind rattled the pane and made his heart pump. If he could turn back time, he'd choose another property as his headquarters. The Jefferson Building impressed clients, but it scared the hell out of him. He'd been terrified of heights since falling from a tree during his childhood, and his office sat forty-one floors above the unforgiving concrete. Acrophobia. That's what the psychiatrist called it. He bristled. That damn reporter from *The Bluewater Tribune* had found out about his acrophobia and printed it in the newspaper. If he ever proved the psychiatrist had leaked the information, he'd sue the doctor and his whole damn practice.

A buzzer startled him. Outside the entry doors, a deliveryman dressed in dark blue waited with a package under his arm. Fieldman narrowed a frustrated brow at Mary's vacant desk before the buzzer sounded a second time.

"Patience," he called out, pushing his chair back.

When Mary finally returned, they would have a discussion about her career aspirations.

He opened the door and let the man inside.

"Fieldman Enterprises?" the man asked.

"You found the right place."

"Here you are." The deliveryman handed over the package. "Cold out there. Winter came early this year."

Fieldman issued an impatient grunt of agreement, wishing the man would hurry.

"I just need you to sign for the package, and I'll get out of your hair."

"Fine. Let's have it. I don't have all day."

The deliveryman brought out a pen and clipboard. Three documents covered the top of the sheet Fieldman needed to sign, leaving only the signature line visible.

"What's this? Are we back in the eighties? I haven't signed with a pen in years."

"Sorry, my machine is on the fritz. Can't do digital signatures today. Please sign."

Fieldman scribbled his name in sloppy cursive and gave the clipboard back to the man, who looked vaguely familiar, though it was difficult to tell with a baseball cap pulled down to his eyebrows.

I've met him. Who is he?

The deliveryman broke Fieldman's train of thought when he removed a gun from his pocket.

"What the hell is this?"

"Don't remember me, do you? I guess I didn't leave a strong impression," the man said. "That's all right. You'll be the one making an impression this evening."

"Look, if you want money, I'll give you whatever you need. My wallet is inside my desk."

"I don't want your money, Mr. Fieldman. Just your attention."

"All right, you have it. I'm listening."

Where the hell was Mary?

"Let's take a walk. How does that sound?"

"Anything you say. Just don't shoot."

The man gestured with the gun. "After you."

Fieldman pushed the stairwell door open, and they stepped inside. The door closed with a finality that echoed off the walls.

"What now?"

"Up the stairs."

"We can't. This is the highest floor."

"I said up the stairs."

The wind gusted so hard that he swore the building had tipped. It whistled beyond the stairwell.

"If I did anything to offend you, allow me to make it up to you."

The man aimed the gun at his head. "Shut up and move."

"You haven't told me what this is about," he said, climbing one step at a time.

"We're going to play a game."

"What kind of game?"

"Don't worry, Mr. Fieldman. You'll enjoy the game. And if you win, I'll let you live."

"This is preposterous. Tell me how I upset you. I'll make things right. You know how much I'm worth, don't you?"

The barrel touched the back of Fieldman's neck, stiffening his joints.

"Walk."

That got him moving again. This time he didn't stop until he stood before a steel exit door that blocked access to the roof. No one could open the door without the code.

"Opening the exit door will sound an alarm. You're aware of that, right?"

"Not if you punch in the passcode. Do it, Mr. Fieldman, and don't screw up. If you enter the wrong code, I'll put the first two bullets through your ear and save the next two for your beautiful wife."

He stammered. "Not my wife. You don't have to hurt my wife."

"Be a good boy and open the door."

Fieldman knew the code by heart, yet he screwed it up three times before he touched the enter button. His fingers wouldn't stop shaking.

"I told you to open the door."

The barrel clanked against his skull.

"Okay, okay."

The moment the door opened, the world spun. Fieldman and the deliveryman stood high above the city, the cars far below like army ants marching in single file. The Jefferson Building dwarfed its neighbors. He had the queer idea that the next building's ledge was close enough to leap to, but it was clear on the other side of the street. And it was cold. Frigid. He thought he understood how much heat the wind stole from the human body, but the gusts on the roof came at 25 to 35 miles per hour. The American flag hanging off the ledge snapped and lay out straight.

He looked again at the black-eyed man with the gun. So familiar, yet he couldn't place the psycho.

"You will follow my orders, sir. If you don't, I'll kill you and pay your wife a visit."

"I'll do anything you say."

"Anything? That's brave of you, considering I haven't discussed the rules of the game."

"What rules?"

The deliveryman gestured with the gun.

"See that ledge? It's wide enough to accommodate your shoe width with a few inches to spare. You will climb over the rail, balance on the ledge, and walk to the corner."

His heart pumped too fast, and a frozen sweat broke out on the back of his neck.

"I can't do that."

"Afraid of heights, Mr. Fieldman? Yes, I remember."

There was no way he could approach the edge of the building without fainting, let alone climb onto the ledge, which appeared impossibly thin. The man had said it was wider than his shoes. It couldn't be.

"Sorry, I can't."

"Fine." The deliveryman aimed the gun at his chest. "Say goodbye, Mr. Fieldman. I'll send your beautiful wife to join you in a matter of hours."

"No, no! Wait. We can work this out."

"There's nothing to work out. Play the game or you and your wife die."

His teeth chattered, the sound rolling in his head like loose bones.

"You don't understand. I'll pass out before I reach the edge."

"The human mind is capable of more than you dream," said the deliveryman. "In times of extreme distress, we summon courage to accomplish the impossible. Believe in yourself."

"It can't be done. The wind."

"You climbed to the top of the world on the backs of others. Now you will prove you can stand on its peak." The man took a step forward. "Get moving. We don't have all day."

Fieldman backed away, moving closer to the ledge without looking. A gust whipped his hair and fluttered his shirt. The wind chill had to be in the teens. He barely felt his fingers and toes, and the cold rushed at him like a freight train.

"Very good. You're almost there."

Reaching behind, he touched the frozen railing. He didn't dare look over his shoulder. If he saw how high up he was, how close he'd come to flipping over the edge, he'd lose his mind.

"You'll have to turn around, Mr. Fieldman. This isn't a trick you wish to perform without looking."

He swallowed. Out of options, he faced his doom. The breath rushed from his chest. It seemed the building had doubled in height. If he stood on tiptoe, he could touch the clouds and the heavens above. So far down. The black dots on the sidewalk might have been people. He wasn't sure.

"Step over the rail. You're wasting time."

"The ledge. It's too thin."

"No, it's not. That's your mind playing tricks on you. Place one foot in front of the other, and you'll have plenty of room. Mind the wind."

"Tell me what I did to you. I'm sorry. Let me fix things."

"I'm giving you a chance to right your wrongs now, sir. It's really not that far. Thirty, forty steps at most. You could accomplish the task in your sleep."

He couldn't do this. Would the crazy man murder his wife over a slight he didn't even remember?

A glowing sign atop the next building read *Coke Adds Life*. So many times he'd walked along the street without looking up at the letters, and now they stood below his gaze. Far below.

"That's it. You're almost to the ledge."

Fieldman stepped over the rail, refusing to let go. Every time the wind blew, it shoved him toward the edge of the building. He reached out with the toe of his shoe. The ledge was too far away.

"Sorry, but you can't hold the rail while you stand on the ledge. Not unless your arms grow another six inches. By the way, I took the liberty of typing your suicide note. Thank you for signing it. Should you fall, the note will explain everything to the police."

Bastard.

Something black whipped toward his head, and he had the impression of a crow taking flight. But crows didn't live atop skyscrapers. He ducked under the roofing tile. If another tile shot off the roof while he balanced on the edge of the building, it would knock him sideways.

One more step. Just a tiny step. The man left him no choice.

He bit his tongue and stuck his foot out until his toe scraped the ledge. Ice coated the concrete.

"It's too slippery!" he shouted over the wind.

"You can do it. I believe in you."

The sole of his shoe found a slice of concrete devoid of ice. Fieldman stepped down and lost his balance. He teetered forward, arms pinwheeling, the polar gusts stealing his screams and pulling them into the swirling dark. A second before he fell off the skyscraper, he threw himself backward. The small of his back struck the rail. Behind him, the crazy man with the gun laughed.

"It won't work if you panic, Mr. Fieldman. Try again."

On numb hands, he pushed himself to his feet, sore and colder than he'd ever been in his life. At the man's command, he walked to the ledge and faced the opposite corner. He felt like a tightrope walker, but circus performers didn't deal with flurries blowing into their faces at warp speed. His eyes watered; tears crystallized on the lids. He refused to look anywhere but straight forward. The man claimed thirty or forty paces. One step every two seconds, and this nightmare would end a minute from now.

"I admire your determination," the man said. "Every journey begins with the first step. Is that how the saying goes? I forget."

Fieldman took that first step without breathing. He put another hesitant foot forward, wary of the slick patches. By the grace of God, he maintained his balance. Another step. Three down, thirty-seven to go. The flurries thickened into a squall, and he was reminded of the *Star Wars* movies, the constellations rushing forth. A crosswind slammed his shoulder and pushed him precariously close to the edge.

"Almost there!" the man shouted.

He blinked and realized he was halfway home. One more step. Then several without stopping. Far below, car horns honked, as if from another dimension.

"Yes, you're doing great. Keep going."

Fieldman walked. He would win this game as he'd defeated every obstacle in life. Ten more steps at most. He was going to make it.

Until his shoe slid on a patch of ice. He screamed for mercy as his legs flew out from under him. Falling backward, he felt his spine and skull smack against the concrete. His hands grasped for the rail, the edge, for anything that would prevent the unthinkable.

But there was nothing to grab.

He was suddenly aware of gravity and the weight of his body as it toppled off the ledge. Then he was weightless, as light as a feather, flying as the birds did.

Fieldman screamed all the way down.

14

A fter identifying Officer Barrett's body, Thomas returned to the station and filled out paperwork. Someone had murdered the police officer in the most bizarre way possible. He was almost willing to believe Barrett had walked into a wasp nest in a warm location, but how had he ended up in the farmer's field?

He leaned out of his office and spotted Aguilar at her desk.

"You still have informants in Harmon?" he asked.

"Not as many as I used to. Want me to call around?"

"Find out about this 315 Royals rumor. Maybe Barrett knew something about gang activity, and that's what got him killed."

"Where would the Royals find wasps?"

"No idea, but if they're moving narcotics into Harmon, we need to work with the police to stop the trafficking."

The inside of his office stayed warm thanks to a corner space heater. The outdated climate control system was another problem with the ancient building. In the winter, the deputies wore sweatshirts over their uniforms or ran heaters under their desks. During the summer, everyone sweated until the building stank like an onion. They needed a new structure, and fast.

Didn't the county realize how much they would save if the sheriff's department moved into an efficient building?

He printed the documents on the Barrett case. Aguilar knocked on his door.

"My informant says the rumors are all over Harmon. The Royals are taking over the drug trade and planning a massive expansion."

"Any idea what they're pushing?"

"Heroin mostly, but they'll sell anything to rebuild their coffers. Losing Troy Dean crippled them."

"When does their shipment arrive?"

"No word on that yet."

"Keep working with your informants," he said, "and get me a time and place. We have to stop them before they supply the city."

"Will do."

Thomas pinched the bridge of his nose. These gangs caused so many issues. How many people had Harmon lost to heroin addiction? The city couldn't afford another wave. Someone had to know more than Aguilar's snitches. He knew who to call.

Rolling his chair back to the computer, Thomas phoned LeVar. The teenager answered on the first ring. He heard a motor in the background.

"Hey, LeVar. Sounds like I caught you in the car. Want me to call you back?"

"Hold on, Shep Dawg. I'm dropping Scout off at her house."

"Hi, Thomas," Scout called in the background.

"Hi, Scout," he said, waiting for LeVar to return.

The car door closed, then LeVar wheeled into the A-frame's driveway and shut off the engine.

"I'm back, Shep. What can I do for you?"

"Sorry to bring up old memories, LeVar, but I need your help."

"If I can help, I will."

"There's a rumor going around Harmon that the 315 Royals are financing operations through the drug trade," said Thomas. "Word is they're bringing in a huge shipment of narcotics. I need to know when and where."

"Hold up, Shep. Do you really think I'd keep that from you if I knew?"

"No, of course you wouldn't, but maybe you can tell me who's running the show for the Royals. You still have contacts in Harmon, don't you?"

"Nah, man. Those days are over. I want nothing to do with that city's problems."

Thomas paused. He'd never heard LeVar speak negatively about Harmon. Sure, the teenager acknowledged the city's many issues and was happy he'd escaped in time, but he wouldn't speak about Harmon in this fashion unless he was upset.

"I understand, LeVar."

"Do you? Look, I just got back from Kane Grove University with Scout. We toured the campus, and I got a first-hand glimpse of what they will offer me next year. The future is bright, dawg. I need to step away from my past."

Thomas shifted his jaw. "I get it. Listen, I realize you don't stay in contact with any of your old crew mates, but if you hear anything, please let me know. This is important."

"You know I will. Don't misunderstand me, Shep. If you want me on a task force to take these people down, just say the word. I'll be there for you. But other than that, I have to put Harmon behind me. Forever."

"Understood. Talk to you when I get home, okay?"

"Yeah."

LeVar ended the call. Thomas stared at the phone. Had he offended the boy? If LeVar couldn't tell him what was happening inside Harmon, could anyone?

Aguilar stepped into the office.

"Did your informant give you more information?" he asked.

"No, but Harmon PD requests our assistance. A potential suicide in the city."

"I'll grab my coat. What do I need to know?"

"Thomas, a man leaped off the top of the Jefferson Building."

LeVar set his face in his hands. He hadn't meant to snap at Thomas, not after everything the sheriff had done for him. If it wasn't for Thomas, Mom would be dead and he'd still be a part of the Harmon Kings. Unless a rival gang member had killed him. He might sit in a jail cell instead of living in a beautiful guest house with his friends steps away.

But he needed them to stop the Harmon talk. Everyone figured he knew what was happening on those streets, as if he kept in touch with the Kings' crew and laughed about old times over a beer. Gang life should have put him in an early grave. Too many mistakes, too many horrible choices. He tried to imagine a life without Scout, Thomas, Chelsey, and Naomi, a life with his mother six feet under, her memory haunting him like a phantasm. He couldn't.

For the past year and a half, he'd made nothing but the right choices. The less he thought about Harmon, the better. If you passed the graveyard at midnight without looking at it, the monsters couldn't hurt you.

Why did he feel so much guilt? Standing up for himself was important. So was helping your friends when you could. He considered calling Thomas back and apologizing for being short. As always, he'd help the sheriff in any way he could, even if it meant entering Harmon again. He just didn't want people to assume he still had connections there.

As he picked up the phone, a mass of ice and snow rolled off the roof and thundered to the ground. Grabbing his jacket, he rushed outside to inspect the avalanche, hoping the winter weather hadn't damaged the roof. The mound stood waist-high beyond his front door. Getting in and out of the guest house would prove challenging until he removed the pile. He snatched a shovel from the closet. The chill bit his hands, and he wished he'd grabbed gloves on the way out. Not surprisingly, the early-season snowfall was dense and wet. It didn't take long before he worked up a sweat.

Ten minutes later, LeVar jammed the shovel into the snow in triumph, as if placing a flag on conquered territory. He caught his breath and smiled over a job well done. Inside Thomas's house, Jack watched him from the window. He lifted a hand and waved to the dog, then stopped. A slow-moving vehicle coasted down the lake road, its brights casting twin beams through the night. It paused outside the A-frame, then continued.

He might be paranoid, but he swore it was the same SUV he'd spotted twice in his mirrors while he drove Scout home from Kane Grove. Before the vehicle disappeared, LeVar ran to the road, huffing and puffing after struggling through the fresh snowpack.

The glowing taillights were all that remained of the vehicle. LeVar bit off a curse.

Someone was following him.

15

The dark drive along the highway between Wolf Lake and Harmon left Thomas tense and disturbed. The Jefferson Building stood forty-one stories tall and wouldn't impress anyone in Manhattan, but in Harmon it was a behemoth ruling over the city. He couldn't imagine anyone leaping off the top. Even if he wanted to commit suicide, sheer terror would stop him from approaching the edge.

"What do we know about this guy?" Thomas asked Aguilar as he drove.

"Christopher Fieldman is worth well over seven figures. He managed a hundred million dollars in accounts for his clients."

"*That* Fieldman? I've read his name in the newspaper hundreds of times. Why would someone that successful kill himself?"

"Suicide rates are high among the ultrawealthy. More money, more problems."

"But to jump off a building that tall . . . I can't picture approaching the ledge, let alone jumping."

Countless city lights glowed like watchful eyes. Thomas entered the business district, aware that 315 Royals territory began two miles down the road. There was no reason to believe the gang had anything to do with the latest tragedy, but they claimed more real estate every month, spreading like a blight.

He parked along the curb behind four Harmon PD cruisers with swirling lights. An ambulance was here as well, but the paramedics had nothing to do. Nobody survived a fall from forty-one stories. Staring up at the Jefferson Building made him dizzy. He couldn't see the top; low-hanging clouds that spat flurries and the occasional snow burst cloaked the roof. The wind almost took his hat, forcing him to hold on with both hands as he lowered his head against the chill.

Chief Pauley greeted them on the sidewalk.

"We meet again," the chief said. "As unsettling as this afternoon's discovery was, this one takes the cake."

"When did this happen?" Thomas asked, walking between Pauley and Aguilar.

"Forty-five minutes ago. Fieldman came within five feet of landing on a woman pushing a baby carriage."

"Good God."

He couldn't pull his gaze from the macabre splatter of red covering the concrete, the mailbox, and the lower portion of the building. Yellow police tape cordoned off the concrete where Fieldman had struck the sidewalk.

"Tell me about it."

"Is there any chance this was an accident? Perhaps he went out to the roof and the wind blew him off. It's gusting hard enough."

"That was my thought too. I mean, who summons the courage to jump off a skyscraper? I hear about people doing it in the big cities but never figured something like this could happen in Harmon. My officers found a suicide note on the guy's desk."

"Can we see the note?" Aguilar asked.

"Absolutely. I'll take you upstairs."

The three officers stepped inside the elevator. Though they rose at impressive speeds, it took two minutes to reach the top floor. The doors opened to a luxurious entrance that read, "Fieldman Enterprises." Two officers dusted for prints and searched for evidence.

"Sheriff Shepherd and Deputy Aguilar, meet Officers Brentwood and Knowles. They're leading the investigation."

Thomas touched the rim of his hat. "Pleased to meet you. Find anything interesting?"

"Fingerprints everywhere," said Brentwood, "but they surely belong to Fieldman and his secretary."

"Where was the secretary when Fieldman committed suicide?" Aguilar asked.

"In the john," said Pauley. "Guess she hides in there to avoid Fieldman while she messages her friends. We interviewed her. She missed the entire event. Brentwood sent her home ten minutes ago."

"I'd like to read the note," Thomas said.

"Of course. Officer Knowles found the letter on Fieldman's desk."

"Fieldman was married, right?"

"Yes, and we're notifying the wife now."

Chief Pauley stood aside as the two officers sought clues that would tell them why Fieldman had jumped, and if the death was a murder instead of a suicide.

Wearing gloves, Thomas and Aguilar leaned over the note and read. It seemed straightforward. Succumbing to the pressures of staying on top, Fieldman had killed himself rather than face an uncertain future. Yet something didn't seem right.

He pointed at the paper. "Fieldman seems almost casual in the letter."

"He does," said Aguilar. "I suppose if he decided ahead of time, he was resigned to the decision."

"Something else bothers me. I can't figure out what it is."

Aguilar poked her tongue against the inside of her cheek. "Huh."

"What do you see?"

"Why would Fieldman print his suicide note, then sign it in sloppy cursive, as though he couldn't be bothered?"

"That's a little strange. Maybe he just wanted to get it over with."

Aguilar spied a printer beside the secretary's desk. "Now I'm curious. Can we send a document to the printer?"

Pauley raised his palms. "Don't see why not."

Thomas typed on the businessman's keyboard and opened a two-page document on the Nightshade County website. After two clicks of the mouse, he sent it to the printer. Aguilar pulled off the pages and set them next to the suicide note.

"These came from different printers," she said. "The paper is different too. Notice the suicide note: cheap, thin paper, the kind you grab off the bargain rack at the office supply store." Aguilar jabbed a finger at the new documents. "This is thick, high-quality stock. Fieldman Enterprises paid a pretty penny for these sheets."

The chief leaned over their shoulders. "I see what you mean."

"Could be Fieldman printed the letter at home and brought it in."

Thomas glanced from Aguilar to Pauley. "We need to find where he printed the note."

16

"I hate these visits," Aguilar said as Thomas drove across the village.

He agreed. Harmon PD had notified Bernadette Fieldman about her husband's death, but now they needed to ask the widow difficult questions in her time of strife. She should be grieving and surrounded by family, not explaining why her successful husband leaped off the Jefferson Building.

"Keep in mind she may not be thinking straight," he said. "We'll take it slow with her. It makes no sense. I remember what you said about too much success creating too many problems, but Christopher Fieldman ruled the city. Every business he formed became a dominant force, and he gave millions to charity."

"He must have had skeletons in the closet. Otherwise, I can't explain the suicide either."

As the cruiser slowed to a stop, he wanted to drive around the block another time and delay the inevitable. Lights glowed inside every window of the brown-brick mansion. A gate blocked access to the driveway. Aguilar followed him to the gate and pressed the speaker button. After they announced their presence, the door swung aside.

The polar wind whipped snow and ice into Thomas's face as he climbed the steps. The front door stood open, and a brown-haired woman in her thirties waited in the entryway. Bernadette Fieldman looked young enough to cheer for the local college. Jagged nails suggested the woman had bitten them since learning of her husband's suicide.

"Mrs. Fieldman, I'm Sheriff Thomas Shepherd, and this is Deputy Veronica Aguilar. We're very sorry for your loss."

She sniffled.

"Please, come in."

Thomas stomped the snow off his boots on the entryway mat.

"Don't worry about the snow," the woman said. "It doesn't matter. Nothing matters anymore." They followed her into a sitting room with a crackling fireplace. Genuine wood, not the gas-powered type. An older woman with a shock of white hair sat beside the fire with a glass of bourbon in her hand. "This is my mother, Francene." She turned to her mother. "The sheriff is here."

Distraught, the older woman simply nodded and gazed down at her drink, as though the mystery of what had happened lay at the bottom of the glass.

"Sit," Bernadette said. "May I get you something to eat or drink? Mom is warming up lasagna."

"That's all right," Thomas said, taking a seat beside Aguilar on a cream-colored couch. He was reminded of his mother's furniture and worried about leaving dirt or water stains on the cushions. "Mrs. Fieldman, did your husband act strangely over the last few weeks?"

"Not at all."

"Was he under added pressure at work?"

"No more than usual. Christopher always had his hand in a new venture. His motto was, *if you're standing still, you're moving backward*. But the pressure wasn't so much that he would . . ." She raked a tissue across her eyes and straightened her shoulders. "Christopher would never kill himself."

She was so sure that Thomas shared a look with Aguilar. Perhaps the woman was deluding herself—such was often the case when a person encountered shocking news—but it was clear she refused to believe otherwise.

"What about medications?" Aguilar asked. "Did your husband begin a new prescription in recent months?"

"No, and he wasn't on antidepressants. The only pill my husband took was a multivitamin every morning."

When Bernadette started crying again, Thomas handed her a box of tissues. Something about the investigation didn't sit right with him. By all accounts, Christopher Fieldman had killed himself. The businessman had even left a suicide note on the table. Thomas kept a copy in his folder.

"Mrs. Fieldman," he said, "I realize this is a terribly difficult time for you, but would you be willing to read your husband's note and tell me if it seems peculiar?"

"Oh, dear God. The police told me Christopher left a suicide note, but it just isn't possible."

"You don't have to read it," Bernadette's mother said from beside the fireplace.

"That's true," said Thomas. "The last thing I want is to further upset you."

Bernadette shot a stiff arm outward and opened her hand. "Give it to me?"

"Are you certain?"

"Yes. I want to read this so-called suicide note." The woman held the paper face down and released another wave of sobs. Then she steeled herself and turned the letter over. Her face morphed from injured desperation to incredulity. "My husband didn't write this."

"How can you be sure?"

"He's more . . . refined than this. Some of the wording . . . I never heard Christopher speak like this."

"But that's his signature, is it not?"

She studied the scribbled name. "Yes, I believe so."

Aguilar gave Thomas a confused glance.

"I'm not an education snob," Bernadette said. "My husband was, but that's another story. Christopher attended Princeton and graduated with honors, and whenever he spoke, he wanted you to know it. He would never talk like this, let alone sign his name to a document worded so poorly. This letter reads like it was written by a high school dropout."

"Are there any other reasons you feel your husband didn't write the letter?"

"For certain. Christopher was petrified of heights. His phobia dated back to when he was a child and fell out of a tree. I'm not talking about a minor fear—it would scare anyone to stand on top of a building—but Christopher couldn't enjoy rollercoasters or Ferris wheels. We rode bicycles last summer, and he refused to cross the overpass. It couldn't have been more than twenty feet to the ground, and there was a fence that prevented people from falling."

"Mrs. Fieldman," Aguilar said. "Do you keep a printer in your home?"

"Why, yes, I do."

"Are you willing to print a document for us?"

"What sort of document?"

"Anything will do. There's something I need to confirm."

An uncomfortable silence settled over the room while Bernadette logged on to a computer down the corridor. The woman's mother sipped her bourbon, lost in thought. Aguilar and Thomas whispered back and forth.

"What do you think?" the deputy asked.

"It doesn't add up. Acrophobia affects many, but it sounds as if Christopher Fieldman's fears were debilitating. How he worked in the Jefferson Building, I'll never understand. Still, a thick pane of glass kept him safe, and he could have pulled the curtain to block the view. Even if he became suicidal, I can't picture him overcoming his fears and jumping off a skyscraper."

"I can't help but believe he—"

Aguilar stopped talking when Bernadette returned with three printed sheets. The woman handed the pages to the deputy. Thomas knew the stock didn't match the paper used in the suicide note.

"This is high-quality stock," Aguilar said. "If I'm not mistaken, it's the same paper used at Fieldman Enterprises."

"Yes, that's correct," Bernadette said. "My husband never stopped working and often brought tasks home with him. If he needed a document printed, he used the same paper at home as he did at the office."

A few possibilities lingered in Thomas's head. Fieldman might have printed the letter elsewhere. A library or copy center, perhaps. But why? He owned state-of-the-art printers at home and at Fieldman Enterprises.

"Was the letter printed on the same paper?" asked Bernadette.

"No," he said.

"That proves my husband didn't commit suicide."

"Mrs. Fieldman, did anyone know about your husband's fear of heights?"

"Sure. Everyone did. His family and friends knew, and the entire city found out after that newspaper reporter printed the story. That angered Christopher to no end."

"Which newspaper?"

"*The Bluewater Tribune.* Christopher talked about suing the reporter and his therapist."

"How can you be certain the therapist leaked the information to the press?"

"Because our family wouldn't treat Christopher that way, and he kept a close-knit circle of friends."

They finished interviewing Bernadette Fieldman and left the house with new questions. Had someone learned about the husband's fear of heights and murdered him in the most terrifying way possible?

17

S cout couldn't wait for the school day to end. The soup kitchen didn't need her today, which meant she could walk to the village center and work with Chelsey and Raven until dinnertime. After yesterday's trip to Kane Grove University, the high school seemed so much smaller than she'd remembered. Would her mother allow her to double up on her studies and graduate a semester early? College seemed like a dream world with endless possibilities.

Snow covered the walkways, slowing her down as she huddled against the elements. The temperature wasn't as frigid as yesterday, and the wind had died down. As was rare this time of year, the sun shone from a crystal-blue sky that raised her spirits even more.

She arrived at the private investigation firm at 3:35.

"There's the future university girl," Raven said when Scout entered the office. "How was school?"

"Long."

"I'll bet. You're excited about college. Don't rush to the finish line. Senior year in high school can be a ton of fun."

Not as fun as scheduling class times, learning new techniques to apply to her career, and hanging out with friends at student lounges. She'd miss her mother, but if she stayed close to home, she could visit whenever she pleased.

And intern with Wolf Lake Consulting. That was another perk of choosing Kane Grove.

Chelsey entered the office carrying a mug of tea. "You look cold. Can I make you something hot to drink?"

"I can make it," Scout said. "Even Mom and Ms. Hopkins trust me to heat water in a kettle."

Raven laughed. "Except my mother won't let you near the stove when she's baking with your mom."

"True."

"Ready for a new investigation?" Chelsey asked.

"Always."

"Well, this is one even the legendary Scout Mourning can't solve."

"Ooh, a challenge. I love challenges."

"Wait until you see the specs." Chelsey waved Scout over to her desk. Raven stood behind them. "We're investigating the death of Officer Shawn Barrett with the Harmon PD."

Scout nodded. A tingle of nervous excitement shot through her chest. Investigating a police officer's death was a humongous responsibility.

"Now, get this: A farmer outside the village discovered the officer in his field yesterday. Barrett was covered in wasp stings, hundreds of them. The medical examiner confirmed the wasp attack."

"Wasp attack? I realize the calendar says it's not winter, but please. I haven't seen a stinging insect since school began."

"Like I said, this is a challenging case. So far, the police haven't figured out how Barrett got to the field or where the wasp attack occurred."

"Heated barn?"

"We thought of that possibility, but no. The barn in question is unheated and wide open. You could freeze a turkey inside and it would stay fresh until Thanksgiving." Chelsey grinned. "Stumped you, didn't we?"

Scout paced back and forth with her thumb and forefinger pinching her chin.

"Not necessarily. Let's assume someone murdered Officer Barrett and dumped him in the farmer's field."

"That's a safe assumption," Raven said. "But where did our theoretical killer find so many wasps?"

"On the internet. You can buy anything online."

"She's right," Raven said.

Chelsey's mouth hung open.

"We're looking for someone who purchased a few dozen wasps over the internet," Scout said. "I say a few dozen because there were a hundred or more stings on the body and wasps sting multiple times."

"You can buy live wasps?" Chelsey asked.

"Certainly. Check out a science catalog. They can't be easy to ship since they grow sluggish or die in cold temperatures. Plus, the post office and major delivery companies might balk. A few dozen wasps in a box could prove dangerous. Was Officer Barrett allergic?"

"Deathly so," Raven said. She pressed her lips together, regretting her words.

"That might be our way to find the killer," Chelsey said. "I'll put the two of you in charge of calling around. Check with every post office and delivery company within fifty miles. If someone ordered live wasps, they should remember."

Scout joined Raven at her desk and grinned to herself. This was a difficult case, but she loved a challenge.

18

U nable to reach Scout after school, LeVar finished his studies and slipped into jogging pants and a light sweatshirt. Using his paycheck from the sheriff's department, he'd purchased a pair of waterproof hiking and running shoes. The treads would cut through the three-inch snow depth without issue.

He locked his phone in an arm patch and donned ear buds. The same old-school hip-hop playlist he'd enjoyed on the way home from Kane Grove energized him for his workout session. Jogging without company made him lonely, but he wanted time alone with his thoughts. Did a responsible person turn his back on his past?

Sure. When your past carried nothing but strife, regrets, and terrible decisions, moving on was a form of self-preservation.

He stepped into the cool outdoors and ran. The first five minutes were always the toughest. He struggled to maintain his pace, and his lungs tried to convince him to go home and rest on the couch. After he passed the five-minute mark, his heart rate adapted. Now he ran without effort, despite the snow under his sneakers. The treads proved up to the task, and soon he was climbing the hill that led from the lakeshore to the state park.

To either side of the trail, shrubs and pricker bushes sagged under the weight of the snow. His breath puffed out clouds.

For a moment, he swore something moved in the woods. He thought about bears again. Glancing around, he only saw the forest. The jog challenged him during the spring and summer, and pushing through the snow made the workout seem like a marathon.

Soon, the ranger's cabin would come into view. Raven was at work, which meant no free hot chocolate awaited him. He continued, hoping Darren would be at the cabin. Darren was always good for fun conversation, and sometimes the ranger put him to work stacking firewood or cleaning debris off the trails. The more time LeVar spent in nature, the more he appreciated its beauty and wondered how he'd survived living in Harmon.

A half mile from the peak, his pace slowed. Even in his new sneakers, he bogged down in the snow yet refused to stop and catch his breath. Not until he climbed the hill. He knew a lot about goal setting and self-development. Stopping would implant failure in his brain, and he'd be more likely to quit next time. So he soldiered on, perspiring despite the chill, his breaths growing shorter.

The crunch of boots on ice pulled his eyes to the forest. He muted the music, expecting to find Darren among the trees. Instead, he saw only long shadows.

"Hello? Someone out there? That you, Darren?"

It might be a hiker walking off the trail. Doing so would get you kicked out of the park if the ranger caught you. His lips curled into a smile.

"Okay, Scout. Quit screwing around. I know it's you."

She was the most likely suspect. The girl loved to pull

pranks, and it would be just like her to hide in the woods and jump out to scare him. But how had she beaten him to the top?

"Scout?"

No reply.

The quiet gave him the creeps. He started up the trail again, hurrying to reach the cabins in case an animal was following him. A silhouetted figure stepped onto the trail and blocked his path.

With the sun in his eyes, he couldn't make out who the person was. The male on the path was too stocky to be Darren, and he wore a winter jacket with the hood pulled over his head, shielding his eyes.

LeVar remembered the SUV following him yesterday, the same vehicle that had coasted past his house after dark.

"Can I help you?"

Unmoving, the figure stared.

"Yo, if you're lost, I'll show you the way back to the cabins."

"You're the one who's lost, LeVar."

That voice. He recognized it. A ghost from his past, the figure stepped into the sunlight. LeVar made out the face and gasped.

"CJ? What the hell are you doing here?"

"Had to go to extreme measures to get your attention. You're a hard person to track down, bro, but I know where you live."

CJ had been a member of the Harmon Kings, and rumor had it he had been furious with LeVar for walking out on them. The gangster kept his hands in his pockets, and LeVar imagined a hidden gun.

"What do you want with me, CJ?"

"Time to repay your debt."

Debt? LeVar took three steps forward and stopped. He stood on alert, and CJ seemed just as cautious. Each was capable of killing the other in a heartbeat, so they stared at one another, like Cold War presidents with fingers poised over the nuclear launch buttons. They'd been friends during the glory days of the Harmon Kings. People changed, and blood was thicker than water. Like the other members, CJ saw LeVar as a traitor. It didn't help that he'd crossed over to the dark side of law enforcement. The police had always been a common enemy for the gang, along with the 315 Royals.

"It doesn't need to go down like this, CJ."

Another step forward. LeVar wished he'd brought his service weapon. In a fair fight, he could match the gangster, but if CJ pulled a weapon . . .

"What's the matter, bro? You shook? Bet you didn't plan on seeing me again. You been ghosting us for a minute."

"Not ghosting you. I bettered my life."

CJ closed the distance between them, and the fiery rage in his eyes made LeVar flinch.

"You abandoned your brothers when we needed you most."

The gangster pulled one hand from his pocket. LeVar's eyes widened. No gun. Not this time. What did CJ hide in the other pocket?

"You owe us," CJ said, poking a finger against LeVar's chest.

"Better remove that finger right now, CJ."

"Or what? You flexin'? If you're feeling froggy, jump."

"This ain't pretend. I know you been following me. That your SUV, bro?"

"What if it is?"

LeVar stood taller. "You mess with me or my friend, and I'll end you."

"Look, ma. The gangster is back. Who's the snow bunny?"

"That's an offensive term. You talk about Scout like that, and we'll have problems."

"Bro, we already have problems. They started the second you walked. So who is this Scout?"

"A friend."

"A friend," CJ mocked in falsetto. "Not even datin' a proper black girl. Hanging around all these white folks in their fancy homes done made you soft."

"Better than risking my life with the Kings. I picked the right time to step away."

"You think Rev was my boy? I wanted that psycho dead just as much as you did. Don't look at me that way. You woulda offed Rev in a second. But like I said, you soft now."

"Test me and you'll learn the hard way. I ain't soft, CJ. You should know that better than anyone."

"Prove it."

"Take your hand out of your pocket, and I'll be happy to."

"Oh, you think I'm packing?" The gangster laughed without mirth. "I don't need a gun to end you, my brother. Never have, never will."

CJ pulled the hand from his pocket. LeVar searched for a bulge in the bulky coat.

"So that's it, is it? We're gonna throw down? I never wanted things to come between us, but you won't let go."

"You're right. I won't let go," said CJ. "I'm not like you. Harmon is my home, not this damn lake."

"Take your best shot. But I'll warn you. Finish the job with one punch, or I'll knock you into next week."

"I came to fight, LeVar, but not with you. Not unless you leave me no choice."

"Stop talking in circles and tell me why you're blocking my way."

The gangster glanced around as if worried someone was listening.

"It's the Royals. They're hanging by a thread, but they won't be for long."

"I don't care about the—"

"Shut your mouth and listen. You always talked too much. Ever since Dean went to prison, they been digging for someone to lead the way. But they broke, LeVar. Out of money. And that means out of ammo."

"Yeah? Word has it they're taking over the drug trade."

"So you *do* keep up with your hometown. Maybe there's hope for my brother after all. They need that green if they want to regain power. And they need a strong leader."

"You volunteering or something, CJ?"

The gangster spat. "Not on my mother's grave would I run with those racist pigs."

"What does this have to do with me?"

"Now's the time to strike and take the Royals out. Once and for all."

An incredulous look came over LeVar's face.

"Are you out of your godforsaken mind? I'm a sheriff's deputy. I can't jump into a gang war."

"Do it for the Kings, LeVar."

"The Kings are dead."

"And whose fault is that? If you won't do it for your family—"

"You ain't my family anymore."

"Then do it for Harmon."

LeVar stuck his hands in his pockets and turned away.

"There you go," said CJ. "Turning your back on your true family again."

"I want the Royals gone just as much as you do."

CJ rounded on him.

"Then do something about it. Stop the Uncle Tom act and come home."

"Don't call me that."

"Ain't it true?" CJ scoffed. "Look at you, living beside the water without a care in the world. Pathetic. If you don't end the Royals, you'll regret your decision."

"Is that a threat?"

"I'm not threatening you, my brother. Just trying to wake you up."

19

Wolf Lake Consulting closed its doors at six o'clock, and the amateur investigators club held its first meeting in two weeks at the ranger's cabin. LeVar helped his sister carry the pizzas from her SUV, their heads lowered as flurries fell through the darkness.

Stepping into the cabin felt wonderful. The sweet scent of the woodstove permeated the interior, and the home was warm enough for shorts and a T-shirt. He considered his decision to attend Kane Grove University and felt surer than ever. Leaving would mean no more amateur investigation meetings, and he couldn't do without the fun.

Darren stoked the flames and tossed a log into the stove. Scout joined LeVar in setting out paper plates. After everyone grabbed food, they convened around the coffee table, Scout and LeVar on the couch, Darren and Raven facing them in chairs.

"What I don't understand is why all of you keep banging on LeVar for bettering his life," Darren said in between bites.

LeVar lifted his chin. "Yeah. Enough already. I ain't your punching bag."

"Nobody is banging on LeVar," Raven said. "All we're saying

is he can have his new life and still hold his head high about where he came from."

"What do I have to be proud of, sis? In what parallel universe is joining a gang a source of pride?"

"Is that all Harmon means to you, boy? You had friends outside the gang."

"None I spent time with after school let out."

"And you loved the city. I remember how excited you got when the Christmas decorations went up after Thanksgiving. Ma would walk you to the center of Harmon so you could point and gawk at the lights. Hell, you met Santa Claus."

"That wasn't Santa."

"How do you know it wasn't?"

"Sis, everyone knows Santa is black, and that dude was ivory white."

Darren rolled his eyes. Scout dropped her face into her hands and shook her head.

"Anyhow, I don't hate Harmon," said LeVar. "The city doesn't embarrass me. I made too many poor choices there, and I can't risk what might happen if I go back."

"He's right," Darren said. "Would you tell an alcoholic it was cool to hang out with his buddies at a bar, even if he promised not to drink?"

"He doesn't have to hang out in Harmon," Raven said, flipping the beaded hair over her shoulder. "All Scout and I want is for LeVar to remember the good, not just the bad. There's a silver lining in every cloud."

"Not according to my meteorology professor," LeVar said, drawing laughter.

"Are you still defending those forecasters? I'd sooner listen to a fortune teller."

"What? Accuracy improves every decade, and the two-day forecast is better than ninety-five percent dependable."

Raven cocked a thumb at her brother. "Listen to Bill Nye, the Science Guy over here." She turned to him. "You can love Harmon and still have everything you've earned the last year and a half."

LeVar lowered his head. "The ghosts of my past won't let me sleep, anyhow." They glanced at him in a question. He blew out a breath. "My boy CJ found me this afternoon."

"Who's CJ?" asked Scout.

"Just a kid I ran with in the Kings."

Darren leaned forward with his elbows on his knees. "He didn't start anything with you, did he?"

"Dude wants to draw me back into gang life."

"See?" Darren looked at the others. "I was right. LeVar knows what he's doing by severing his past."

Raven lowered her voice. "What did he want?"

"The Kings are no longer, but there are enough members scattered around that they want to hit the Royals one last time."

"Don't you dare," Darren said.

"Bro, as if I would. That life is behind me. For some, the war with the Royals never ends."

"I'm sorry," Raven said. "I didn't know."

"Me neither," said Scout, rubbing his shoulder. "But like Raven told you, there was more to Harmon than your time with the Kings."

"But it ain't the mayor waiting for me with open arms. The Kings wait at the gates, and they want their boy back."

Darren snapped his fingers. "I say we investigate CJ and find out what his intentions are."

"Nah, man. Leave CJ be."

"Are you sure? It pays to know what you're up against."

"CJ was my dawg. I can't do him like that."

"All right," Raven said. "So we won't look into CJ. Do we plan to eat pizza all night, or should we begin the meeting?"

"Are we waiting for Chelsey?"

"She's spending the evening with Thomas. Wedding planning."

"More pizza for me then."

"LeVar," Raven said, raising her voice.

"All right, I'll leave you a slice."

"I vote that we begin and eat at the same time," said Scout, "before LeVar goes through both pizzas."

"All in favor say aye," said Darren.

They all agreed.

"If we're not taking on a new investigation," Raven said, "we should concentrate on the Barrett case. With WLC, the sheriff's department, and Harmon PD all searching for evidence, this is one we can solve if we share information. Darren, what can you tell us about the Harmon PD?"

The state park ranger chewed over his words for a moment. "There were problems with the Harmon PD back when I patrolled in Syracuse."

Scout turned her head toward Darren. "What kinds of problems?"

"Whispers of corruption. There's a long-standing rumor that a few officers accepted payola from the gangs to look the other way."

"From the 315 Royals?"

"And the Kings." Darren glanced at LeVar. "Sorry."

"Nothing I didn't hear about back in the day," said LeVar. "But that's all I can say about it. If any cops took money from the Kings, I wasn't in on the transaction."

"Scout and I researched websites where you can purchase live wasps," Raven said. "We also called a bunch of post offices and package delivery services in the area. Nobody recalled transporting wasps, but we still have three quarters of the list to work through."

"You can buy wasps on the internet?"

"Oh, yeah," Scout said. "You can buy just about any insect from a science supply company."

"Weird." He lifted his chin at Darren. "Ever hear corruption rumors about Officer Shawn Barrett?"

"Never," Darren said. "I'm not saying everything was on the up and up, but never did anyone mention Barrett taking payola."

"We always knew there were dirty cops in Harmon, but it still sucks to hear it."

"Nothing was ever proven. As I said, it was all rumor. The bigger question is how someone imported a few dozen wasps and killed a police officer."

"The person who did it knew Officer Barrett was allergic," Scout said. "People survive swarmings if they get medical treatment in time. The killer trapped Barrett, unleashed the wasps, and waited for the officer to die before he dumped him in the country."

"What a horrible way to die," Raven said, staring at her sneaker.

"Bet," LeVar said. "We'll track the evidence and find the lunatic who did this."

"One problem. Not every science supply website agreed to help us. Customer confidentiality. Without a warrant, a lot of these places won't help."

"You'd think they would," said Scout. "It looks bad for them if people are using their website to kill people."

"I'll bring it up to Shep," said LeVar. "He can pull strings we can't."

Raven nodded. "In the meantime, Scout and I will visit area zoos and entomologists."

"Where will you find an entomologist?" Darren asked.

"Universities. Kane Grove has a program, and I'm sure Scout doesn't need an excuse to visit the campus again."

"Can't wait," Scout said.

"LeVar, are you willing to work with Harmon PD if it comes to it?"

"Yeah, I can do that," he said. "We're on the same side now."

But if the 315 Royals were responsible for killing Officer Barrett, LeVar worried he'd get caught between three warring armies—the police, the Royals, and what remained of CJ's Kings.

20

S aturday morning dawned gray and icy. The wind slithered through the man's jacket as he stuffed the plastic sheeting into black garbage bags. After he finished, he vacuumed and dusted the room, wiping down every surface Officer Barrett might have touched. Then he tore up the carpet the dead man had lain on and dragged it out to his truck.

He stuffed the bags and rug into the bed. Closing the gate, he fired the engine and drove to the county dump. As long as you paid a fee, nobody checked the contents of your garbage. With the cold chewing on his extremities, the man tossed the bags into the center of the pile, where they blended with the detritus and became part of an unsolvable puzzle. He dropped the rug into the stinking, festering pit and brushed off his hands.

At the exit, he paid his five dollars and drove off. A small price to rid himself of the evidence. The connecting plastic sheets had cost the most, and it seemed a waste to spend so much money for twenty-four hours of use. But at least that bastard was dead. Good riddance, Barrett.

When he entered Harmon, he grabbed breakfast at the diner. Greasy eggs, bacon, home fries, and buttered toast. The breakfast of champions. The food left him satiated, yet there was so much work to be done. An endless supply of enemies awaited his wrath.

The events of the last week made him want to clear his head. Instead of driving home, he stopped at the city park and strolled around the perimeter. Only a few brave souls joined him on his trek. Most people were gutless and refused to exercise when the temperature dropped into the thirties. They didn't experience life the way he did. All his adult years, he'd been a difference maker, and yet so many fought him tooth and nail. Did they think he wouldn't seek revenge?

He walked with sunglasses covering his eyes and his hands in his pockets. The black frames shielded his eyes from the wind and made him difficult to identify. Not that he was doing anything wrong, but people always caused him problems.

After three laps, he became bored. Playground equipment grew out of the snow. Three children ran among the swings and climbed up and down steps that led to a wooden fort. A boy reached the top and leaped off, not needing to ride the slide down. Brave child. Unlike Christopher Fieldman. That chicken-shit would have soiled himself standing five feet off the ground.

The man chuckled and settled on a metal bench that held November's breath. Extending his legs, he stretched and crossed them at the ankles, wiggling his feet as he enjoyed the morning. He recalled his childhood swing set and playing on it until the bars grew too rusty to support his weight.

Even in his early years, he'd understood his power. He was the largest boy in the neighborhood. Not fat nor muscular. Country strong, his mother had called him. When another boy was on the park's playground equipment and he wanted to use it, he shoved the other kid off and dared him to do something about it. He ruled the playground, the schoolyard, and the class-room. Nobody messed with him, not until a high school teacher called him out for bullying. The bitch sent a letter to his mother, and the principal stepped in, threatening suspensions if he didn't reform his ways. Both the teacher and principal found their tires flat a week later. They knew he'd done the deed, but could they prove it? He was too smart to get caught.

In his junior year, he'd flunked the mathematics final. His teacher paid the price that summer. On the way home, he detoured to the teacher's house, which he'd looked up in the phone book, and hurled a rock through the window. That's what everyone got for telling him he wasn't good enough for their ridiculous standards.

He yawned and imagined ruling over this playground. Twenty-five years ago, he would have.

As he huddled inside his coat, a bald man watching the children play walked toward him. Now what in the hell did this jerk want?

"Can I help you?" he asked without acknowledging the man with a glance.

"Yeah," baldy said. "You're staring at my kids."

"Just enjoying the morning."

"There are reports of a weird guy creeping around the park and watching children."

He chuckled. "Well, it's not me."

"But I saw you looking at my boy and girls."

Sick of the direction the conversation had taken, he stood. Baldy suddenly realized the stranger in the park outstripped him by six inches. Though he kept himself in shape, he was a runt in the stranger's shadow.

"Are you calling me a child molester?"

He shoved Baldy by the shoulder. The children stopped to watch, their mouths hanging open. Their father wasn't Superman, and they saw that now. He was going to get himself hurt by opening his mouth.

"I, uh, never suggested you were. Hey, we just had a misunderstanding. All I'm doing is protecting my children. You can't be too careful these days."

The man leaned forward so only Baldy could hear and whispered, "You know what you are? You're a pussy."

The father gulped. "I don't want trouble."

"Then you shouldn't start trouble."

"D-don't push me, all right?"

"You mean like this?" He shoved the smaller man and knocked him back a step. "How would you like me to kick your teeth in while your precious kids watch? Want me to make them scream, '*Daddy, Daddy, please don't die*'?"

"Hey, uh, this doesn't need to get physical. We're grown adults."

The man snickered. "From my point of view, I'm the only grown adult in the park."

"If. . . if you hit me, I'll call the police."

Now the bully stared straight down at his adversary. "Go ahead and call the police. I double-dare you. Because if you do, I'll find where you live and beat the life out of you in front of your wife and kids. They'll see me in their nightmares after your funeral. Sound like a plan?"

The runt turned and ran back to his children. Casting wild-eyed glances over his shoulder, he rustled them into a minivan parked near the entrance.

Following, the man slipped into his truck and turned onto the road. He kept the minivan in his sights, staying two blocks behind so the father didn't see. Five minutes of driving later, the man coasted past a prissy suburban home with a snowman in the yard and the minivan in the driveway. He memorized the address.

Before he pulled away, he caught someone jerking the curtain shut. Good. The punk understood his place in life.

The stranger hadn't decided what to do. Should he bang on the door and tell the wife her gutless husband had given him the finger and driven off like a coward? Or should he be truthful? When someone disrespected him, they deserved payback.

It was then he noticed a face peeking between the curtains. The little boy who'd climbed on the playground equipment. The child's eyes held the true meaning of fear. He understood who his father was—not larger than life, but a small man who couldn't defend his children.

All he had to do was walk to the door, yank the bald man into the yard, and beat him senseless. Show the punk what happened to anyone who got in his way.

The man grinned and winked at the boy, then slid a finger across his throat like a faux knife.

The gesture said, *I'll come back later*.

He drove away.

21

Returning from Kane Grove University, Raven drove along the highway with Scout in the passenger's seat. She'd never seen the teen so enthusiastic. Walking through the college and speaking with professors had given the girl a new perspective on her future. Unfortunately, they'd struck out talking to the entomologist. The professor appeared stumped when Raven asked about a wasp attack in late November. The man agreed with her: The only explanation was that the attack had occurred indoors. After the first frost, he rarely saw hornets or wasps, and those he encountered were usually inside his house and hiding from the cold. After the snow fell, you didn't expect to see another stinging insect until spring.

"I hoped the professor could shed light on the investigation," Raven said, "but it appears we're nowhere closer to untangling this knot than we were before."

Scout adjusted the seatbelt. "It's still possible the killer ordered the wasps and had them delivered. How long will it take to call the rest of the companies?"

"If we hustle, we'll finish by late afternoon. Tell you what.

When we get back to the office, let's split the list. You take half, I'll take the other."

"Deal."

When they arrived at Wolf Lake Consulting, Chelsey was sitting across the kitchen table from Officer Barrett's wife. Trix Barrett rose as Raven and Scout entered.

"These are two of my partners," Chelsey said. "You've met Raven Hopkins, and this is Scout Mourning. Scout is a high school intern, but don't let her age fool you. She's one of my most valued investigators."

"And I'm chopped liver," Raven said.

The self-deprecation made Trix laugh, and Raven wondered if this was the first time the widow had smiled since her husband went missing.

"Hardly. Raven is as fine an investigator as you'll ever encounter."

"I'm very sorry for your loss, Mrs. Barrett."

"Thank you, and please call me Trix," the woman said.

"As I told Trix," said Chelsey, "Wolf Lake Consulting is prepared to return her money."

Trix held up a hand. "I won't have that. You support the justice system, just as Shawn did. You found him. Now I want you to tell me who did this to him."

Raven took Trix's hand and sat her down. "Are you positive this was homicide?"

"There's no doubt in my mind."

As Scout leaned against the counter and observed, Chelsey asked, "Who knew about your husband's allergy?"

"Plenty of people."

"His fellow officers?"

"Of course. Chief Pauley required every officer to train using an EpiPen. Shawn carried his own from March until October, but why would he need it now?"

"What about Wilson Manfredini?" Raven asked. "Did he know about your husband's allergy?"

"I suppose it's possible, but I couldn't guess how. All our neighbors were aware, along with Shawn's friends and family."

"Did Shawn have issues with a neighbor?"

"Heavens no. We live in a supportive community, and everyone loved having a police officer in the neighborhood. Made them feel secure."

Chelsey set a hand on Trix's arm. "I want you to understand this will become uncomfortable. If you want us to move forward, everyone Shawn knew will be a suspect."

Trix lifted her head. "Nothing could be more uncomfortable than facing how Shawn died. I'm prepared."

"As you wish. We'll continue with the investigation."

As Chelsey led Trix to the door, Raven noticed the discomfort on Scout's face. Investigating mysteries put the teenager on a permanent high, but the girl rarely encountered victims and saw their pain firsthand.

"Don't let it get you down, Scout," she said. "That's the reality of what we do. If you want to work in law enforcement, you'll have to face the dark side."

"How do you stop it from getting to you?"

"We don't, and nobody gets used to it. But it drives me to catch criminals so they never kill again."

While Chelsey worked at her computer, Raven and Scout sat at their desks and called every post office and delivery company on the list. When the clock rolled past two, she crossed off the last number and threw up her hands.

"Total strikeout," she said. Scout set her pen down and nodded in agreement.

They'd called everyone, and nobody remembered transporting live wasps. Most of the people thought she was crazy for asking. Who ordered stinging insects?

"I suppose it's possible the killer ordered the wasps using a delivery company outside the county," said Scout.

"We can't contact every company in the state."

The teenager rocked in her chair. "What if the killer planned the attack ahead of time and collected a nest over the summer?"

"Is that feasible?"

"He'd need to know how to care for the wasps and keep them alive. That would require a large tank, ventilation, and a way to contain the wasps so they didn't sting him."

"Then we're looking for Dr. Doolittle."

"I have an idea," Chelsey said.

"Let's hear it."

"Scout, can you open Photoshop and create a fake business card?"

"Yeah, sure," Scout said. "What do you need?"

"Grab a sample from an exterminator's website and create a local address and phone number."

"Want your name on the front?"

"Make a fake name. How about Gwen Burgess?"

Raven snorted. "You look like a Gwen Burgess. What's the plan?"

As Scout designed the card, Chelsey dragged a sweatshirt over her head.

"Gwen Burgess, the new exterminator in town, is about to pay Wilson Manfredini a visit."

"Thomas doesn't want us running surveillance on Manfredini. He'll freak if he finds out."

"So we won't tell Thomas."

"Not a terrific idea."

"Until you come up with something better, it's all we have."

AT 3:05 P.M., Chelsey stopped her Honda Civic up the road from Wilson Manfredini's house and walked to his residence. No sooner did she push the bell than the door whipped open, and a man who outweighed her by a hundred pounds stared bullets into her eyes.

"Who the hell are you?"

"Gwen Burgess, Burgess Extermination," Chelsey said, handing him a card.

"I ain't got any bugs."

"Not now, of course you don't. But wait until spring."

The man spat into the snow. "If I see a bug, I'll call you during the spring. Until then, get the—"

"Sir, this won't take a moment, and you don't even need to accompany me outside. I realize it's freezing for November. All I'm gonna do is check the likely places bees, hornets, and wasps build nests and make sure you're free and clear."

She watched his face when she mentioned wasps. His mouth twitched, but that wasn't a sure-fire sign that he'd killed Officer Barrett.

"Ain't no nests out there. Can't you see it's been snowing?"

"They build nests through the fall. This is the perfect time to remove the nests, because the little monsters are asleep and won't attack. But if you wait until spring . . ."

"Yeah, yeah, I get it, but I'm not paying."

"You don't have to pay a dime, sir. We're the city's new extermination team, and we're running a promotional offer in which we inspect the exterior of your home for free, no strings attached."

"Free?"

"That's right. All I ask is you spread the word to your friends if you value our service."

"Fine, but make it quick."

He slammed the door in her face. Real nice guy.

Chelsey followed the driveway around the house and entered the backyard. From the corner of her eye, she caught Manfredini spying through the window. She pretended not to notice.

Honestly, she didn't know what she was looking for. Where did bees and wasps build nests? Some stinging insects burrowed holes in the ground. She'd found out the hard way while mowing once. Shining a flashlight, she examined the trees bordering the yard. A mass of dead leaves might have been the beginnings of a nest, but a furry animal or bird was probably responsible.

Turning to leave, she spotted something beneath the deck. It lay against a wooden post, shielded by the overhead boards. Yes, that was a nest. It might have belonged to wasps or hornets, but she wasn't an expert. She snapped a picture with her phone, then edged away. Though it couldn't be warmer than 35 degrees, she envisioned a swarm darting out of the opening and attacking.

She gave a thumbs up at the window.

Manfredini's glare followed her from the yard to the sidewalk.

22

The sun was almost down when the man exited the grocery store with a paper bag tucked under his arm. This must be his lucky day. As he opened the trunk, he glimpsed none other than Trix Barrett arriving. He kept his head down and waited for her to pass. The widow had a phone plastered to her ear and seemed to talk to a friend or family member.

"Forget what the newspapers reported," the woman said, aiming a key fob at her car. "Someone murdered Shawn. No, I'm not deluding myself. It wasn't an accident." After the other person on the phone argued, Trix ground her teeth. "I'll prove it. The police are looking into Shawn's death, as is the sheriff, and I hired a private investigation team. Yes, really. Wolf Lake Consulting. Have you heard of them? They're the best PI firm in the region."

Trix faded from earshot. He considered following her into the store to learn more, but he'd gained all the information he needed. Wolf Lake Consulting. He might have laughed the conversation away, yet he knew enough to respect the firm's investigators. They'd solved too many crimes for him to consider them a mere nuisance. He would need to deal with the issue. As he had everyone who'd gotten in his way, he'd push them until they backed off. And they would back off or pay with their lives.

A catalog of names opened in his head as he drove the truck across town. Chelsey something or other, a black woman named Raven, and her gangster brother. Wasn't there a young teenage girl working at the office? Oh, and a former cop from the Syracuse PD. He had to be extra careful of that one.

Stomping on the gas, he raced around a slow-moving hatchback, not caring that he'd crossed the double line. The idiot wailed his horn, and the man left him behind.

Darkness poured across Wolf Lake when he parked across the street from the converted home where the investigators worked. With the holiday season fast approaching, vehicles lined the curb, and people hustled from one shop to the next, eager to escape the deepening chill. The lights were on inside the old house. White LED lighting shone like stars through the windows.

He waited fifteen minutes before the door opened and a woman bundled in a winter coat, hat, and mittens descended the steps and skated on shaky legs and outstretched arms across the parking lot. This would be Raven. He didn't know the woman's address, but he intended to find out. Right now.

A Nissan Rogue backed out of the parking spot, turned right past the lot, and headed toward the edge of the village. He executed a three-point turn and followed, staying a few blocks behind. Did she live in the village? She looked like a city girl, but the highway to Harmon was in the opposite direction. Down neighborhood streets she drove, the houses becoming more sparse with every passing minute. The lake came into view. It would be two months before the surface froze, but ice chunks and slush floated like flotsam close to the shore. Did this Raven person live along the lake?

When she reached the lake road, she turned right, then took a quick left and ascended a hill. Her tires spun on the ice, and his breath caught. If she skidded into the ditch, he could end this now. The man would offer to drag her SUV onto the road, and when she let her guard down, he'd snap her neck and leave her in the woods. Nobody was looking.

But she righted the Rogue and continued up the hill, passing a tiny housing development that overlooked the water. Where was she going?

After the SUV fishtailed a second time, the woman turned left into the state park. He idled short of the parking lot and watched as she stomped through the snow and unlocked the door to the ranger's cabin. He should have known. Darren Holt had left the Syracuse PD to run the park, and apparently Raven was his lover.

Two birds. One stone.

He would eliminate both threats tonight.

THIS TIME of year depressed Raven. It wasn't yet suppertime, and the sun had disappeared below the distant terrain. The nights would only grow longer until a few days before Christmas. She longed for May and June when the days stretched forever and the promise of warmer days lay ahead.

The Rogue's tires slipped and slid on the frozen slush leading up the hill between the lake road and Wolf Lake State Park. LeVar's advice rang in her head. She needed snow tires before winter hit with full force. As she fishtailed, she spotted the twin beams of a pickup truck in her mirrors. They reflected blinding light and made her wish the person would back off and let her reach her destination. The truck crept closer. She'd first noticed the vehicle on the village outskirts.

With a frustrated grunt, she swung the wheel and entered the parking lot outside the visitor's center. Darren's pickup stood beside a snow-covered path. She searched the mirrors for the truck that had followed her. Strange that it hadn't appeared.

On her way across the campgrounds, a motor pulled her attention to the road. A red truck roared past, kicking up a hazy trail of snow. Anyone following the driver would need to run their windshield wipers to see the road.

The door opened into the cabin and the heat from the wood-stove caressed her body, thawing her face and hands.

"Darren?"

He didn't answer.

She peeled off the hat and gloves and stuck them down the sleeve of her jacket, which she hung in the closet. After kicking off her boots, she hurried to the woodstove and sat beside the vent, rubbing her hands and socked feet until the chill abated. While she warmed herself, a thudding sound came from outside. She pulled the curtains aside from the window and caught sight of Darren carrying three chopped logs. Raven beat him to the door and opened it for him. His eyes widened in surprise.

"Good timing," he said, placing the logs on a stand they kept next to the stove.

"I saw your arms were full."

"Appreciate it." Darren removed his coat and placed it beside Raven's in the closet. "How did work go today?"

"Scout and I phoned everyone, but nobody recalled a delivery of live wasps."

"And that's a package they would remember."

"Definitely. She thinks maybe the killer—"

"If it's a killer."

"—Right—that he saved the nest during the warm months and kept the wasps in a heated enclosure."

"That's a lot of effort just to keep stinging bugs alive."

"But if he intended to use them as murder weapons, it was worth the effort." She cupped her elbows with her hands and bounced on her toes, still feeling the rush of outdoor air that had entered the cabin when she let Darren inside. "Trix Barrett stopped by the office. Even after her husband's body showed up, she wants us to continue investigating."

"I'm happy to help. Sure, I retired from the force, but I'll do anything to support the family of a murdered officer. Hell, I'll work pro bono."

"Get used to it since we don't pay you."

Darren laughed. "I keep forgetting." She leaned against his chest and he kissed her forehead. "I missed you today."

"Missed you too. Chelsey and I figured you'd make an appearance."

He blew the hair off his brow. "Wish I could have. Damn Gregory Rose and his wife went hiking and left the trail. Rose got them to Lucifer Falls before she complained about the cold. The loudmouth figured he could lead them through the woods and find a shortcut back to the cabins. Twenty minutes later, he ran into the hill and realized there was no way they could safely climb through the ice and snow. I had to toss a rope down and pull them back to the trail."

"Mr. Rose seems more trouble than he's worth."

"I'll remember the next time he wants to rent a cabin. But that wasn't all. Instead of using the park's grills, he dragged his own across the clearing and lit the coals beside the forest."

Raven's mouth fell open. "What?"

"One spark could have burned half the forest. Despite the snow, this is the driest time of year. No leaves on the trees, low humidity, gusty winds. The entire park is kindling."

"What was he thinking?"

"Obviously, he wasn't. Rose didn't want to use our grills

because, quote, he didn't want other people's germs, and it's too blustery in the clearing, end quote."

"Darren, kick him out. If he raises a stink, just give the money back to him. He's not worth the trouble."

Darren lowered his head. "I know, but I don't want to be a hardass. Wolf Lake State Park has a reputation. Ever since that doctor dug bones out of the creek bed, the park has become the butt of too many jokes."

"I like it when you're a hardass."

She slapped his backside.

"Well now, someone is frisky."

"Dinner first, then playtime."

"If you insist."

She pressed her lips against his, eager to feel his body against hers. Pitch black pressed against the windows.

23

In the dead of night, when the jagged brush of one's imagination turned dreams into nightmares, Raven awoke in a state of confusion. A slapping, smacking sound came from beyond the cabin walls, as though someone were clapping hands or snapping branches over a knee. She had the impression that she'd overslept and Darren was working outside, yet it was still dark beyond the drawn curtains. Under the blankets, Darren's form created a lumpy outline against the black.

She blinked, her thoughts still muddled inside a brain that was two-thirds asleep and begging for rest. The covers moved, and Darren sat up and glanced at her.

"What is that?" he asked.

The snapping grew louder. Before the smoke reached her nostrils, he threw the covers aside and said, "Fire," then pulled his clothes over his body and slipped on boots. She ran to the window and saw the eerie orange glow advancing like the gates of hell. The blaze pulled itself through the trees, feeding on the dry wood, expanding, growing more confident in its advance.

There was no time to think. With the fire still in the forest but coming their way, she dressed and grabbed her phone.

"Call 911," he said, but she was one step ahead of him.

The dispatcher recognized her voice and urged her to get out of the cabin and save herself. A home and its belongings could be replaced. Flesh and bone were a different story.

"The fire department is on its way," she called to him, taking the phone with her. "Sheriff's department should be right behind."

Darren only nodded. He was out the door and unraveling a hose along the side of the cabin. She opened the faucet with frozen hands, only half-aware she'd neglected to grab her coat and mittens. The water bellowed forth. He directed the spray at the trees beyond the forest's edge. The blaze hissed, and smoke billowed with the rage of a dragon.

And still the fire advanced. Two rows of trees lay between the forest and the clearing. The night wind gusted into her face and foretold the unthinkable. Once the blaze grew and reached the nearest trees, the gale would be strong enough to carry sparks and drop them on the ranger's cabin. How long before the inferno caught their home and burned it to cinders?

With growing desperation, Darren directed the stream left and right. For every area where he thwarted the fire, another was consumed by it.

"I can't stop it," he said. "Wake the Roses and get them out of the cabin."

"If we work together—"

"Just do it!"

She sprinted across the snowpack. Above, the moon tracked across the sky. A blue lunar glow reflected off the icy terrain.

Her fist rose to pound on the door just as it swung open. Mrs. Rose, dressed in a thick cotton robe and furry slippers, peered out with slitted, sleepy eyes. She glimpsed the fire and screamed to her husband, who shot out of bed as if someone had doused him with a bucket of ice water.

Which gave Raven an idea. She would grab a bucket from the closet and help Darren battle the fire. They didn't need to win the battle by themselves, only keep the flames at bay until the fire department arrived.

"Grab your husband and evacuate the cabin," she said. "Don't worry about your belongings. Just go."

She bobbed her head in understanding as Gregory Rose tossed clothes and items into a suitcase behind her.

"Mr. Rose, please," she said.

"I won't lose everything we brought because of your incompetence," he growled, refusing to obey.

With no time to argue, Raven ran to the ranger's cabin and filled a bucket in the sink. While Darren fought an unwinnable battle against the fire, Raven hurled the bucket's contents against a tree trunk. She couldn't drive the fire back, but at least she could soak the trunks and make it harder for the fire to spread into the clearing.

"Stay back," Darren said, but she wouldn't listen.

She continued to race from the sink to the fire until her arms and legs grew weary. The effort paid dividends, but her energy reserves were depleted.

"Let me," he said, wrestling the bucket from her hand. "Here. Aim the spray wherever the fire catches."

She pointed the hose while Darren hurried to refill the bucket. To her horror, the wind kicked up and carried a firefly-spark above her head. It landed on the cabin's roof. She prayed it wouldn't catch. A second later, a larger ember took to the air and struck the outer wall with a *thunk*. Battling the fire grew more dangerous. Those sparks and embers could easily land in their hair or on their clothes.

Had the Roses abandoned the cabin? She didn't dare pull her attention from the advancing fire. The snow sizzled at the edge of the clearing. The wind caught more sparks and dropped them in a deadly rain upon the cabin. She smelled smoke behind her. It could have been from the wood stove. It could have been their home burning to the ground.

To Raven's shock, Mrs. Rose ran by with another bucket of water. She must have entered the ranger's cabin and found it in the closet. With a huff, the husband joined her, but not before chastising his wife for helping. They needed to care for themselves, not worry about the ranger.

With four people battling the fire, the advance slowed. Inch by inch, it claimed the outer edge of the forest and spat embers upon the clearing. If only the wind would die.

"Mr. and Mrs. Rose," Darren said, "stand back. I won't let you risk your lives."

That was all Mr. Rose needed. He hooked his wife's elbow and dragged her across the clearing. Their buckets lay where they'd dropped them.

Raven gritted her teeth. Had the Roses battled beside them a few minutes longer, they might have turned back the advance. Now the fire roared with glee, sensing their weakened states.

Her eyes watered, and she hacked and coughed as sooty air filled her nostrils. They were out of time. If they didn't flee, they would die saving the cabin. Seeing Darren hurl water against the tree trunks despite his exhaustion buoyed her to stay and fight. There was no winning this war, only delaying the inevitable.

A burning ember landed on Darren's arm. He yelled and brushed it off. She checked him over, but the skin wasn't blistered, thank goodness. As she pointed the water at the tree line, sirens rose behind them. A bell accompanied the wails; the fire department had arrived. Two cruisers from the sheriff's department followed the firetrucks into the parking lot.

Darren waved a hand over his head. "Over here!"

As if the emergency workers didn't smell the smoke or see

the dancing flames. Once the firefighters arrived with their high-powered hoses, the tide shifted. They drove the fire back until it was little more than a smoking, hissing cloud.

She collapsed to her knees in the snow, which had partially melted and turned to mud because of the heat. Darren helped her up and supported her. Ash and soot covered his face and hair. She looked no better.

Chelsey ran from her car and hugged them both. Thomas was there with Deputy Lambert. When they confirmed she and Darren were all right, they made way for the fire chief, who pawed around the outskirts of the forest.

"How did the fire start?" Thomas asked.

"Can't be sure," said Darren, "but I have an idea."

He glanced back at Gregory Rose and his wife in the parking lot. They huddled together in a blanket.

The cabin was spared. Except for a few smoking coals on the roof, which a firefighter brushed away before dousing the cabin's exterior, there was nothing to worry about. Had the wind blown in the opposite direction, they would have lost the forest.

Raven and Darren held each other close, thankful to be alive. What if they hadn't woken up in time?

The fire chief motioned to Darren. "Could you come over here? I need to show you something."

Darren did as the man asked, and she followed him into the trees.

"Found how the fire started," the chief said. "See the coals beneath the ash? Someone dumped their grill in the woods. It must have smoldered until the wind picked up. The dead leaves caught fire, then the fallen branches, then the trees. You could have lost everything."

Darren pressed his lips together. She couldn't contain her fury. Had he not grasped her elbow, she would have marched over to the Roses and thanked them for their carelessness. Idiots.

"Thank you for saving the forest and the cabin," Darren said.

"How do you want to pursue the matter, Ranger Holt? One could argue this is arson."

Thomas cocked an eyebrow.

"Let me think it over."

Darren stared at Gregory Rose. The pompous man didn't seem to care.

24

N ow it was Raven's turn to hold Darren back. He wanted to chew a hole in Gregory Rose, who was already dragging their belongings from the car back to the cabin. If the man believed he was staying another night at the campground, he had another thing coming.

"Think before you bite his head off," she said.

"We could have lost our belongings. Hell, we might have died in the fire if you hadn't woken up in time."

"The smoke detectors would have saved us."

Darren replied with a grunt.

"Anyhow, we don't have proof Mr. Rose started the fire."

"We don't? Besides us, who else is staying in the park? I told him to keep the grill away from the trees, and he disobeyed a direct order. Gregory Rose and his wife need to go. All these acres of forestland." Darren swept an arm over the horizon. "One shift of the wind, and they'd all vanish because of his idiocy. That's it. I'm laying into him."

"Darren, don't."

"And after I have my say, I'll let Thomas and the fire chief have a turn. If they want to charge him with arson, I won't stand in their way."

Raven gave Thomas and Chelsey a flustered look and hurried after her boyfriend. The sheriff joined her, worried that Darren was angry enough to turn the encounter physical.

"Slow down, Darren," Thomas said, striding alongside the ranger.

"All I'm going to do is talk to the guy," Darren said.

"Take a breath. If he's guilty, we'll handle the situation."

Gregory Rose emerged from the cabin and folded his arms. His wife cowered behind him.

"I don't know why you're angry at me, Ranger," Rose said. "I helped for as long as I could, but I wasn't about to risk my wife's life saving your park."

"Are you kidding me?" Darren stood two inches taller than Rose and was almost chest to chest with the man. "I warned you to keep the grill away from the forest, and you dumped hot coals on a bed of dry leaves. What on earth did you think would happen?"

"Stop right there. I did nothing of the sort."

"You started your grill last evening. You're the only guests in the park."

"But I didn't. After you cussed me out and told me to stay near the cabin, I said screw it. It was too damn cold to stand in the wind. I ordered sandwiches from the village deli. Didn't you see the car pull into the parking lot?"

"If you expect me to believe you're innocent—"

"I *am* innocent. Tell him, honey. Did I grill last evening?"

The wife shook her head. "Gregory said it was too cold, and I agreed with him. It was my idea to call out for food."

"Then whose coals were in the forest?" Darren asked.

"Not ours," Rose said. "I swear on my parents' graves. Look, you can inspect my grill. It's clean as a whistle."

"Show me."

With Raven and Chelsey behind him, Darren stomped into the cabin. The portable grill stood against the wall. There wasn't a speck of ash to be found in the container. The man could have cleaned the grill with a cloth, but it looked brand new.

"It's never been used," Rose said, finishing Darren's thought. "Besides, would I put a hot grill inside our cabin and risk our lives?"

Darren wiped a hand across his mouth.

"If I find out you're lying, I'll call the fire chief myself."

"We're not lying. Hey, if you want us to leave, refund our money and we'll pack the car."

Raven met Darren's eyes. This was their chance to rid themselves of the Roses.

"That's unnecessary," he said, making her heart sink. "If you say you're innocent, I'll take your word for it."

Thomas lifted his palms in question. Did Darren want the sheriff to press the matter?

"We'll leave them be," said Darren. "Mr. and Mrs. Rose have been through enough, and they helped us fight the fire."

"Ranger Holt," Rose said, stopping them in their tracks. Raven braced herself. Undoubtedly, the arrogant man wanted to give them a piece of his tiny mind. Yet he didn't. "My wife and I heard someone outside our cabin after midnight. We thought it was you. Apparently, we aren't the only people inside the campgrounds."

Thomas turned to Darren. "Maybe we have an arsonist after all." The sheriff raised his chin at Rose. "Where was this person?"

"He came around the east side of the cabin, right past that window."

Rose pointed to the left, and his wife nodded in agreement.

"Stay in your cabin the rest of the night," Darren said. "If you hear anything, call me."

Raven and Darren followed Thomas around the east side of the cabin. Yes, there were tracks in the snow. Dozens of them. The firefighters had rushed this way, as had Thomas and Lambert and the guy who'd delivered food from the deli. Even Darren and Raven had walked back and forth through the snow.

"Some of these tracks belong to your arsonist," Thomas said.

"Why would anyone want to burn down the forest?" Chelsey asked.

"Perhaps he didn't." The sheriff glanced from the forest to the cabin. "This might have been directed at you."

Who would burn their cabin?

"Whoever it was went through a lot of trouble," said Darren. "By dumping hot coals, he made it appear as if a camper was responsible. I can say with reasonable certainty that the Roses didn't do this."

"Then who?"

Raven bit her tongue. "Yesterday after the sun went down, I noticed someone following me from the village to the park."

Darren spun to face her. "Why didn't you tell me?"

"Because I didn't think there was a reason to worry. It was just a guy in a red truck, and he drove past after I parked."

"Did you see his face?"

"Not really. I was worried about the snow and ice."

"Whoever dumped the coals, my cameras should have caught him."

He had placed cameras around the campground after a rash of burglaries.

Lambert finished conferring with the fire chief and joined the others inside the cabin. Raven sat beside Darren as he accessed the security camera recording on his computer.

Chelsey, Thomas, and his deputy leaned over the chairs for a closer look.

"Rose said after midnight, correct?" Darren asked.

"That's right," Raven said.

She had to hand it to Gregory Rose. His estimation proved true. At 12:06 a.m., headlights flashed across the parking lot.

"Damn. He knew enough to avoid the camera overlooking the parking lot."

"Or he got lucky."

"I don't believe in luck."

A minute later, a shadow drifted across the exterior of the cabin, and a man wearing a bulky winter coat strode past with a metal bucket in hand. He wore the hood over his head.

"That's our man," Thomas said.

"Smile for the camera," said Lambert, squeezing the back of Darren's chair with impatience.

The arsonist kept his head down on his way to the tree line. He shook the coals out of the bucket and onto the leaves, then adjusted his hood and started back the way he'd come. This time, the sheriff and his deputy almost scrambled over Darren and Raven to see the man's face.

"He knows where the cameras are," Darren said, sitting back.

The figure vanished from the security feed. Headlights swept across the lot.

"I couldn't see a face," Chelsey said. "What would you estimate his height at? I'd say six feet, give or take an inch."

"Fair estimation," said Lambert. "We're looking for a six-foot-tall man in a black, bulky winter coat with a hood. Doesn't help much, does it?"

"And he's aware of the camera locations," Thomas said. "He scoped you out during the planning phase. The question is, why does he want to kill you?"

25

B reakfast scents mingled with the woodstove inside the ranger's cabin. Raven tried to convince herself the burning stench was the bread she'd left too long in the toaster, but one glance out the window reminded her of how close they'd come to dying last night. The blackened husks of trees, the few that remained standing, loomed in the forest like demon creatures. Even the trees that the fire had spared wore ugly scars. Chunks of bark were missing, and a humongous swath of charred earth lay where snow once covered the ground. Though she harbored no love for winter, she wished for six inches of snow, anything to mask the scorched soil.

"I thought about it all night," she said to Darren, "and I can't understand why anyone would do this. The camera footage proves it was arson, but was it meant for us or the park?"

"There are plenty of sick people, and this time of year brings out the worst in them. Could be a depressed, angry person who wanted to show his rage. I can't explain why anyone would start a forest fire, but people do."

Raven forked a piece of fresh pineapple past her lips. "We

have to catch him, Darren. This should be the focus of our investigation club."

"But we're not playing games. This is real life."

She rounded on him and set her fists on her hips. "Since when has investigating been a game to any of us? We saved Deputy Aguilar from a serial killer."

Darren lowered his head. "I know, and I'm sorry. That's just my frustration talking. I love this park and everything about it. The idea that someone would try to burn it down angers me beyond reason."

A car door slammed in the parking lot, and a motor started. Raven walked to the window and parted the curtains.

"The Roses are leaving."

"Good riddance. I feel bad that I accused them, but I won't miss Gregory Rose."

"He still had four days remaining on his stay."

"I'll refund the balance to his credit card. In fact, I'll just delete all the charges. They went through hell. I can't charge them in good faith."

She rubbed his shoulders. "You're a kind man, Darren Holt."

He touched her hand. "Someone doesn't think so."

"Yeah? Well, the arsonist is wrong, and I'll kick his ass all over Wolf Lake for thinking otherwise." She paced across the cabin. "Besides, the fire might have been directed at me."

"Ah, the red truck."

"I should have gotten the make and model."

"License plate would have helped a tad."

"Don't remind me."

As she cursed herself for not paying attention to the trailing vehicle, her phone rang. She read LeVar's name on the screen and answered, putting him on speakerphone.

"Y'all good up there?" he asked. "Can't believe someone started a fire in the woods."

"We're all right, LeVar. Thank you for asking."

"Anything I can do?"

"Are you free later this afternoon?"

"I can be. What do you need?"

"Darren and I need to clear away the dead, charred wood," she said. "It's nothing but future kindling."

"*Aight*. How's two o'clock?"

"Two o'clock works for us."

"Hey, is the ridge trail open? Scout and I planned to run from the house to the cabin this morning, but I didn't want to get halfway up and find you'd closed the trail off."

"The ridge trail is open," Darren said from across the room. "But don't come to the cabin. Once you hit the top of the hill, you'll be close to where the fire started. Too dangerous."

"Got it. We'll turn around before we hit the top."

"You heard all that?" LeVar asked, knotting his shoelaces.

"The top of the trail is closed," Scout said. "I can't get over someone trying to burn down the forest. What an absolute sicko."

"And according to Thomas, the arsonist looked away from the cameras. What does that tell you?"

"Inside job? Someone who'd stayed at the campgrounds before?"

"That's a theory worth pursuing."

Seated at their feet, Jack grinned. The dog knew he was going for a jog with the others. They never brought a leash, as the loyal pup wasn't prone to running off. He stuck by his family, always grateful for the people who'd rescued him from the woods and taken him into their homes. Even so, LeVar considered bringing the leash this time.

"You don't trust Jack?" Scout asked.

"I wonder if he'll sniff where the fire occurred and want to check it out."

"Dogs are smarter than that. They stay away from fires. Same thing with wolves."

Wolves. LeVar looked at Scout knowingly, and all she did was grin.

He took her advice and left the leash behind. They stepped into the freezing outdoors. He considered adding a layer to his clothes, but he didn't want to risk overheating. Still, his teeth chattered as they rounded the lake, with Scout leading the way on the narrow trail.

After ten minutes of uphill running, he finally warmed up and hit his stride. Scout must have too, because she kept a pace that would have impressed him during the summer, let alone in three inches of snow.

"Smell that?" she asked.

The wind blew dusty snow down the terrain, carrying an ashen scent.

"Yeah."

"Horrible, isn't it?"

"Ain't like after a barbecue. Can you imagine if the fire spread and killed all the animals that call the park home?"

"Isn't that the plot to *Bambi*?"

His throat closed up. "If you make me cry, I'll abandon you in the woods."

"As if. I'm faster than you, LeVar."

He chuckled. "Not on your best day."

"Is that a challenge?"

"Scout, I don't think we should—"

She took off running. He sprinted to catch up, shielding his eyes as her sneakers kicked up snow. The girl glanced over her shoulder, saw him, and ran faster. He hit another gear and closed the distance. She amazed him. Last spring, no one had believed she would ever walk again, and now she appeared ready to join the high school cross-country team.

They laughed like children rejoicing on a snow day. Without question, she was the best friend he'd ever had, and he hoped they would stay together forever.

But fear wormed through his chest as she ran up the hill. CJ. If the gangster leaped into the open, he wouldn't have enough time to defend Scout. CJ was his brother from another mother, as they'd once referred to each other. Would the boy kill LeVar and Scout because he'd abandoned the Harmon Kings and caused their downfall?

"Slow up for a second," he said.

"Can't keep up?" She grinned back at him.

"It ain't that. Remember what I told you about CJ? This is where he found me."

She tried to appear confident, but the caution in her eyes belied her. The girl slowed to a jog and allowed LeVar to run past. Jack barked and glanced back at them. The dog stayed several strides ahead, always vigilant and protective.

The trees rustled in the forest, and Jack stopped. The dog's hackles rose, and he growled from deep in his diaphragm. LeVar and Scout stood behind the enormous pup.

"What is it?" she asked.

"Someone is in the woods." He cupped his mouth with his hands and called out. "CJ? That you? We don't want trouble."

The sound stopped, and nothing moved in the forest. LeVar sensed someone hiding behind an old tree deep in the woods. Jack took a step in that direction, growling louder.

"He wouldn't react that way to a deer or rabbit," she said. "A bear maybe."

"That's no bear out there."

"Darren?" she called.

Jack wouldn't act this way around Darren either.

"We should turn back," he said.

"What if it's the arsonist coming back to finish the job?"

That thought had occurred to him, but he felt uncomfortable voicing it. Only a lunatic would set a beautiful forest on fire.

Unless it was personal. If the arsonist wanted Raven and Darren dead, he might target LeVar as well. And Scout. Why?

A man edged out from behind the tree. He stood taller than CJ and wore a bulky black jacket with a hood pulled over his head. Exactly as Raven and Darren had described.

LeVar lifted his phone to dial Darren's number as Jack shot off like a bullet and ran after the arsonist, barking.

"Jack, no!" LeVar reached for the dog's collar, but he was too late. If the man carried a gun, he would shoot Jack. "Go to the cabin and get Darren."

"I'm not leaving you," she said.

"Please, Scout. There's no time."

She wouldn't listen. He took off after Jack, with Scout hurrying to catch up. Whenever he ran at full speed, she struggled to keep pace.

But he was no match for Jack. The dog ran like the wind, barking, growling, snapping at the air. Jack and LeVar were gaining on the arsonist, who struggled through the forest. Whoever the man was, he ran almost as fast as LeVar. Not fast enough. Given enough time, the former gang member would catch him.

When LeVar was five steps behind the arsonist, the man looked back from inside his hood and widened his eyes. The psycho sprinted faster, surprising LeVar with his speed.

"The ledge!" Scout shouted from behind.

"What?"

"The cliff! LeVar, slow down!"

He realized with a start how close he was to the cliff. LeVar skidded to a stop, but his sneakers kept sliding. He grabbed a tree to keep himself from slipping over the edge. Jack snapped at the man.

The arsonist never stopped running. He yelled and fell off the cliff, legs kicking, arms reaching for tree branches which lay beyond his grasp.

Beside Jack, LeVar peered over the cliff as the man plunged into the frigid lake. He disappeared with a splash.

"Where is he?" Scout asked from behind.

"He didn't come up. I don't see him anywhere."

"Who was he? Did you get a look at his face?"

LeVar shook his head and brushed sweaty dreadlocks off his forehead. Below, the water churned, driven by the winter wind. The lake temperature couldn't be warmer than 40 degrees. Anyone who fell in would experience hypothermia within minutes.

"Don't know who he was, but he's dead now."

26

S tanding still in the snow made LeVar shiver. He was still sweaty from running, and the wind cut through his bones, reminding him he wasn't dressed for winter. Scout jogged in place to stay warm, and Jack stood at attention, as if the arsonist might reappear at any second.

Darren, Raven, and Thomas walked along the cliff's ledge and searched for the missing man. In the lake, two divers with the state police scoured the water.

"I can't imagine anyone surviving," LeVar said to Thomas. "The water is too cold."

"Tell me again what he looked like."

"It was impossible to make out his face with the hood pulled over his head, but he was white and wore a beard."

"Age?"

"Couldn't tell you, but he ran almost as fast as me. Another hundred yards, and I would have caught him."

"So we know he's in shape."

"Bulky black winter coat," Darren said, returning to LeVar and Thomas. "Just like the guy on the park cameras."

"It has to be the same person," Raven said, bouncing on her

toes. She draped an arm around Scout as they combined body heat. "He came back to finish the job."

"Can't say I'd wish drowning in chilly waters on anyone, but he did try to burn us out of house and home."

"He must have parked nearby," LeVar said.

"That's true," said Thomas. "Raven, you said a red pickup truck followed you home?"

Her teeth chattered. "That's correct."

"I'll contact dispatch and get another cruiser out here. If this guy left his truck down the road, we'll find it."

LeVar rubbed his arms. "If you don't mind, Scout and I should head back. We're dressed to exercise, not stand around in the cold."

"I'll drive you home," Darren said. "You and Scout take Jack up to the cabin and hang out until I finish."

"Thanks, Darren. Come on, boy."

Jack woofed and padded over to LeVar and Scout. They squeezed between the trees and found their way to the trail. What else could go wrong? The last time he'd jogged to the park, CJ had tried to convince him to fight the Royals. This time, they'd encountered the man who tried to burn the forest.

Scout shivered.

"You cold?" he asked, wondering if he should put an arm around her shoulders. He was never sure how to act around her anymore or what was appropriate.

"A little."

"Your teeth are chattering."

Clouds puffed out of her mouth. "That's the first time I ever watched someone die. At least I assume he's dead."

"He never surfaced. I expected him to pop up along the shore and climb out before the sheriff's department arrived."

"I realize he was a terrible person, but it still disturbs me. Maybe I'm not cut out for law enforcement."

"Is this the same Scout Mourning?"

She lifted a shoulder. "Between seeing what Officer Barrett's wife is dealing with and the arsonist drowning in front of us, I've gotten a new perspective."

"It's a reality check. Don't let it scare you off, Scout. Think of what Mrs. Barrett's life would be like if she didn't have people like us working to catch her husband's killer."

"I suppose you're right."

The cabin appeared through the woods. Just in time. Scout released a relieved breath and picked up her pace. LeVar opened the door and let Jack trot inside. The woodstove was running. The first thing he did was peel off his sweatshirt and drape it over a chair.

"Oh, that's so nice," she said, prying off her running sneakers and removing her socks. She placed them beside the stove to dry and stood in front of the furnace, rubbing her hands together. "Do you mind if I take my leggings off? They're soaking wet."

"Nah, do what you gotta do." She slid her shorts down her thighs, and he spun around. "Yo, girl. I'm in the room with you."

"Relax. I'm wearing leggings under my shorts."

"Yeah, but . . . hold up. I'll change in the bathroom while you do your thing. Tell me when you're decent."

LeVar entered the bathroom, twisted the lock, and leaned with his back against the door. What would Raven think if she returned and found them stripping off their clothes? He had to remind himself his friend was sixteen now.

And quite pretty.

Hold the phone, bruh. This is Scout you're thinking about.

Heat built in his cheeks. While he waited for her to tell him the coast was clear, he pulled off his shorts and jogging pants, then dragged the shorts up and over his hips. They were damp, but he couldn't sit around in his Batman boxers with Scout in the room.

"I'm decent!" she called.

He closed his eyes and whispered, "Please, let her be dressed in shorts. Help me out here, God. Your boy is trying to do right."

Squinting his eyes, he stared at himself in the mirror. He opened the door.

She sprawled in front of the woodstove with a throw pillow under her head. Jack lay on his side, snoring. Her leggings hung off a chair beside her sweatshirt. Like LeVar, she wore running shorts and a T-shirt. He stood outside the bathroom door, looking for some way to keep himself busy. Maybe he'd straighten up after Raven. She could be a slob.

"Warm up beside the fire," Scout said, scooting over to give him room.

"I'm good."

"LeVar, your lips are blue."

"Are they? It might just be the lighting in here."

He emptied the dish rack and placed a loaf of bread in the cupboard. Inside the refrigerator, he spotted leftover pizza from their meeting.

"I could go for cold pizza," he called to her. "How about you?"

"Did you say cold pizza? I'm down."

He plated their lunches. As he handed her a dish, the heat from the woodstove thawed his legs. Keeping a few feet between them, he sat on the floor and crunched on the crust. Paul and Brothers made the best crust this side of New York City.

"They make a mean pizza," he said. "It blows away any I've tried in Syracuse and Harmon."

"The only pizza I've eaten came from Wolf Lake and Ithaca."

His jaw dropped. "Are you for real? Until you eat pizza from New York City or Jersey, you haven't lived."

"I hear Chicago makes a great crust."

He choked on a crumb and smacked himself in the chest.

"The only people who think Chicago makes great pizza are Chicagoans."

"What's so great about New York pizza?"

"Girl, you need to get religion. One of these days, we're hitting the Big Apple and you'll taste the difference. It's the water. That's what I hear."

"Ew. I wouldn't eat crust made with water from the Hudson River."

"I don't know where the water comes from. Might be holy water."

She punched his shoulder and chuckled. "You jerk."

That got him laughing too. The door opened and Raven paused in the entryway.

"We're right here," he said. "Stole the rest of your pizza."

"Better you than me," said Raven. "Cheese goes straight to my hips."

Raven eyed them as if she suspected they'd been doing more than sitting around the woodstove. Darren entered the cabin behind her and stomped off his boots.

"What's the verdict?" LeVar asked.

Darren brushed off his coat. "The divers never found a body, but the lake is a hundred feet deep beneath the cliffs, and the current might have dragged the guy toward the center. Either way, he didn't surface. You two ready to head home?"

"Ready when you are."

LeVar and Scout grabbed their clothes and slipped into their sneakers. He hoped the truck was warm. Jack padded over to join them.

"Be back in a bit," Darren said, kissing Raven's cheek.

As the ranger drove toward the lake road, LeVar stared at the water. He couldn't imagine falling into the lake at this time of year. Nobody would have survived.

27

The man burst out of the lake with a deep-throated gasp. He couldn't feel his arms and hands, and only a trickle of sensation ran down his legs. Even in the shallows, he was in danger of drowning if he didn't prop himself upright. Dying of hypothermia or drowning—neither appealed to him.

On lacerated elbows, he dragged himself across the rocky bottom toward the shoreline. The rocks tore away bits of his skin. Blood welled to the surface.

I'm too cold to bleed.

The thought made him laugh maniacally. He summoned enough strength to pull himself onto the shore and lie on his back, panting. Puffy clouds with black bottoms swam across the blue sky and thickened by the minute. It would snow soon, but that was the least of his concerns. He didn't intend to freeze to death.

His hands were rubbery and useless. Attempts to pull off his shoes proved futile, yet he had to remove his clothes. The combination of cold and wet would kill him. His body temperature hovered at a dangerous level.

With a groan, he jammed the heel of his shoe against a rock and pushed down. The footwear came off too slowly. The effort drained his energy. Yes, this was it. After murdering a police officer and Harmon's most successful businessman, he would die after fleeing from two teenagers and a dog. It was enough to make him laugh at the unforgiving sky.

The wind gusted across the lake and his body rippled with goosebumps. His flesh was an odd mix of pallid and pink, sure signs of impending frostbite. With both shoes off, he used his toes, which held no sensation, to rip off his socks. A broken nail cut through the skin on the back of his calf and he didn't even feel it, though blood poured from the open wound. His bones ached. Landing in the water after jumping off the cliff had jostled his insides. He would ache for days. Once his blood flow returned to normal—if he survived—bruises would form across his body in a patchwork of agony.

His eyelids fluttered. No, he couldn't allow himself to fall asleep. Slapping himself across the face, he fought to his knees and elbows. A modicum of sensation returned. Just a trickle. Enough to confirm he was alive.

Teeth chattering, he worked his pants and underwear off, then the sodden jacket and shirt. Water poured off the clothes and formed puddles on the rocks. Steps away, the lake smashed against the shore and sprayed him with frigid shards.

He made it to his feet and lost his balance. His knees struck the bed of rocks and he cried out. Pain was better than numbness. More blood drizzled off his body.

Above the lake, a cottage on stilts grew out of an incline. A staircase covered with ice led to the home. If he regained his ability to walk, he could reach the steps in a minute. The stairs seemed miles away.

"Move," he ordered his body.

His arms carried the brunt of the work, dragging him toward

the stairs. His bare feet tingled with pins and needles. He kept his balance and limped, heedless of the jagged stones tearing the soles of his feet. His hands rubbed his arms, willing the blood to return. Naked, he wondered if anyone had eyes on him. He must be quite the sight, stumbling toward the stairs with a heap of clothes lying on the shore. Just a little longer. There would be a change of clothes in the cottage. And blessed heat. If he survived that long.

He clutched the rail for support. The old wood left splinters in his hands, but he wouldn't have known without seeing the slivers jutting through the top layer of flesh. The epidermis. He'd learned that term in biology class many moons ago. Why the word came back to him as he battled the elements, he couldn't guess.

The climb seemed to take hours, though he reached the top a minute later. If the homeowner spotted him, the sheriff's department would come. Nobody stood at the picture frame window along the back of the house.

It occurred to him he had no way to unlock the door without breaking the window, but when he tested the knob, it turned without effort. A miracle. Yet an unlocked door suggested the person who owned the house was home. Even along Wolf Lake, people locked their doors when they left during the day. You never knew when a naked psychopath would drag himself out of the frigid waters and smash a window. That made him laugh again. He was delirious, half out of his mind.

The door drifted open on well-oiled hinges. Silence met him at the entrance. A kitchen with a linoleum floor stood before him. The antique table held one chair.

A mix of water and blood dripped off his skin and left smudges. The floor didn't creak as he padded across the room, the feeling slowly returning to his body. Though he heard the vent blowing heated air into the home, the warmth hadn't reached his bones.

Somewhere in the house, a toilet flushed. He threw himself against the wall, prepared to kill the owner. No witnesses. As far as the authorities were concerned, he'd drowned in the lake or perished in the cold. By all rights, he should be dead.

A door closed at the end of a hallway. He leaned around the corner and confirmed no one was in the corridor.

The first room he encountered held a queen-size bed and a dresser. Hurrying, he rummaged through the drawers and removed socks, underwear, and a large pair of men's sweatpants. He discovered a long-sleeve shirt and a bulky sweatshirt and took those too. He had to get out of there before the person returned.

Shoes. He needed something for his feet.

The closet held nothing of use. He winced when the door squeaked. Backtracking, he hurried toward the kitchen. On his way, he glimpsed two leather work boots in the front entryway. He paused outside the living room and ensured he was still alone. Still naked and with the clothes tucked under his arm, he hobbled to the boots and grabbed them.

A thud came from down the hall. He hurried into the clothes, slipping the socks on first, then the underwear and sweatpants. He struggled into the boots, which were a size too small for his feet. No matter. He would make do.

As he pulled the shirt and sweatshirt over his head, footsteps approached the corridor. He hurried out the front door and found himself on the road leading from the lake road to the state park. His truck was down the hill and parked on an incline behind a stand of trees.

Houses stood on either side of the cottage. If he lingered, someone would spot him. A siren jolted him to his full height.

His eyes darted left and right. It was coming from the bottom of the hill and heading his way.

Now he played a game of chicken, running down the icy hill, betting he would reach his truck before he encountered the cruiser. The boots slipped on the snow, and he envisioned his pickup sliding down the icy rise and smashing across the road.

The siren grew louder. He pumped his arms and legs. Faster. No time for pain.

He caught sight of his truck behind the thicket. Had he not known it was there, he never would have seen it from the road. Racing up the rise, boots sliding on the treacherous terrain, he reached the pickup just before the cruiser rolled past.

Panting, he lay on his back and grinned at the sky.

Keep moving.

Before another sheriff's deputy arrived, he climbed into the cab and slammed the door. Keys. The damn keys had been in his jacket pocket. Now they probably lay at the bottom of Wolf Lake.

No problem. He kicked the plastic panel below the steering column and wrenched it off. His fingertips were still half-numb as he pushed the clutch sideways. The engine started.

The truck fishtailed until the tires caught the macadam. The grin of a hyena curled his lips.

He was death-proof.

28

U pon entering the guest house, LeVar turned on the space heater and peeled off his still damp shorts and underwear. He tossed them in the hamper before realizing anyone could see him through the window. And by anyone, he meant Scout. She was next door and changing clothes.

The investigation club had called an impromptu meeting and would soon arrive. The other investigators wanted more information about CJ. He wasn't sure what to tell them.

For all he knew, CJ wanted him dead, though the boy hadn't attacked him when he had the chance. He wouldn't see the boy coming if CJ decided murder was the only option. Yet he was certain CJ had nothing to do with the fire, nor was he the man they'd chased today.

LeVar trembled as he stepped under the hot spray of the shower. He kept the bathroom door locked in case Scout returned. Alone inside the cabin, she'd stood next to him in nothing but leggings to cover her lower body. Well, her underwear too. At least he hoped so. Were they too comfortable around each other? She looked every bit like a teenager now, and he was about to turn twenty. He needed to be careful for both their sakes.

As he lathered his body with soap, his muscles released pent-up tension. The spray thawed his bones and made him feel human again. It also reminded him that he'd watched a man plunge off a cliff into the chilly waters of Wolf Lake. What were the chances he'd survived? The cold alone would kill him. That the arsonist hadn't burst out of the lake and sucked air into his lungs told LeVar the man had drowned. He'd gotten what he deserved for setting fire to the campgrounds.

The investigators were wrong about CJ. Even if the Kings wanted to kill LeVar and they'd sent the boy to execute him, CJ didn't have a beef with Darren and Raven, and he wouldn't consort with a bearded, middle-aged Caucasian arsonist. None of the Kings would.

But LeVar had to be certain before he convinced the others. Stepping into a dry pair of sweatpants, he called CJ's phone while he yanked a shirt over his head.

"You finally decide I'm right about taking out the Royals?" CJ asked as a way of greeting his former friend.

"I'm not about to walk into another gang war."

"Then why are you calling me? Until you do right by your brothers, you're dead to me."

"CJ, I need to know if you were on the trail today."

"Nah, man. We had words. No reason for me to follow you again. Believe me, you'll see me coming next time."

"That another threat?"

"The Kings make promises, not threats. You remember."

"You're telling me the truth, right?"

"Hundred percent. Got no reason to lie to you, my brother from another mother."

LeVar grinned. "You remember."

"Course I do. We go way back, but not as far as the Kings. I've known my boys longer than you, and Harmon even longer. Those are where my loyalties lie." CJ paused. "Why you asking me about the trail? What's going on?"

"Not sure if you heard, but someone set fire to the park last night. White guy with a beard. Ring a bell?"

"Ain't got nothing to do with me. Why would I burn down a park?"

"If you say you weren't there, I believe you. Same guy returned today, and I chased after him."

"Catch him?"

"Almost."

"The old LeVar would have. You're gettin' slow, my brother. Livin' with rich folk will do that to you."

"The guy jumped off the cliff and landed in the lake."

CJ chuckled. "Well, he's dead. White people are crazy. Don't know what you see in them."

"We need to talk," said LeVar. "Are the remaining members of the Kings targeting me?"

"You alive, ain't you?"

"Yeah."

"Then we ain't."

CJ hung up.

LeVar stared at the phone for a long time. Could he trust CJ? He wanted to believe his old friend, but people didn't walk away from gang life without trouble. For the past year and a half, he'd expected to turn a corner and find a gun aimed between his eyes. Rev, the insane leader of the Kings, had tried to kill him before the police arrested the gangster.

A truck pulled into Thomas's driveway. Darren was back, and he had Raven with him. While they crossed the yard, Scout exited her kitchen and joined them. He opened the door.

"Hustle," he said. "You're letting the heat out."

"You sound more like Ma every day," Raven said, kissing his cheek.

"Come in. Should we order food?"

"Better get to the heart of the matter," Darren said. "I don't feel comfortable leaving the park unattended."

"I hear that."

Scout wore a hooded Kane Grove University sweatshirt.

"Where'd you get the hoodie?" he asked.

"The village sporting goods shop carries KGU football gear."

"Oh, you're even referring to the school as KGU now. Why don't you just get it over with and apply?"

"Maybe I will," she said wearing a smile.

They gathered around the card table. LeVar turned the heater to face them.

"All right, LeVar," Darren said. "I want the truth. Were the Harmon Kings and that CJ kid behind the arson?"

"No way."

"But the guy you chased showed up in the same spot as CJ."

"I told you, bro. This guy was middle-aged and bearded. Caucasian. I didn't get a good look at his face, but he sure as hell wasn't CJ."

"You need to be one hundred percent positive," said Raven. "We can't take any chances."

"CJ isn't trying to kill me."

"Rev did."

"But CJ isn't a psycho. Listen, if the Kings want me dead, they'll come at me directly, and they sure as hell won't waste time setting fires in parks."

"Isn't it possible the Kings targeted Raven because she's your sister?" Scout asked.

"That's a good point, LeVar," Darren said.

LeVar stuffed his hands in his pockets and looked down.

"Rev might have, but CJ wouldn't, and it seems the other members of the Kings listen to him."

"What about this guy you chased? Is it safe to assume he's dead?"

"You know how cold that water is."

Darren nodded. "And he never broke the surface."

"He could have swum underwater," Scout said. "Once he reached the other side of the cliff, you wouldn't see him."

"It's a long way to shore."

"I'm uncomfortable assuming he drowned," said Raven. "After what we went through last night, I won't sleep right for months. I say we focus our investigation on the arsonist."

"What about catching Officer Barrett's killer?" asked Scout.

"We'll get him, but an arsonist can kill many with one fire. Until the authorities drag his body from the lake, we need to assume he's alive."

"All right," Darren said. "Thomas's deputies and the state police are going door to door along the lake and asking if anyone spotted this guy. I say we drive up and down that road until we find his vehicle. If it's the same man who tailgated Raven, we're searching for a red pickup."

"We should split up," LeVar said. "Raven, you go with Darren. Scout and I will take my Chrysler."

"What about my Rogue?" Raven asked. "It's an SUV."

"Unlike you, I'm responsible and own snow tires."

29

Working on three hours of sleep, Sheriff Thomas Shepherd directed the cruiser along the icy road leading down from the state park. Deputy Aguilar had joined him, while Lambert assisted the state police in following the arsonist's tracks through the woods. Both his hands gripped the wheel; it wouldn't take long for his tires to lose traction on untreated blacktop.

Whatever Aguilar was drinking made his mouth water.

"What is that, a smoothie?"

"My secret formula for staying sharp after a rough night of sleep."

"Didn't sleep well last night?"

"I grabbed five hours. Not sure why I kept waking up."

"You made out better than me," he said. "When I arrived home after the fire, it was almost time to wake up."

"But you're the boss man, Thomas. Isn't that what Lambert calls you?"

"Your point?"

"You can set your hours. We can hold down the fort while you catch up on rest."

"But I'm the *sheriff*. Nightshade County is my responsibility."

"That doesn't mean you need to join the Justice League. Take care of yourself. Nothing heals a body like sleep."

He rubbed the sand from his eyes. "So what's this secret formula?"

"Try it," she said, handing him the bottle. "Don't worry, I don't have the plague."

"I'm not trying it until you tell me what's in it."

"What are you, three years old?"

He took the thermos and drank a mouthful.

"Whoa, that's fantastic."

"Right?"

"Now will you reveal your formula?"

"It's not too different from the smoothies I blend at work," she said. "Frozen fruit, spinach, vanilla and protein powder. After a rough night, I add a tablespoon of pure cacao and two teaspoons of lion's mane mushroom powder."

"That's . . . different."

"The cacao and lion's mane give me an energy boost and a positive mindset. You want more?"

"No, but text the ingredients to Chelsey. She's running to the store later."

Aguilar examined the homes beside the lake.

"If our fugitive survived, you'd think someone would have seen him by now."

"Yeah, and if he's somewhere in the lake, we might never find him."

At that moment, the cruiser's radio crackled. Aguilar reached for the receiver. The dispatcher's voice rang over the speaker in bursts of static.

"Baxter Reyes, at 1242 State Park Hill, requests the sheriff's department. He found bloody footprints in his hallway and the front door unlocked."

Thomas glanced at Aguilar and reversed course. The address was a quarter mile behind them. A squat man with a dark complexion answered the door.

"Mr. Reyes? Nightshade County Sheriff's Department."

"Come in, come in," the man said.

Thomas entered the living room and ran his gaze over the interior. The bookshelf on the far wall held a few dozen classic fiction tomes. Across from the shelf sat a couch with a folded afghan on top. A splotch on the olive-green carpet looked like blood.

"You told dispatch you found your front door unlocked and footprints in the hallway?" Thomas asked.

"And blood, yes."

"You didn't cut yourself?"

"It's not my blood, Sheriff. I was in my study and working on the computer when I heard the front door close. After I came out, I saw the footprints."

"Show us."

Thomas and Aguilar followed the man to the edge of the hallway, where he stopped and pointed. The man hadn't exaggerated. Bloody footprints led down the corridor and into an open bedroom.

"The footprints begin in the kitchen," Reyes said. "I neglected to lock the back door. That's how the person got inside."

"You didn't see the man?" Aguilar asked.

"No. Whoever it was ran off before I checked."

"Did you touch the back door?"

"Well, yes. I locked it."

"Is anything missing from the house?"

"No valuables. I left a fifty-dollar bill on the nightstand, and it's still there. Call me crazy, but I think the person stole clothes from my dresser drawer. Here, I'll show you." Reyes led them into the bedroom. "See where the footprints end in front of the dresser?"

Aguilar crouched and studied a discoloration on the handle.

"Does that look like blood to you?" she asked Thomas.

"It does."

Aguilar slipped gloves over her hands, and Thomas followed suit.

"Oh, and I kept a pair of leather boots by the front door. They're gone too."

Thomas removed his phone. "I'll call Chief Pauley. We could use support from Harmon PD."

While they awaited the officers, Thomas opened the drawers.

"Notice any clothes missing?" he asked.

"Maybe. There was a sweatshirt in the middle drawer, but I don't see it anymore."

"Anything else?"

"It's possible he stole socks and underwear. I have too many as it is."

"Thank you, Mr. Reyes. Please do your best not to touch anything until Harmon PD arrives and dusts for prints."

Twenty minutes later, a squad car stopped at the end of the driveway. Aguilar peeked out the window.

"It's our friends from the skyscraper," she said.

Thomas walked to the pane. "Officers Knowles and Brentwood?"

"Isn't that them?"

"Looks like them to me."

Both officers appeared haggard and rushed.

"Sorry for making you wait," Knowles said. "We arrived for shift just before you called."

"No worries."

"What do you need us to do?"

"Dust the back door and kitchen for prints. The intruder came in through the kitchen and left blood everywhere."

"Think it's the guy who fell off the cliff?" Brentwood asked.

"Well, this person arrived barefoot and possibly naked. He stole clothes from the bedroom and a pair of boots."

"A prowler?"

"Doubtful. He didn't touch the fifty bucks on the nightstand."

While the Harmon PD officers worked in the kitchen, Aguilar dusted the dresser drawer for prints.

"I found more than a dozen," she said, chewing her lip. "They're smeared. I don't figure they'll help us."

"Plus, most probably belong to Mr. Reyes."

"True."

Thomas captured a blood sample in the hallway. After he finished, he measured the footprints and took photographs. The edge of his yellow evidence marker held a ruler, lending perspective.

Brentwood and Knowles appeared in the hallway.

"We pulled multiple prints off the back door and the kitchen wall," said Brentwood. "Want us to check the stairs? The foot-prints lead from the shore up the steps."

"If you would be so kind."

Brentwood tipped his cap, and Knowles led his fellow officer into the kitchen. Aguilar leaned against the bedroom doorway.

"Did you notice that?" she asked.

"Notice what?"

"Neither of them wore gloves."

Thomas smacked his forehead.

"Wonderful. They contaminated the scene. Now we'll have to work around the homeowner's and officers' prints."

"I hate to snitch on another law enforcement officer, but Chief Pauley needs to speak to them."

"I'll handle it. For now, play nice and ensure they don't screw up again."

An officer's radio squawked from the kitchen. Knowles returned to the hallway.

"Sorry, Sheriff, but the chief called us back to Harmon," said Knowles. "There was an incident involving the 315 Royals."

Brentwood stood behind Knowles with his thumbs hooked in his belt loops.

"No problem," Thomas said. "We'll take it from here."

The question was how he'd separate everyone's prints from the arsonist's.

30

S tanding at the window inside the ranger's cabin, Raven couldn't stay warm. Beyond the property, skeletal black trees reached skyward with gangling claws. She knew all too well about anxiety affecting someone after a break-in. How was this different? A psychopath had invaded their paradise and set the woods on fire. To make matters worse, she'd learned the arsonist had survived the leap off the cliff and broken into a lake house down the road. He'd come back.

"Thanks, deputy," Darren said from the kitchen. "I'll tell her."

She turned to him after the call ended. "Was that Aguilar?"

"Here's what we know: Someone broke into Baxter Reyes's house. The intruder left wet, bloody footprints and stole clothes from the owner's dresser drawer."

"That has to be our guy. He changed clothes so he didn't freeze to death."

"Thomas and Aguilar discovered the soaked clothing on the shore. The black winter jacket matches the description your brother gave."

The two investigation teams had spent the last couple of

hours searching for a red pickup truck. Darren had spotted tire tracks in the snow close to Reyes's lake house. The state police were attempting to identify the tires from the treads.

"He's still alive," she said. "How did he survive the fall?"

"The lake saved him, but the clock was ticking. If he'd stayed in the water a few minutes longer, he wouldn't have made it."

"What else did Thomas and Aguilar find?"

"Fingerprints on the doorknob. The ones on the dresser were too smudged."

Raven's face brightened. "If he's in the system, they'll identify him."

"Problem is Harmon PD contaminated the scene. Neither officer wore gloves."

"Are you serious?"

Darren pushed the air down with his hands.

"Don't lose faith. Aguilar is the best at what she does. She'll separate the prints from the officers'." He walked over and touched her cheek. "Come away from the window. You'll make yourself crazy if you stare at those trees."

She bit her lip. The sun would set in three hours. How would she sleep tonight?

"He didn't finish the job. That's why he returned to the trail before LeVar chased him away."

"That would be incredibly brazen. The arsonist has to know everyone expects him to try again."

"I doubt the man cares. He wants me dead. Remember, it was me he followed."

"If he's the same guy who tailgated you."

"He is. I can sense it."

He stroked the hair away from her cheeks and said, "That's why I intend to catch him tonight."

"Not without my help."

"I can handle it, Raven. You sleep while I run surveillance on the camp. If he returns, I'll nail him."

"Darren, I won't get a wink of sleep knowing he's out there and you're searching for him. Let me help."

"I can't. You just recovered from a concussion."

"And I'm a hundred percent healthy."

"It's not worth the risk."

She poked a finger against his chest. "Don't play the role of macho superhero with me. It doesn't suit you. I don't care how many surveillance missions you've led. Chelsey and I have run our share."

He sighed. "You're not making this easy."

"You should expect that of me."

"I do. Look, if you insist on working, you'll do so from inside. I don't want you out in the cold. It's supposed to drop into the teens overnight."

"Don't ask me to stay in the cabin by myself."

"I have a different idea in mind," he said. "All the guest cabins are vacant. Let's set you up in one of those. The arsonist will expect us to be home."

"Why a guest cabin?"

"They're back from the tree line. Even if he sets another fire, you'll have plenty of time to escape. A lot more than you will if you stay here."

She walked away. "You're handling me with kid's gloves. That's not like you."

"Listen, you can run surveillance from a cabin. We'll set up your laptop so you can monitor the trail cameras. If you spot anybody, alert me over the radio or send a text." As she watched him from the corner of her eye, he huffed. "Okay, you can go after him too, provided you're armed."

"Trust me, I will be."

"Speaking of running surveillance with Chelsey, why don't you ask her to help? I'll feel better if you aren't alone."

"I intend to ask Chelsey, but not because I'm afraid of working alone." She turned her gaze to the window. "Darren, what if this is the same guy who killed Officer Barrett?"

"What makes you think he is?"

"Why else would he target me? He found out WLC is working for Trix Barrett."

"That's a possibility."

"Shoot," she said. "What if he goes after the others? LeVar, Scout, and Chelsey need to know."

"So we'll tell them, but don't jump to conclusions. You've caught your share of criminals over the years. This might be someone from your past."

"Mark Benson is in jail."

Mark Benson, Buck's cousin, had stalked Raven and her mother before the investigators and sheriff's department tracked him down.

"Then someone else. Keep your mind open to every possibility."

She checked her gun and made sure it was ready. Minutes passed in seconds.

Night was coming.

31

L ight faded outside Thomas's office window as he pried off his hat and gloves and set his coat on a rack. Though he'd enjoyed working beside Chelsey at her business, he and Aguilar needed to run the fingerprints through AFIS, the Automated Fingerprint Identification System, and that required they work from the sheriff's department this afternoon and evening, no matter how uncomfortable the temperature was inside.

Heat blew into the room, but the forced air barely fluttered the cobwebs hanging off the vents. Which reminded him he needed to dust the grates.

While Aguilar fed the prints through the system, he loaded a digital map on his computer and measured the distance between the cliff and Baxter Reyes's home. The readout confirmed it was four hundred and twenty yards, a little less than a quarter of a mile. That was a long distance to swim in wintry temperatures. The arsonist must be strong and agile to stay ahead of LeVar and traverse the icy waters.

Wrapped in a coat, Chelsey crossed the sidewalk and opened the entry doors. Her head was huddled inside the neck of her jacket as she walked down the hallway. Aguilar greeted her and said Thomas was in his office.

"Finishing early today?" he asked.

Chelsey was always the last person to leave the investigation firm.

"Taking a break before I work late. Raven called and asked me to run a stakeout at the park."

"You really think the arsonist will return? He almost drowned and froze to death this afternoon."

"The odds are long, but it pays to be safe."

"Lambert is working the overnight shift. I'll make sure he checks on you. Do you need a deputy?"

"Don't see why. Between Darren, Raven, and me, we'll see the guy if he shows up."

"Chelsey, if the cameras catch anything in the park—I don't care if it turns out to be a deer—I want you to call the department."

"We will." Chelsey fixed her eyes on his desk. "What are you working on?"

"Besides measuring the distance between the cliffs and Baxter Reyes's house—it's four hundred and twenty yards, in case you're wondering—I'm going over this suicide note the Harmon PD found."

"The Christopher Fieldman case?"

"That's right. Harmon PD is handling the investigation, but they asked us to help."

"I can't turn on the news without hearing about his suicide. He owned the city of Harmon. What is so suspicious about the note?"

"A few things. The paper stock is inferior quality, not the kind Fieldman used at home and in his office. Also, the wording seems clunky. His wife pointed it out to me. I'm comparing the note to a letter he wrote last week for his staff. It's like two different people composed them."

"That's understandable if he was suicidal."

"But what if he wasn't suicidal?" he asked.

"You suspect someone threw him off the Jefferson Building?"

Thomas wasn't sure what to believe, but he felt uncomfortable with Harmon PD ruling the death a suicide.

"That's what I intend to find out."

She leaned over the desk and kissed his lips. "I'm heading home to take care of the pets and grab a few hours of shuteye. We might end up pulling an all-nighter."

"Please be safe and call me if you change your mind about the deputy."

After she left, he rocked back in his chair with copies of both letters in his hands. As Bernadette Fieldman had stated, the suicide note seemed written by a different person. His eyes darted to the computer screen and the terrain between the ranger's cabin and Baxter Reyes's address. The investigations had nothing to do with one another, right?

He tapped his fingers on the desk and studied the papers. Raven believed the man who'd killed Officer Shawn Barrett was the arsonist. Burning the forest was his attempt to eliminate her from the picture. Would he go after Chelsey, LeVar, and Scout?

What did this have to do with the Fieldman suicide? Nothing, as far as he could determine.

"Sheriff."

Thomas jumped, not hearing Aguilar enter his office.

"Yes, deputy."

"I have bad news. The prints came back. They belong to Officers Brentwood and Knowles."

"I was afraid of that."

"There are two additional prints, but I confirmed one belongs to the homeowner."

"And the other?"

"Too smudged to send through AFIS."

"Like the prints on the dresser drawer. That leaves us at square one." Thomas scratched his head. "I'll call Chief Pauley."

"I hope he doesn't suspend the officers. They screwed up, but everyone deserves a second chance, especially around the holidays."

"You did your best, Aguilar. Let me know if you're able to pull a legible print out of the smudges."

He expected she wouldn't. Aguilar was an expert at pulling prints, not to mention a perfectionist. If another usable print existed, she would already have it in her possession.

Pauley answered with a grunt. Thomas didn't blame him. The chief had lost an officer and friend in Shawn Barrett, and the media remained in an uproar over the Christopher Fieldman suicide. After he told Pauley about the officers not wearing gloves, the chief sounded as if he were chewing nails.

"I apologize for my officers, Sheriff. Hopefully, they won't be my problem for much longer. Rumor has it Brentwood wants to work in Buffalo, and Knowles wants out of the force. Can't say I'll miss either. They produce sloppy work, and I'm afraid one of them will botch key evidence and wreck an investigation."

"I didn't want to tell you."

"No, I'm glad you did. I'll talk to the officers and ensure nothing like that happens again. Were you able to pull a usable print?"

"Every print we put through the system belonged to Reyes or the officers."

"Dammit. Because of my men, your arsonist is running free."

"We'll catch him, Chief," Thomas said.

"I owe you one. If you need support, I'll send you everything you need. And next time, I'll make sure it's someone besides Brentwood and Knowles."

"Before we finish up, do you have an opinion on Christopher Fieldman's suicide letter?"

"As Deputy Aguilar pointed out, the paper stock is different. Of course, Fieldman could have printed the letter anywhere. It sure looks like a suicide."

"Yes, but the grammar and syntax don't match Fieldman's company notes. Did you receive the office memo I sent you?"

"I did, and the differences made me wonder as well. My lead detective is working on the investigation. Let me get with her and call you back."

"Thank you, Chief."

"And again, I apologize about my men. They'll answer for this screw up."

32

I n the dim light of a corner lamp, LeVar hunched over the computer and put the final touches on a term paper. If he aced his finals, he would earn a 4.0 GPA for the second time. During high school, he'd never studied, and his grades suffered. All he'd cared about was the Harmon Kings.

The space heater worked overtime to keep the front room comfortable. He didn't want to guess how high the energy bill would be this month. Thomas deserved more money, but LeVar already gave the sheriff half his paycheck. Maybe he should talk to Ruth Sims at The Broken Yolk about picking up more hours, especially with the holidays approaching.

Outside the window, darkness concealed the lake. Wind rattled the glass and blew snow against the pane. If it was this cold before Thanksgiving, what would January bring?

A tap on the door made him flinch. He checked the clock. It was almost eleven, too late for Scout or Naomi to visit. He thought about his service weapon in the bedroom.

Standing, he stared down the gloomy hallway toward the front door. A curtain over the window prevented him from identifying the person.

"Hello?"

He was exposed. Had a ghost from his past returned? If the Harmon Kings wanted to kill him, he couldn't watch his own back twenty-four hours a day. His imagination conjured a bullet blasting through the door and striking him in the chest.

The tapping came again, quiet enough to avoid drawing attention from the neighbors. LeVar walked along the wall, staying out of the way in case the intruder had a gun.

"Who is it?"

"Open the door."

LeVar closed his eyes and knocked his head against the wall. CJ. Should he let his old friend inside? He thought of Thomas looking out the window and spotting the gangster.

"Get inside before someone sees."

CJ entered. As before, his hands were jammed deep inside the pockets of his black winter coat.

Like the jacket the arsonist wore.

"Are you crazy?" he asked. "The sheriff lives in the A-frame."

"That's why I tried to be quiet."

"You shouldn't be here."

"I can't visit my brother no more? Not welcome under his roof? You changed, bro."

LeVar peeked between the curtains. The kitchen light shone in Thomas's house. He led CJ into the front room and shut off his computer monitor. The gangster took in the surroundings and whistled.

"Damn, LeVar. This is sweet. How much does this place run?"

"More than I can afford."

"Seems you're living large to me."

"Take your hands out of your pockets."

CJ pulled out his hands and raised them.

"You still worried I'll put a bullet in you? When did you get so paranoid?"

"Around the time I joined the Kings. Never knew who wanted your spot and was willing to pull a trigger to steal it. Turn out your pockets."

"Seriously?"

"Either that, or I'll do it for you."

"You and what army?"

He strode up to CJ and patted down the jacket, locking eyes with him the entire time.

"All right, dawg. You're clean. Now tell me why you're here."

Though he'd checked for weapons, LeVar winced when CJ removed his jacket and draped it over a chair.

"Mind if I sit, or don't you want my dirt on your furniture?"

"Stop. My home is your home. You're still my brother."

"Don't seem like it." CJ plopped onto the couch. "Here all right?"

He pulled a chair from the card table and sat on it backwards.

"Make yourself comfortable. Out with it. You didn't drive all the way here for a social call."

"I'm giving you one last chance, LeVar."

"One last chance at what?"

CJ frowned. "To hit the Royals. This is the time. With Dean gone, they're disorganized. They've never been this ripe for the picking."

"I told you I'm a county sheriff's deputy. Not gonna jump into a gang war. That ain't my life, not anymore."

CJ sat forward with his elbows on his knees.

"Don't you care? If the Royals take over the drug trade, they'll regain power. Hell, with us gone, they'll have even more. Nobody will stand in their way."

"What's that to me?"

"Damn, LeVar," CJ said. "You really *did* turn your back on your city."

"I saved myself."

He clapped his hands with mock enthusiasm.

"And moved into the burbs with whitey."

"You know what your problem is, CJ? You're a racist."

"How the hell am I a racist?"

"You judge everyone by skin color and look down on me because some of my friends are white."

"From where I sit, all of your friends are white. Just because you got it good don't mean you can't care about your people. Hey, if you won't do it for the street, do it for your new boys—those cops you call friends. As an officer of the law, don't you care about the drug trade?"

"Course I do, but I'm not starting a gang war." LeVar lifted his chin. "Tell me about the drug shipment. When is it coming in?"

"I don't know, and that's the God's honest truth."

"What are they pushing?"

"Heroin." CJ noticed the blood draining from LeVar's face. "That's right, bro. The same stuff that almost killed your ma."

"How do you know about my mother?"

"We all knew, LeVar. Everyone did. Think about it: thousands of more heroin addicts shooting up, crowding the soup kitchen, stumbling around like zombies. That what you want for Harmon?"

LeVar crossed his arms. "Getting the boys back together and firing bullets at the Royals won't make Harmon safer."

"Better than letting them take over the city."

LeVar pinched the bridge of his nose.

"All right, CJ. I'll help you."

The gangster grinned and extended his arm, encouraging LeVar to bump fists.

"But not as a member of the Kings."

CJ pulled his hand back.

"What are you saying?"

"This is a job for law enforcement." When CJ rolled his eyes, LeVar grabbed his arm. "Look at me, CJ. I love you. You're the smartest kid I ever met. If anyone should have run the show, it was you, but it's time you gave up the streets and stopped blaming the police for your problems."

"I can't do that."

"You have to, unless you want to die before you escape your twenties. Think of the difference you can make for Harmon."

"The cops, huh? You're asking a lot, my brother."

"Let me introduce you to Sheriff Shepherd."

"He the autistic guy?"

"Asperger's, yeah. He's also the kindest person I've ever known."

"What's he know about gangs?"

LeVar blinked. "Besides dealing with the Kings and Royals? Dude spent ten years working the streets with the LAPD. He ate a bullet during a drive-by."

CJ appeared distrustful yet resigned. "And this Sheriff Shepherd will do right by Harmon?"

"He volunteers at the soup kitchen, which is probably more than you can say."

"I do plenty for my city."

"Then prove it. But I warn you: We'll have to bring in Harmon PD."

The boy turned away. "Not those pigs."

"There's no choice. You want to stop the Royals or not?"

CJ rubbed his face.

"If that's the way it has to be, then let's go for it. But if the cops do us dirty, the Kings will take matters into our own hands."

33

L ong after darkness settled over the lake, the man stood on a ridge overlooking the valley and pulled black gloves over his hands. Combustible fury raged inside his body. The Wolf Lake Consulting investigators were proving to be a problem.

They'd pushed him to the brink. His only choice was to kill the forest ranger and Raven Hopkins, then murder the two teenagers.

With binoculars pressed to his eyes, he glassed the state park. The forest concealed the ranger's cabin, yet he saw its lights beyond the trees. Nobody was moving.

He checked his watch: five minutes after midnight. It had taken all his will to contain himself this afternoon while he waited for night to return. Surely, the sheriff's department and investigators anticipated he'd set another fire. But two nights in a row? They probably expected him to hide under the radar until things calmed down. That wasn't his way. By morning, they would all be dead.

The man climbed into his truck. Snow crunched as the tires ground it into dust. When he returned to the village, he stopped at a twenty-four-hour gas station and pulled two containers from the back of the cab. A hood concealed his face. He didn't worry about the police identifying his license plates on the camera feed overlooking the pumps. Before entering the village, he'd plastered snow and ice over the front and rear plates. If the authorities were looking for a red pickup, he wished them luck. There were thousands of trucks like his in the county. Besides, the clerk inside the store wouldn't think twice about a customer filling containers. Gasoline was the one accelerant that didn't draw attention. This time of year, people needed fuel for snow-blowers.

He shut off the pump and pulled himself into the cab. Turning out of the parking lot, he drove to Wolf Lake State Park.

34

———

Raven and Chelsey lay on twin beds, Chelsey facing the east windows of the cabin, Raven the south windows and front door. The time ticked past midnight, and the fire starter hadn't returned to the state park.

The lights were off. Because of the bright moon outside, they would be invisible to prying eyes. The only light inside the cabin came from the space heater's faint orange glow. The supplemental heat source kept the cabin comfortable, which was more than Raven could say for Darren's hiding spot on the hill. She felt guilty and wanted to join her boyfriend, but he refused her help.

"No movement in the forest," Chelsey said.

Raven nodded and raised binoculars to her eyes. For a stakeout, this was cozy. They had all the amenities of home at their disposal—the heater, a laptop that displayed camera views from around the campground and kept them connected to the world, and more snacks than either woman could eat. Chelsey's cooler contained drinks and sandwiches from the deli. It seemed more like a picnic than a stakeout.

"Imagine if all our missions were this comfortable," she said.

"I'm not sure how we could pull that off."

"Here's an idea: Let's purchase a bus, gut the inside, and add a refrigerator."

"Why not install a bar while we're at it?"

"Now you're talking."

Chelsey rolled her eyes.

Raven crawled further down the bed until she was two steps from the window. She'd never stayed up this late to watch the forest. Night held a secretive beauty that the sun couldn't capture.

She spoke into the radio. "You there, Darren?"

He didn't reply until her third attempt. Were the batteries dying? It shouldn't be this difficult to reach someone a hundred yards away.

"I got you loud and clear," he said.

"How's the weather up there?"

"Nice. Now you're taunting me. Enjoying your Club Med surveillance mission?"

"It's pretty sweet. You could do the same and hide in a cabin."

"I want to be outside if and when this guy returns."

"Your choice, but don't complain about the cold."

She craned her neck and looked up the hill. He remained invisible, which was a good thing. According to Darren, he was holed up behind a snowbank. The poor guy had to be freezing. How long had he been out there? She wished he would stop the heroics and hide in a cabin. How much better could his view be?

PERCHED on a hillock overlooking the campgrounds, Ranger Darren Holt studied the clearing through his binoculars. The snow reflected eerie blue moonlight. Beyond the clearing, deep shadows pooled in the forest. Trees surrounded Darren as he crouched behind a snowbank, a white blanket tossed over his head and shoulders, more to conceal his presence than to keep him warm. Still, he was thankful for the blanket. Condensation clouds rolled off his lips; he wiggled his toes and fingers to keep them from going numb. It had to be in the teens, if not colder.

Darren had worked his share of uncomfortable stakeouts with the Syracuse PD, but never in temperatures this chilly. Once, he'd shared an abandoned apartment building with a fellow officer while waiting for a drug deal to go down across the street. He'd thought that was frigid, but the temperature was in the twenties that night, and the building shielded him from the wind.

This was the true meaning of cold. Crouching low, he shifted his weight back and forth to keep his blood flowing. It made no sense to him that the arsonist would return one night after setting fire to the forest—the psychopath needed to recover after jumping into the lake—but Raven was sure the man would come, and he'd learned to trust her instincts.

He could see cabin number four, which housed Raven and Chelsey. The lights were off, but the ones in the ranger's cabin spread bright rectangles across the clearing. If the arsonist struck, he'd set fire to the trees beside the cabin. They'd ignite easily. Every tree along the clearing was little more than charcoal waiting for a match.

"Raven, where did you go?" he said into the radio.

A few seconds passed, then, "We're still here. See anything?"

"Nothing yet. How about from your vantage point?"

"Quiet."

"It's almost one in the morning. I doubt he'll return tonight."

"Give him another hour."

Easy for her to say. She wasn't the one kneeling in the snow.

"Another hour it is. Then we'll call it a night."

"Deal."

He set the radio in his pocket and looked through the binoculars. Forest stretched for as far as the lenses carried him. Nothing moved in the shadows, not even deer. The animals had decided it was too chilly to forage for food.

Darren sat and placed his back against the bank. It felt nice to stretch his legs. His knees popped and crunched like potato chips. He blinked and stared up at the mass of stars as the moon tracked across the horizon, taking the lunar glow with it. This next hour would be the longest of the mission. He needed to stretch his muscles, but he couldn't risk standing.

With a groan, he turned onto his stomach and lay flat with the blanket covering his body. He peered out from the opening, searching for signs of the arsonist. Pools of black bled through the woods.

A shadow darted from one tree to the next. He shifted the binoculars. Was that his imagination? One could grow punchy after several hours of surveillance.

He edged out from behind the bank, keeping the blanket over his head and shoulders. Again he searched the forest and found nothing.

The shadow moved to another tree. This time he was certain it was a man. The silhouette stood upright and hid behind the trunk.

Darren checked his gun. The arsonist had returned, and he was heading toward the cabins. How would he warn Raven and Chelsey without alerting the intruder? He pressed the radio's call button several times to get their attention and whispered into the speaker.

"Raven. He's here."

No one replied. A sharp odor reached his nose.

Gasoline.

35

"Darren, come in."

Raven fiddled with the radio, removed the batteries, and stuck them back in the compartment. For the last five minutes, she'd failed to contact the ranger.

"He's not answering," she said to Chelsey.

"Maybe the radio died."

"Try yours."

Chelsey did, but Darren didn't reply.

"Nope."

"I'm worried. Something isn't right."

Raven climbed off the bed and pulled on her jacket.

"You aren't walking up that hill, are you?" Chelsey asked.

"What choice do I have?"

"Send him a text."

That made the most sense, but Raven's instinct warned her the radio was the least of their worries. She squinted into the night.

"I don't think we're alone."

Chelsey crawled off the other bed and joined her at the window.

"I'll get my jacket."

As Chelsey dressed for the cold, Raven slipped her hands into a pair of gloves and wrapped a scarf around her neck. She stopped and sniffed the air.

"What's that smell? Is that gasoline?"

Chelsey's eyes widened.

Raven opened the door just as a shadow ran past the trees. Footfalls trailed down the hill and raced through the snow. Darren was coming. Did he know the man was carrying a container of fuel?

Chelsey split off and circled around the opposite side of the cabin. The chill stiffened Raven's joints and made it difficult to move in silence. Her boots scuffed through the snow, her breath blowing back into her face and freezing on contact.

She could almost make out the man's face. He hadn't seen her yet and was busy dousing the trees with gasoline. Now and then his eyes darted to the ranger's cabin, fixated on the light glowing through the window. He never saw his attacker approaching from behind.

"Darren, no!" Raven yelled a second before the man struck a match.

Flames exploded, pushing Darren backward. The arsonist turned and saw the ranger. To Raven's horror, the man pulled a gun.

Darren wrestled the man down and knocked the weapon from his hand as she sprinted to help. Chelsey reversed course, driven away by the fire. Smoke puffed and strangled the air.

The arsonist turned Darren over and fought his way to the top. He threw a punch, but the ranger blocked it with his forearm and covered up. Seeing her boyfriend in trouble, she grabbed the psycho from behind and yanked him off. He whirled around. She made out a bearded face hidden deep inside a hood.

Before Raven could stop the arsonist, he struck another match. The flame caught residues of fuel coating his leather gloves. Fire engulfed his hands as Raven dove out of harm's way. Screaming, the man dropped to the ground and rolled, plunging his gloved hands into the snow. As she crawled to her feet, the inferno burst upward and knocked her over.

Darren scrambled away. Chelsey pulled her gun and fired at the fleeing man. The bullet ricocheted off a tree before the flames formed a wall between them.

"Call 911!" Raven yelled.

Chelsey phoned the emergency hotline.

Darren would have raced after the arsonist, but Raven grabbed his arm.

"Are you insane? You'll never make it through the fire."

He appeared determined to try until she dragged him away. Darren regained his senses and retrieved the hose. She cranked the faucet.

"The Wolf Lake Fire Department is on the way." Chelsey said. "Did you see his face?"

Raven shook her head. She'd had a chance to catch the madman and let him get away.

36

The dashboard clock read two in the morning when Thomas stopped his truck in front of the state park visitor's center. Deputy Lambert was already there and questioning Darren. He spotted Chelsey with Raven outside the ranger's cabin.

Déjà vu struck him as he crossed the clearing. Firefighters drenched the trees closest to the cabin. The fire was out, but smoke covered the landscape in a toxic mist. He ducked his face inside his jacket and coughed. Lambert left Darren and came over to meet him.

"What do we have, deputy?"

"The arsonist set fire to the trees a half hour ago," Lambert said. "Darren almost caught him, but the flames got in the way. Chelsey says she fired her gun and missed."

"Did anyone recognize the guy?"

"Nobody got a good look at his face. Raven repeated what LeVar told you. White male, bearded, an inch or two shorter than Darren."

"That's not much to go on."

"We finally got a break. When the arsonist tried to set Raven on fire, the flame caught his gloves. He must have sustained burns. They heard him screaming."

"I understand he used gasoline."

"That's correct," Lambert said. "He carried two containers and left them behind. They exploded in the fire. The inspector is looking over the remains."

"All right. We'll call every gas station in the county and check the security cameras. We're searching for a white, bearded male in his thirties or forties. This guy filled two containers at the pump. Concentrate on anyone driving a red pickup truck."

"I'll contact our office."

Thomas joined the others and pulled Chelsey and Raven into hugs.

"You're unharmed?"

"Darren is getting his breath back," Raven said, "but we came out of the attack unscathed."

"I trust the fire didn't reach the cabins."

"No, we turned it back. Thankfully, the fire department arrived in time."

"What about you?" he asked Chelsey. "Did you inhale smoke?"

"I'm all right," she said. "Just a little shook up."

"Did this guy say anything that would help you recognize his voice?"

"Not until he screamed. By then, the fire blocked us from reaching him. That's how he escaped."

He groaned in frustration.

"First he leaped off a cliff into a frigid lake and survived, and tonight he set himself on fire and got away. Lady Luck can't stay on his side forever."

Raven led Darren into the cabin and sat him at the kitchen table. An emergency worker followed them inside. Though Darren protested, the paramedic convinced him to accept oxygen until his lungs cleared. Every several seconds, the ranger removed the mask and coughed.

"Stop acting stubborn," Raven said. "You're not too tough to ask for help."

"You're one to talk," Darren said. His voice sounded hollow and alien through the mask. To Raven's chagrin, he pulled the oxygen away from his mouth. "Thomas . . . the arsonist." Darren coughed again. "He knew how to fight."

The sheriff kneeled beside Darren. "Martial arts?"

"I'm not sure. Grappling technique. He got off his back in a hurry and took me by surprise. Reminded me of everything I learned on the force."

Thomas shifted his jaw. A cop? He checked the recordings. As expected, the arsonist had avoided the cameras and approached through the forest. They would find his tracks, and perhaps that would help the sheriff's department catch the man. It also lent credence to Thomas's theory: The arsonist knew about the camp's security system. How did he know so much about Darren's cameras?

Lambert entered the cabin and joined him at the computer.

"I picked up his tracks two hundred yards down the hill. The fire melted the snow on top of the ridge."

"Good work."

Lambert narrowed his eyes. "I hope you have something warmer than that jacket. The wind chill is below zero."

"I'll get by."

"Why don't you stop at the house before we track his path?"

"Because he's already a half hour ahead of us. Let's go."

"Take my sweatshirt," Chelsey said, removing her jacket. "I'll be inside the rest of the night. You need it more than me."

He kissed her.

"I appreciate it."

"Please be careful. Those trees could fall at any second."

"I will."

"And try to stay warm."

Thomas wondered how that was possible as he stepped into the crisp night air. Lambert was dressed for the cold, yet the deputy shuffled his feet, battling to generate heat.

They set off into the forest. The madman's tracks led through the pitch black.

HE TRIPPED in the entryway and stumbled into the living room, moaning, cursing, biting his tongue and drawing blood. The gloves hadn't saved his hands from the fire. Bits of leather joined the skin hanging in opaque flaps. On the verge of bursting, a blister the size of an eyeball rose off his palm.

The man limped into the kitchen and fell against the counter. Using his elbow, he nudged the faucet and got the water flowing. How would he test the temperature? He placed his elbow in the water and waited until it felt lukewarm.

Before the arsonist could talk himself out of it, he shoved his hands under the flow and screamed. The agony was worse than anything he'd experienced in his life, more painful than driving a nail through his thumb. He wanted to yank his hands away from the water. But he couldn't. He had to stop the burning.

After he finished, he hobbled to the bathroom and searched for an appropriate medication for burns. There was nothing. He returned to the kitchen, pried the pantry open with his foot, and located a box of plastic sandwich bags. Carefully, he slid the bags over his hands. They would protect his flesh until he sought a doctor.

But where? Every physician would be on the lookout for a man with burned hands.

He slumped to the floor and sat with his back against the cabinet.

"I'll kill them all. They did this to me."

The man ground his teeth. He knew who to blame. That bitch Raven Hopkins and her ranger boyfriend. The other woman was Chelsey Byrd; he'd recognized her from the Wolf Lake Consulting website. First he would kill Raven, then Darren and Chelsey. After that, he would murder those punk teenagers, LeVar Hopkins and Scout Mourning, and punish them for sticking their noses in his business.

Lowering his head, he stared at his plastic-covered hands. He couldn't go to work like this. How would he hide the burns? Heck, how would he sleep tonight? He felt as if the flames still engulfed his flesh.

Too close. He might have died tonight, had it not been for his quick thinking.

"Stop, drop, and roll," he said with a maniacal laugh.

The most arduous task was accessing the ibuprofen. Without hands, it seemed impossible to open the bottle. He stomped the container until it snapped apart. On his knees, he inhaled two capsules and swallowed.

Yes, he would make them pay. All of them.

37

Thomas was already at the sheriff's department when Deputy Aguilar arrived at 5:50 a.m. She passed his office without noticing him, set a thermos on her desk, then did a double take.

"You were here all night, weren't you?" she asked.

He rubbed his tired eyes in answer.

"Why, Thomas? You should have let the midnight crew handle the investigation."

"We let the arsonist get away again."

"Don't move a muscle. I'll make you one of my energy smoothies."

"Aguilar, you don't have to."

"Nuh-uh. Don't talk back. If you insist on abusing your body, at least feed your mind."

He turned his gaze back to the computer screen. For a second, he thought he was seeing in triplicate, but three prints stared back at him. One belonged to Baxter Reyes, the others to Officers Brentwood and Knowles. Though he trusted Aguilar's ability, he needed to be sure the smudged prints couldn't be read.

Finally, he sat back in frustration. The arsonist had evaded them again, this time thanks to shoddy police work.

Aguilar set the smoothie in front of him and sat.

"You look perturbed," she said.

"It's more than a lack of sleep. I can't understand how this fugitive broke into a house and left no usable prints."

She sipped from a mason jar and watched him over the lid. "We would have found his prints if the officers hadn't screwed up. The bigger question is why he returned and set a second fire. He had to assume Darren and Raven would be ready for him."

"And he knew the locations of the cameras." Thomas drank another gulp. He had to admit the concoction granted him energy. Suddenly, he sat up and clapped his hands together. "That's it. The security cameras."

"What about them?"

"Area law enforcement officers know about Darren's cameras. They tap into his feed. Aguilar, maybe we have the arsonist's fingerprints after all."

She shifted her chair toward the desk.

"Are you suggesting the unsub is a police officer?"

"It makes sense. Did Knowles and Brentwood dust for prints? I didn't monitor their activity."

"Oh, Thomas, be careful. We won't make friends with the Harmon PD by accusing their officers."

"Put the facts together," he said. "The person who killed Officer Shawn Barrett knew about his allergy."

"And he knew Barrett had taken an alternate route home to avoid traffic."

"Harmon PD watches the feed from the state park, the same as we do. Raven believes the arsonist pursued her because she's working for Trix Barrett."

"If Knowles or Brentwood killed Shawn Barrett, they would purposely screw up the evidence."

"Exactly. Now we just have to prove it."

Aguilar looked up in thought. "Raven and LeVar each described a bearded man in a black winter coat. Officer Ferris Knowles has a beard."

"But Brentwood doesn't. What are the chances Knowles drives a red pickup truck?" He turned to his computer and punched the officer's information into the system. "There it is. A red Toyota Tundra."

"Slow down, Thomas. Knowles looks like our guy, but we need to be sure. All of this might be coincidental."

Thomas couldn't slow down. He sent the officer's picture to Raven and LeVar and typed, *Does this look like the guy you saw?*

LeVar's reply came a minute later.

Shep, that might be him. Big dude. Who is he?

Thomas wasn't ready to commit.

Just a suspect. Will let you know after I learn more.

It took longer for Raven to get back to him. No surprise. She'd stayed up late. Like LeVar, she agreed the bearded man might be the arsonist.

Thomas and Aguilar spent the morning looking into Officer Ferris Knowles. Nothing stood out, except Chief Pauley had reprimanded Knowles for roughing up a driver he caught speeding. Time passed too quickly. The clock ticked past ten, and Thomas worried that Knowles, if he was the arsonist, would go after the Wolf Lake Consulting investigators after sunset.

He brought two junior deputies into the investigation, warning them not to utter a word about Knowles to anyone outside the office. They needed to keep this in-house until they were sure.

Aguilar kept staring at the officer's financial records while she worked at her desk. Thomas left his office and joined her.

"What's on your mind?" he asked.

"Last year, Knowles bought a house valued at almost

$300,000 in a posh neighborhood overlooking Harmon, yet he only pulls $70,000. He never made detective."

"LeVar thinks a few Harmon PD cops were on the take. They accepted money from the 315 Royals to look the other way."

"What if Officer Barrett found out about Knowles and threatened to turn him in?"

"If the two men had issues," he said, "Barrett might have told his wife about his suspicions."

Another idea occurred to Thomas, and he dialed Chief Pauley.

"Chief, I'm wondering if I can speak to Officer Knowles about the evidence he gathered."

"Knowles must figure I'm angry about yesterday," Pauley said.

"Why?"

"He called in sick, but I'm not buying his 24-hour-flu story. He's a chronic liar."

Thomas raised a thumb at Aguilar and mouthed, "Knowles called in sick."

"You mentioned Knowles and Brentwood were applying for new jobs."

"That's the rumor."

"Any idea where Knowles applied?"

Pauley said, "Not that I believe it, but Knowles boasted he wanted to get into commercial real estate and become a power mogul. The idiot always fancied himself as rich."

"Like Christopher Fieldman."

The chief chuckled. "Yeah, that's a good one. Like Christopher Fieldman." Pauley stopped laughing. "What are you suggesting, Sheriff? Do you think Officer Knowles had something to do with Fieldman's death?"

"I don't want to jump to conclusions, but Knowles botched the investigation yesterday, and that's something a veteran officer wouldn't do. He matches the description of the man who set fire to the state park. Did Knowles get along with Officer Barrett?"

"No." Pauley sounded troubled. "They were constantly at odds. Barrett told me he had something on Knowles, but he didn't want to say what it was until he proved it."

"Could it have something to do with the 315 Royals?"

"I'd hate to say so, but it might."

"Contact me if you hear from Knowles today."

"You're leaving me with troubled thoughts, Sheriff."

"I hope to God I'm wrong." Thomas ended the call and turned to Aguilar. "We need to speak to Trix Barrett."

"I'll go."

"Tell me if her husband suspected Knowles. I'll contact the WLC crew and warn them."

38

A dense gray canopy lay over Nightshade County as LeVar took the Harmon exit and cruised into the city. Since last night's encounter with CJ, nightmares about his mother had consumed him. Images of Ma jamming a needle into her arm made him skittish.

When he passed the adult video store, he searched for gang members and spotted three he didn't recognize lingering near the door. A hooker worked the corner, but the Royals had lost most of their prostitutes after Troy Dean went to prison.

A white, tattooed boy with a shaved head watched the Chrysler Limited coast past. He tapped his partners on the shoulder and nodded at the car. They recognized the former enforcer of the Harmon Kings.

A block down the road, LeVar pulled to the curb and dialed CJ's cell.

"Come to your senses, LeVar?" CJ asked.

"Meet me outside the bar."

"The same one we ruled during the glory days?"

"That one."

"Give me ten minutes."

"If you're not there in fifteen, I'm outta here."

LeVar ended the call and wheeled into a municipal parking lot across the street. He paid five dollars to the attendant, who eyed the teen with wariness. The tavern stood halfway down the block. He took a bench outside and shoved his hands into his pockets, shivering against the chill. It would snow soon. He felt it in his bones.

Five minutes later, the SUV that had trailed him out of Kane Grove University stopped at the curb. CJ hopped out.

"What's so important that you called me here?" the boy asked.

"Are you willing to hit the Royals?"

CJ's eyes brightened. "Now we're cooking with fire. I'll call the boys and—"

"With the police."

The gangster lowered his head. "Shit."

"It's the only way. Take it or leave it."

"Then I suppose I don't have a choice." CJ plopped down beside LeVar and stared at the sky. "I should expect this from a cop. You changed when you became a deputy, LeVar."

"Nah. I changed the second Rev took over the Kings, but it's all good. I believe life happens for you, not to you. That was my wake-up call to get out of Harmon and take care of Ma."

"That ain't a reason to hate your city or your brothers."

He shrugged. "It ain't hate. I just can't be here anymore."

"Yet you're in Harmon now."

"To set things right. You say you support the city. Show me."

CJ eyed LeVar for a long time before agreeing.

"Come with me."

They traversed the crisscrossing streets, passing through alleyways strewn with garbage, cutting through the city park, which housed the only grass for blocks. An elderly man in a beige jacket huddled on the sidewalk outside a consignment shop. A paper bag concealed a bottle. The man glanced up at CJ with pitiful, bloodshot eyes.

"Give me the bottle, Isaac," the boy said.

"It keeps me warm."

"The hell it does." Without asking again, CJ took the bottle and handed the man a ten-dollar bill. "Get something healthy to eat. If I find out you bought liquor, I'll come back for you."

The boy's charity impressed LeVar, but he wasn't ready to believe CJ had turned a new leaf. They continued walking until LeVar knew where they were going. The soup kitchen.

They rounded a corner, and two boys hanging out in front of the kitchen came into view. Like the gangster he'd passed in front of the adult video store, these two had shaved heads and tattoos up and down their arms. He chewed his lip.

"What are they doing here?"

"It's like I been telling you," CJ said. "They're taking over the city."

"Why hang out in front of the soup kitchen?"

"They sell drugs and recruit. But not for long."

Before LeVar could stop CJ, the boy strode up to the two gangsters.

"You best get steppin' unless you want trouble."

One skinhead lifted his chin. "Who's gonna make us move? There's two of us and one of you."

LeVar pushed himself in front of CJ. "I'll make you move."

The smaller of the two gangsters shrugged with indifference, but his partner grabbed him by the arm and whispered into his ear. LeVar knew they were talking about him.

"I'm telling you," the bigger kid said, "that's him. That's LeVar."

"The dude who ran the Kings?"

"He didn't run them, but yeah."

LeVar took another step forward, and the gangsters scattered, though the smaller kid shot hateful glances over his shoulder. The kid would be back.

CJ set his hands on his hips. "That was cool, but what happens next time when you aren't here to help? They come all the time, intimidating families who show up looking for food. A lot of people don't come no more on account of the Royals."

LeVar patted CJ on the chest. "I'm glad you brought me here. Let's go inside."

The boy appeared uncertain.

"That might be a bad idea, LeVar. The woman who runs the place don't take kindly to gang members."

"Don't worry. I'll introduce you."

The door was locked, but two knocks brought the owner to the entrance. Mora Canterbury smiled upon seeing LeVar. The grin melted away when her eyes landed on CJ.

"It's okay, Ms. Canterbury. CJ is with me."

She stood aside and let them in, then locked and bolted the door. Polycarbonate panels hung over the windows. Those were new.

"Mora Canterbury, meet CJ. CJ, meet Mora Canterbury."

Mora shook the boy's hand but still seemed uneasy.

"CJ and I go way back," LeVar said. "He wants what's best for the city. You can trust him."

"The two of you chased away those gangsters?" she asked.

"CJ did. I just stood there and looked pretty."

The quip caused Canterbury to relax and break into a smile.

"Well, I appreciate it. If it isn't those two, it's the others. White skinheads. Racist and violent."

"You're aware they recruit people who visit the kitchen?"

"I had my suspicions, but not much I can do about it. They're here all the time. It would help if more men worked in the kitchen."

"Ms. Canterbury, if any gang member gives you trouble, I want you to call me."

"You can call me too," CJ said, puffing out his chest. The boy gave Mora his number. "And you can call the sheriff's department or Harmon PD."

LeVar glanced at CJ in shock before he shook the cobwebs loose.

"What CJ said. You're responsible for keeping families fed, and we won't let the Royals drive them away." LeVar gestured at the windows. "The polycarbonate panels are a good start, but you need a sturdier door. Next time the sheriff and our crew volunteer, we'll talk to you about options. You shouldn't have to worry about anyone breaking in."

"Thank you, LeVar," she said. "And you too, CJ."

LeVar shuffled his feet. This was his home.

Had he made a mistake by abandoning Harmon?

39

Trix Baxter stared at her reflection and gasped. It seemed her hair had grayed overnight. She raked a brush through the snarls and stopped, hearing Shawn's voice in her head.

"You look beautiful, Trix. Stop worrying."

Yet she was right to worry. For years she'd feared something would happen to Shawn on the job, that a gangster's bullet might strike him dead, or an arrest gone wrong might result in a fight he wouldn't survive. Such was the life of a police officer's spouse. And now he was gone forever.

A tear rolled down her cheek. She needed to stay brave. Shawn would have wanted it that way.

She sniffled and closed the medicine cabinet. As she entered the hallway, the doorbell rang. Who could that be? She wasn't expecting visitors.

Trix paused outside the living room and waited until the man at the door showed his face. She furrowed her brow. What was Officer Ferris Knowles doing here? He wore his uniform and a cap pulled over his head. While she contemplated whether to answer—she despised Knowles and so had Shawn—he glanced up and down the street as if searching for someone. Or worried the neighbors were looking.

She pushed that thought away. As much as she disliked the officer, he enforced the law and had nothing to hide, right?

After the second ring, she decided to find out what he wanted. Shawn had told her a story about Knowles using excessive force on a speeder who refused to respect his authority. She had always believed her husband possessed more information on the officer, secrets that might get the man fired, but Shawn talked little about his coworkers. Was he here to pay his respects, or did he have an ulterior motive? Perhaps he wanted to find out what Shawn had told her.

Nevertheless, Trix didn't trust the man. If she allowed him in her house, she would record everything he said, just in case she needed to bring the information to Chief Pauley. She couldn't imagine what that would be, only that the officer at the door was slippery as grease on an eel.

She opened the voice recorder application on her phone and started it. So Knowles wouldn't notice, she set the phone on the bookshelf between two tomes and laid it face down. Another impatient ring of the doorbell got her moving.

"Coming," she called. She opened the door and peered out at the man. "What may I do for you, Officer Knowles?"

"Hi, Trix," he said, lowering his head. "I realize I haven't stopped by to express my condolences. Shawn was a good friend." When she lifted an eyebrow, he said, "Sure, we had our issues over the years. It's a high-pressure job, and sometimes we say things we don't mean, but we were a lot closer over the last few months. Anyway, I just wanted to say how sorry I am."

"Thank you. Will that be all?"

"Don't be that way. Shawn wouldn't want us at odds. Look, the reason I'm here is I think I know who hurt your husband. Are you willing to let me inside so I can tell you what I know?"

"I suppose," she said, opening the door and standing aside.

He strode through the entryway and studied the room. She noticed he hadn't removed his gloves, and he cast uncomfortable glances at the blaze in the fireplace. Did he suspect she was recording him? How would he know?

"Please sit," said Trix. "May I get you something to drink? I just made a pot of coffee."

"That's gracious of you. Thanks."

She left him alone, worrying he'd snoop behind her back and locate the phone. Her ears tuned to his every movement as she opened the cupboard and removed two mugs. She took the cream from the refrigerator and grabbed the sugar.

"I like mine black," he said.

She whirled around, heart racing. He stood at the kitchen entrance. How had he sneaked up on her without her hearing?

"My apologies," said the officer. "I didn't mean to startle you. Can't imagine what you're going through, being alone in the house. I'm happy to check on you if it will make your feel more secure."

To her confusion, he still wore his winter gloves.

"Are you cold, Officer Knowles? I can turn up the heat."

"That's unnecessary. I'll only be a few minutes." He offered his help. "Ah, let me."

She handed the mugs to him, and he carried them into the living room.

"On second thought," he said, "A teaspoon of sugar would be great. I didn't sleep well and could use the energy. Nightmares about Shawn."

Trix returned for the sugar but felt uncomfortable leaving him alone with the drinks. Why? When she returned, he sat in Shawn's favorite lounge chair with an ankle balanced on a knee. He raised his mug to her.

"To Shawn."

She repeated his toast and gulped her coffee.

"So you wanted to tell me about your suspicions," she said. "You don't believe the wasp attack was a coincidence?"

He raised his palms. "How could it be? Where would any of us run into wasps this time of year?" The officer leaned forward with his elbows on his knees and whispered conspiratorially, "I think Shawn ran afoul of the 315 Royals."

"Are you're suggesting my husband accepted a payoff from a gang?"

"Not at all. Shawn was righteous, the finest officer I ever worked alongside, but his unwillingness to cooperate may have gotten him into trouble." A bout of vertigo caused Trix to touch her head. "Are you all right, Trix?"

"Yes," she said uncertainly. "I haven't eaten today."

"Drink your coffee. I find coffee cures headaches and dizziness."

She took another sip. "You believe the Royals murdered my husband?"

"I do. I've gathered evidence, but I'm not ready to approach Chief Pauley. Not until I'm certain."

The floor pitched, and she grabbed the arm of the couch to keep from falling.

"Something is wrong," she said.

He shot off the chair. "The blood is draining from your face, Trix. If it was something I said, I apologize. This is too much, too soon."

She waved a hand in front of her face. "No . . . I . . . I think I'm sick."

"Don't worry. My truck is right outside. I'll drive you to the hospital."

Her instinct sent a warning from the back of her clouded mind. Why was he driving his personal vehicle while on shift, and why hadn't he removed his gloves?

She toppled forward and landed in his arms. Then the outdoor air touched her exposed skin. She was weightless, floating through the sky.

The truck door slammed as she slumped against the seat.

Her last thought was, *He's going to kill me.*

40

Indecision gripped LeVar after he returned to the guest house beside the lake. This morning's trip to Harmon had surprised him. It wasn't just CJ who wanted to defend the city. He did as well. The Royals intimidating people at the soup kitchen angered him to no end. Something had to be done about the gang before they forced the kitchen to close its doors. What would the poor, homeless, and starving do for meals?

He stared at the term paper on his computer monitor but couldn't concentrate. Did a happy medium exist between putting his former home behind him and helping the city rid itself of the Royals?

The door opened.

"Scout, that you?"

"It's me," his mother said. She entered the front room and ran her gaze over the surroundings. "I like what you've done to the place. Cozy."

"That's because of the space heater. This room is a freezer when the wind blows." He glanced at her and pulled his eyes away. Pictures of Ma with a needle in her arm haunted his memory. "Baking with Ms. Mourning today?"

"No. I just thought I'd stop by and ask about Thanksgiving."

"Sure. What's up?"

"Thomas is hosting, but with everyone he invited, I'm worried there won't be enough room. Could we borrow your chairs? I'm bringing a folding table from my basement."

"Yeah, that's fine. Need help getting it here?"

"Buck will carry it." She sat beside LeVar and took his hands in hers. "What's bothering you? You haven't seemed yourself."

He didn't want to tell her the heroin trade had reminded him of days gone by.

"Someone opened my eyes in Harmon today."

She held his eyes. "It better not have been CJ. Yes, I heard from the others that he visited."

"It was him." When she twisted her mouth, he touched her shoulder. "He's changed, Ma. CJ isn't the banger he was back in the day."

"Once a King, always a King," she said.

"Really? Do you feel that way about me too?"

"Of course not. You grew up and realized what was important."

"Then you should afford CJ the same courtesy." There was no way to soften the blow. He lowered his head. "Ma, the Royals are importing heroin into Harmon."

"Fool, there's already heroin in the city."

"Not this much," he said. "They're taking over downtown. CJ and I chased them away from the soup kitchen earlier."

"Are you crazy? What if one of them had a gun?"

"I'm a deputy with the Nightshade County Sheriff's Department. It's my duty to maintain law and order."

"Don't give me that bull. You weren't on shift. This was just LeVar trying to save the world."

"I have to do something, Ma. They're recruiting members

outside the soup kitchen. Pretty soon they'll start selling drugs at the door. Is that what you want?"

She turned to him. "Listen to me, boy. I know what this is about. You hear the word heroin, and suddenly you're the new sheriff in town. Stopping a drug shipment won't change what I did. That was my choice, my decision. You can't turn back time and save your stupid old mother."

"But I can make it so another kid doesn't grow up with his parents shooting up and buying drugs with grocery money. It's not too late to stop the Royals."

"And then what? What happens when the next gang fills the void and does the same?"

"I'll cross that bridge when I come to it."

"This is a job for the sheriff's department and Harmon PD," she said. "Have you talked to Thomas?"

"I will."

"Don't you work for the sheriff's department today?"

"At three o'clock."

"Then that's the time to talk to the sheriff. And what about CJ? Will he stand back and allow the authorities to do their jobs, or will he fire his gun at anything that moves?"

"CJ has connections in the city. He'll serve as our informant."

She gave him a doubtful look. "If you turn the task over to the police, I'm all for helping the people of Harmon. You promise you'll talk to Thomas before you run off and do something rash?"

"I swear."

She patted his knee.

"Then I support you. But I prefer you not involve yourself."

"Why's that?"

"There's no sense dredging up old ghosts, LeVar. You did the right thing by leaving the city. Don't let it coax you back."

41

Deputy Aguilar stopped her cruiser in the driveway beside Trix Barrett's car. A light shone in the living room, barely visible behind translucent curtains. She recalled her first visit to the house. The widow's grief had been fresh and jagged then, and it had taken willpower for the deputy to hold it together.

There were five stages of grief—denial, anger, bargaining, depression, and acceptance. She'd witnessed the first two on the day the sheriff's department discovered Officer Shawn Barrett's body outside the village, bloated with hundreds of wasp stings.

She knocked on the door and received no response. Glancing at the window, she pressed the doorbell and waited. The sheriff's theory that Officer Knowles was the arsonist, as well as Christopher Fieldman's killer, seemed like a shot in the dark, but she'd learned to trust Thomas's intuition over the years. That Knowles had been at odds with Officer Barrett was common knowledge inside the Harmon PD. If Knowles was the killer, would he go after Trix?

Nevertheless, Aguilar wanted the widow to tell her everything she knew about her husband's difficulties with Knowles.

The deputy rang the doorbell a second time and stood on tiptoe, searching for movement in the house. After nobody answered, she knocked on the neighbors' doors. Trix Barrett wasn't visiting, and no one had seen her today.

Something felt off as she returned to the home. The car was here, the lights were on, and it was awfully chilly for a walk. Maybe the poor woman had needed to escape the home and clear her head. Aguilar knew she had kids. They weren't here either. Weird. She contacted the sheriff on the radio.

"Yeah, Thomas, I'm outside the house, but no one is answering. Trix Barrett's car is in the driveway, but the neighbors don't recall seeing her today. What do you want me to do?"

"Can you see inside?"

"There's a curtain over the living room window. I can't make out much. Should I enter the home?"

Thomas contemplated the decision before answering. Though Aguilar grew increasingly worried about Mrs. Barrett, law enforcement was conservative about entering a house uninvited. She had no proof Trix was injured or dying.

"Not yet," he finally said. "Contact the relatives. Maybe someone picked her up and took her shopping. She probably needed to get out of the house."

Aguilar walked to the cruiser and slid behind the wheel. She gave the house another glance, her paranoia growing by the second. All appeared well, especially if she accepted Thomas's assumption that a family member had picked up Trix.

As she backed out of the driveway, she noticed tire tracks in the snow along the curb. A truck had stopped here. The tracks appeared fresh.

Officer Ferris Knowles's red Toyota Tundra?

On a whim, she stepped out of the cruiser and dialed the widow's number. A phone rang inside the house, but no one answered.

"Thomas," she said into the radio, "her cell is ringing inside. I don't like that she didn't take it with her. Should I enter now?"

"Do it. If we catch hell from the county, I'll take the blame."

Aguilar tested the knob and found the door unlocked. Curious. Trix Barrett might not be of sound mind, but would she forget to lock the door after her husband's murder?

"Mrs. Barrett? Nightshade County Sheriff's Department. I'm entering the house."

After waiting for a reply, she walked into the living room and called again. A brief search led her to Trix's cell on the bookshelf. Realizing the phone might be evidence, she donned gloves before touching anything.

"Mrs. Barret? Trix? If you're hurt, call out and I'll come to you."

No reply. Two half-consumed mugs of coffee sat on a table between the couch and a lounge chair. The aroma of coffee drifted from the kitchen. She touched the mugs and found them warm. The pot on the kitchen counter billowed steam. Whoever had been there left in a hurry.

TWO HOURS PASSED before Aguilar reached Trix Barrett's sister Claudia. The sister had taken the kids skiing, and now they were at her house, drinking hot chocolate and warming up.

"No," Claudia said, "that isn't like Trix to leave without taking her phone, and I can't imagine who picked her up."

"If she was going somewhere, would she contact you?"

"Absolutely. I'm supposed to drop the kids off in an hour." Claudia lowered her voice. "I won't say anything to the children, but should I worry?"

"Not yet. There may be a logical explanation. If Trix contacts you, get back to me."

"I will."

Aguilar grew more unsettled. She'd returned to the widow's house to check if the woman had come back. While she waited, Thomas sent a cruiser past Officer Knowles's house, but nothing appeared out of the ordinary. He hadn't answered when they knocked.

Light faded as the afternoon wore on. The sheriff wanted her to stay at the house, but there was nothing for her to do. Another cruiser pulled behind hers. LeVar had started his shift and arrived to relieve her.

"Still no word from the family?" he asked.

"The aunt sounded concerned. She has the kids and is supposed to bring them home. As long as Trix Barrett remains missing, there's no one to look after the children."

"Thomas wants me to take the phone to WLC. If you're willing to stay on for a few extra hours, he'd like you to work with Chelsey to retrieve the data. Scout is there too, and you know she's a whiz at that kind of thing."

She didn't want to leave the house alone, as if doing so were giving up on Trix, but snooping through her phone might lend a clue as to her disappearance. Officer Knowles was involved, but could she prove it?

Aguilar followed LeVar into Wolf Lake and stopped behind the private investigation firm. She could see Chelsey, Raven, and Scout through the windows. Everyone was working overtime to figure out where Trix Barrett was.

Before climbing out of the vehicle, she gave the aunt one more call. Still no word from Trix, and a child was crying in the background.

She wouldn't allow the kids to lose both parents in the same week.

42

L eVar sat down to work with Aguilar and the WLC team. Having met Officer Shawn Barrett at the community college, he felt like he knew the man and his family, and he would do anything to find the missing widow.

Though Chelsey led the team, everyone looked to Scout for instructions. Nobody understood data better than Scout, and she showed them how to find hidden files on the phone. So far, the investigators had encountered nothing of note.

He was staring over Raven's shoulder and offering a suggestion when his own phone buzzed. Recognizing the sender as CJ, he stepped away to read the message.

It's done.

What did the boy mean?

What's done, CJ?

The plan is in place. I contacted the Harmon Chief of Police. They're moving on the Royals.

He wasn't sure how to react. On one hand, he was proud of CJ for speaking to Chief Pauley instead of taking matters into his own hands. On the other, the investigation was moving too quickly. It seemed rushed. A moment after he messaged CJ, his phone rang. It was Thomas.

"I need you back at the office, LeVar," the sheriff said.

"Give me five minutes."

The boy raced across town. Thomas had sounded harried on the phone. When he entered the department, he found the sheriff waiting for him in his office.

"Close the door," Thomas said.

LeVar did as he was told. Was he in trouble? Thomas preferred open-door meetings.

"What's going on?"

"This boy from the Kings, CJ. Would he lead the police astray?"

"The old CJ might have, but I trust him."

"You're aware he called Chief Pauley about the Royals?"

"Yeah, he told me."

"Apparently your friend keeps his ear tuned to the city's underground because he found out the first shipment is going down in less than an hour."

He sat forward. "Already?"

"Chief Pauley wants our help. I need to know something, LeVar. If I put you on the team, will your feelings about Harmon affect your actions? From everything I've heard, you want nothing to do with the city."

"I place my duty above my feelings, Shep. And anyway, I want to eradicate the Royals and stop the heroin shipment before it reaches the city."

"That's all I need to hear. They want you in Harmon now. I'll give you the specifics."

LeVar's body hummed with anxiousness. He could save Harmon, wipe out the Royals, and prevent many people from becoming addicted. He called Chief Pauley from inside the cruiser and received his instructions. No one needed to tell

LeVar how dangerous this mission was. The Royals armed themselves with automatic weapons, and the police would be outgunned.

But LeVar Hopkins was a nightmare for every existing Royal. And now he intended to finish the job.

~

"THESE CALLS ARE EXPLAINABLE," Scout said, running a pen over the computer screen.

The monitor displayed a list of calls to Trix Barrett's phones and those she'd initiated.

"The first two are to the aunt who took the children," Chelsey said, "and the other three went to her mother. We already determined the call from this morning came from a tele-marketer."

"So nothing out of the ordinary," Raven said, folding her arms. "What about the low-memory warning from three hours ago?"

"That could be a lot of things," Aguilar said. "She may have opened too many apps at once, or the phone might have a failing memory chip."

Scout wasn't so sure. She pulled up the app usage history.

"That's weird," the girl said. "Trix Barrett opened a voice recorder application."

"Was she dictating to herself?" Chelsey asked.

"If she was, she forgot to close the application. It recorded until she ran low on data." She sifted through the files and found the recording. "Let's hear what she said."

Instead of dictation, she heard footsteps crossing the floor, then a doorbell ringing.

"Did Trix Barrett start the recording by accident?" Aguilar asked.

"I don't think so."

A deep-voiced male spoke to the woman. Scout reversed the recording and increased the volume. Running the file through a filter eliminated a distracting hum in the background.

"They're talking about Shawn Barrett," Raven said, sitting forward. "Turn it up."

The unknown man accepted coffee before the conversation shifted to the 315 Royals. He seemed to suggest Officer Barrett had taken payola from the gang, and Trix sounded offended. Then the woman's voice changed. She sounded sick and complained she hadn't eaten.

"This is our kidnapper, the guy who took Trix Barrett," Chelsey said. "Is she talking to Officer Knowles?"

"I've never heard the man speak," said Aguilar, "but I know someone who has. Send the recording to Chief Pauley."

"No can do. Pauley and the Harmon PD are moving on the 315 Royals."

"Is that why Thomas called LeVar into the office?"

Worry creased Raven's brow, and Scout bit a nail. The teen didn't want to imagine LeVar facing the most notorious gang in the county.

On the recording, the unknown man promised to rush Trix to the hospital. Silence pervaded the room. The microphone caught a vehicle door slamming outside, then a motor firing.

"That's a loud engine. I can buy that it's a Toyota Tacoma. Scout, play the recording again."

She replayed the footage. Yes, that sounded like a pickup truck's motor.

"We have to get this recording to Thomas," Scout said. "If he can confirm the unknown man is Officer Knowles, we'll know he's the killer. Should I send the recording to the sheriff's department?"

Chelsey nodded. "Send it."

The file uploaded halfway and stopped. Aguilar and Raven cursed in concert.

"What's wrong?" Chelsey asked. "Why won't the file upload?"

"Could be a lot of things," said Scout. "Network congestion, a problem with the server."

"Give me the phone," Raven said. "I'll drive it over. No sense fighting technology when I can be there in five minutes."

Chelsey agreed and handed the phone to her partner. "Don't forget about the construction project on the edge of the village. Take the back roads."

"Gotcha. I'll call you as soon as we verify the voice."

Scout returned to work. She'd copied enough data to keep the team busy for the next hour.

Yet she couldn't take her mind off LeVar.

Please let him be all right.

43

Raven forgot how extensive the construction project was. On her way out of the village, she ran into a blockade with *ROAD CLOSED* written in black letters against an orange background. She needed to reverse course and hop on Prentice Road if she wanted to reach the sheriff's department.

She felt rushed. With Trix Barrett missing and almost certainly abducted, time was running out. There was already one Barrett dead this week. What would become of Trix? Would the authorities find her in the country, bloated and stung to death by wasps, or worse yet, thrown off a skyscraper?

She kicked the accelerator and ran through a stop sign. A check of the mirrors showed no police following her. Not that she didn't have an excuse for rushing. This was an emergency.

As she turned onto Prentice Road, she spotted a cruiser a half-mile behind and closing fast. She checked the speedometer and slowed from 70 to 55 mph. This wasn't the time to argue with the police about her urgency to reach the sheriff's department. Maybe the officer hadn't caught her speeding and was rushing to the interstate to join the team in Harmon.

No such luck. Whirling lights flashed, and the cruiser pulled up on her bumper.

"Not now," she muttered, stopping along the shoulder.

Darkness fell over the land, and she couldn't make out the officer behind the wheel. She prayed it was someone she knew.

Raven reached for Trix Barrett's phone and drew in a breath. It wasn't in her pocket. She ran her hand over the seat, thinking the phone must have fallen out of her pocket, but it wasn't behind her. The recording was her only proof that she had a reason to speed. Her own phone lay in the cup holder, connected to a USB cable and recharging.

Her fingers felt for Barrett's phone. Where was it? Under the seat?

In the mirrors, the cruiser's door opened and a booted foot landed on the pavement. The vehicle's headlamps, set to bright, blinded Raven and prevented her from identifying the officer.

She stopped pawing for the phone. If a police officer approached your window and found you pawing for something under the seat, he might suspect you had a weapon. Better to set her hands on the wheel, sit still, and explain the situation.

She lowered the window. Cold, damp air rushed into her Nissan Rogue.

When the man approached, his face backlit by the head-lamps, she said, "Officer, I'm working for Sheriff Shepherd. I need to—"

A jolt of electricity made her limbs stiffen. She lost control of her body and slumped forward, her head colliding with the wheel. A stun gun.

The door opened. The officer grabbed Raven under the arms.

Her heels dragged along the snowy macadam.

～

"THAT FILE IS INTERESTING," Chelsey said, peering over Scout's shoulder.

The teenager continued to prove her worth. Chelsey knew how to pull data from a phone, but the girl operated on a higher level. Whatever the Wolf Lake Consulting team understood how to do, Scout could accomplish in a quarter of the time. Plus, she'd learned tricks Chelsey had never heard of. The girl was just an intern, and New York State law didn't allow WLC to hire her for another nine years. By then, Scout would have her own office with the FBI. She couldn't imagine what the private investigation firm would accomplish with Scout working full time.

"That's another voice recording," the girl said. "It's five months old. Looks like she deleted it. Want me to retrieve the file?"

"Probably unnecessary."

Chelsey bit her lip and stared at the clock. What was taking Raven and Thomas so long? They should have contacted Harmon PD by now and verified if the man on the recording was Officer Knowles. The Harmon PD office operated with a bare-bones staff; most of its officers were in the field, preparing to encounter the Royals.

Impatient, she dialed Harmon PD dispatch, which put her through to Chief Pauley's phone.

"No, I've heard nothing from Sheriff Shepherd since he agreed to send us one of his deputies," Pauley said. "We're up against it tonight. Besides our operation, we lost a cruiser. Someone stole the vehicle while it was parked along the curb in Harmon. Probably a carjacker with the Royals."

"Keep your line open, Chief. Thomas has a recording you need to hear."

After the call ended, she drummed her fingers on the desk. Aguilar needed to join Thomas at the office, and Scout couldn't work alone. Every minute on the clock ticked by in the blink of an eye, and no one had heard from Raven.

At last, the phone rang. Thomas's name appeared on the screen.

"Thomas, thank goodness. Did Harmon PD identify the voice?"

"Raven never arrived," he said.

Terror like a moth's wings fluttered in her chest. Raven should have reached his office ten minutes ago.

"Something is wrong. Can you send a cruiser to look for her?"

"I'll go," Aguilar said, grabbing her belongings.

Chelsey mouthed, "Thank you." She wanted to search for Raven, but someone needed to take care of Scout. No chance she could take the girl with her. A gut feeling warned her Raven's and Trix Barrett's disappearances weren't coincidences.

She did her best to keep her voice calm when she addressed Scout, not wanting to alarm the teen.

"Do you want me to drive you home, or would you prefer to stay and work?"

"I'm still going through the data," said Scout.

"No problem. I'll call your mother and have her sit with you."

"You're worried about Raven, aren't you?"

"I'm sure she's fine."

"Take me with you."

"I can't. I promised your mother never to leave you alone in the office or place you in harm's way."

"But if something happened to Raven—"

"Nothing happened to Raven. We'll figure out where she is and have a laugh over this. I'm sure the construction slowed her down."

But the road crews weren't working this evening, and no

amount of closures explained why Raven hadn't reached the sheriff's department by now.

Naomi Mourning agreed to drive to the office and watch Scout. The woman must have heard the worry in Chelsey's voice because she promised to hurry.

Chelsey dialed Raven's phone. It rang without an answer.

Had Trix Barrett's abductor taken Raven too?

The black sky merged with the landscape, and there was nothing the streetlights could do to drive back the darkness.

Chelsey crisscrossed side streets on the edge of the village until she found Prentice Road. Despite the stifling darkness, she spotted the abandoned Nissan Rogue on the shoulder, its headlights dimmed and windows fogged up from the night air. She climbed out of her car and rushed to examine the vehicle, her mind racing with desperation.

The driver's side window was down, but there was no sign of forced entry. The backseat contained nothing out of place, save for a few used tissues in the footwell on the driver's side. Fear lanced through her body. She backed away from the SUV and cast a glance down the road, but all she could see were vast fields stretching in both directions.

Chelsey crouched and peered into the car, a sense of dread welling up inside her. That's when she spotted it: Trix Barrett's phone slipping out from under the driver's seat. She recognized the blue case and the crack over the screen. Panic coursed through her veins. Raven hadn't made it to the sheriff's station. A trail of footprints led away from the Rogue, disappearing beside a pair of tire tracks that appeared to come from a police cruiser.

Officer Ferris Knowles had Raven.

44

It was after seven, the darkness complete when LeVar arrived in Harmon in his deputy uniform. Over two dozen officers with the Harmon PD gathered inside the conference room, where Chief Pauley laid out what they knew about the Royals moving heroin into the city.

CJ was there. Though several officers eyed the teenage gangster with disdain, they listened when he told the police where and when the drug trade would occur.

The officers in the room exchanged uneasy glances. Sure, they had intel on the Royals, but could they trust the information provided by a kid who ran with a rival gang? After all, CJ was a wild card—he might set them up for disaster.

Chief Pauley cleared his throat and addressed CJ.

"Are you sure about this? We need to know that we can trust you."

CJ nodded and looked him in the eye.

"I've never been more sure of anything in my life. I'm here because I want to make things right."

The chief seemed to accept this answer, and he directed his officers to their assignments. They split into two units—one team would be posted in a building across the street from the adult video store while another would wait nearby in an unmarked van.

LeVar's hands clenched into fists. He trusted CJ, but if the intel fell through, the police would turn on him. The teams arrived at the store, but there was no sign of the Royals or their heroin. Nothing moved outside the building. The lights were out, and even the few prostitutes who worked for the Royals had abandoned the corner.

LeVar waited with CJ in Pauley's squad car, scanning every passing vehicle.

Chief Pauley radioed orders that the officers should stick to their posts.

As LeVar's legs pulsed with nervous energy, a moving truck with *Jasper's Play Things* scrawled across the side rounded the corner and pulled up behind the adult video store. The driver's window rolled down, and a white-haired man in his mid-fifties stepped out. He was dressed in pristine black slacks and a navy-blue vest.

Pauley grabbed his radio.

"We've got action. Large truck behind the store. Move out."

"This is it," LeVar said under his breath. He grabbed CJ by the arm and they crept out of the squad car.

The police moved like wraiths, swimming through the darkness unseen as they closed in on the front of the building. More circled around the other side as the van backed into position.

Tires shrieked. The Royals had spotted them.

In an explosion of fury and shrapnel, the moving truck burst through a chain-link fence as officers dove out of the way. Bullets pinged off the back of the truck to no effect.

His heart in his throat, LeVar looked around for CJ but didn't see him. As he searched the street, Pauley grabbed his arm.

"Back in the vehicle, Hopkins."

Squad cars roared after the truck, their sirens wailing through Harmon's deserted streets as they followed the Royals into an industrial complex on the north side of the city. LeVar could see gang members shifting cargo from a truck to a black Camaro. Were they forcing the police to chase two different rabbits and catch none?

Pauley radioed for backup as he kept pace with the truck and Camaro, the vehicles weaving around abandoned warehouses and desolate parking lots until they reached a dead-end alleyway. The driver of the moving truck slammed the brakes, reversed, and turned around as two police cars formed a blockade and trapped the gangsters.

The Camaro's driver overestimated his ability. LeVar cringed as the skinhead behind the wheel veered left and attempted to squeeze between the cruisers. No room. Metal met metal in a rain of sparks.

LeVar leaped out of the vehicle with Pauley. The officers drew their weapons, crouching beneath the cruisers for protection in case the Royals were packing automatic weapons. The night turned deathly quiet. Everyone waited to see if the chase would end in peaceful arrests or in a massacre.

With each passing beat of the night's heart, the skinhead gangsters slowly stepped out of the truck, their hands raised in surrender. The Camaro driver, his face a mask of blood, tried to leap over the hood of a squad car. LeVar and another officer threw him to the ground. The other Royals followed suit, dropping to their knees with their hands behind their heads.

The deputy stared at the unknown man dressed in navy-blue.

"Who's the penguin?" he asked.

The chief said, "Brad Marloni. He leads a crime syndicate out of Albany, but I never expected to encounter him in

Harmon. Thanks to your buddy, we took down two gangs in one night."

He watched as Pauley approached the Royals, his gun still drawn. He barked orders at the criminals and read their rights before the officers cuffed them. As the deputy searched the darkness, he worried about CJ. What had become of him? He wasn't among the gang members, and he hadn't caught up to Pauley's squad car. His heart pounding, the deputy pressed through the crowd and called to CJ. No answer. He cupped his hands around his mouth and yelled more loudly, drawing glares from officers who didn't trust him or his gangster friend. To some cops, LeVar would always be the enforcer for the Harmon Kings and nothing else.

"CJ, where you at?"

"Behind you."

The whispered voice made LeVar spin around. CJ emerged from behind a dumpster knocked cockeyed by the moving truck.

LeVar looked at the sky and exhaled.

"What, were you worried about me, bro?" CJ asked, grinning. "It will take more than these racist pushers to take me out."

"You scared me, little brother. Where did you run off to?"

"I recognized the Camaro down the road and figured the driver was waiting for the delivery to go down. As soon as I took off after the car, everything went haywire."

LeVar laughed. "Did you think you'd catch the Camaro on foot?"

"Almost did. I'm as fast as the wind."

LeVar smiled and shook his head, amazed at CJ. He placed a hand on the young man's shoulder and looked into his eyes. "You'd make one helluva cop."

CJ laughed. "Me? A cop? No way, dude."

"Why not?" LeVar said. "You've got the instincts and the heart, not to mention the crazy streak."

CJ dropped his gaze to the ground as he considered LeVar's words. When he looked up again, he was no longer smiling.

"I don't want to be a cop. I want to teach."

LeVar frowned in confusion but nodded for CJ to continue.

"I've seen what goes on in this city," CJ said, gesturing around him at the crime scene and its aftermath of broken dreams. "And I know if kids had access to education, maybe they wouldn't end up like these guys—involved with gangs or drugs or whatever else is out there on these streets." He paused, jaw clenched tight as he thought about how he could use his influence to make a difference in people's lives.

"I want to help those who couldn't help themselves," CJ said. His voice had grown stronger. LeVar saw the fire in his eyes.

"That's a noble ambition," LeVar said, "but you know it takes money to make an impact." He paused and studied the young man, wondering if he was up for the challenge. "You sure you're up for this? The world gets mighty heavy when you put it on your shoulders."

CJ nodded. "Hundred percent," he said. "And I'm willing to do whatever it takes to make it happen. For me and for Harmon."

LeVar smiled and clapped him on the shoulder again.

"Then let me help," he said. "I'll talk with my advisor at Kane Grove University and see what options they have for you."

CJ ran a thumb over his chin. A wave of gratitude swept over LeVar. How far could one person's generosity take a city? Based on CJ's metamorphosis, anything was possible.

"I owe you one," CJ said. He turned and glanced at the police, many of whom continued to glare at him with suspicion. "I better hop. This ain't my party."

LeVar bumped fists with CJ.

"I owe *you*, my brother. You didn't have to help us."

"I didn't, LeVar. I helped my city."

45

R aven came awake, confusion thick in her mind. It took a few blinks before the reality of her predicament set in. Someone had tied her to a beam in a damp and dusty cellar. Panic raced through her veins. She tugged against the bindings, but the knots held her firm.

A lingering dirt scent as ancient as time permeated the air. The mildewed walls were made of concrete blocks and crumbling in spots. A solitary bulb swung like a hanging man from the ceiling, casting dim light that failed to reach the rusted washer and dryer before her. An abandoned house?

As she struggled, a demented laugh came from the darkness. Officer Ferris Knowles stepped into the light, his face a mask of rage.

"Big-shot private investigator," he said, his mouth twisting in disdain. "I have to hand it to you. You figured out I killed Officer Barrett and kidnapped Trix."

"Where is she?"

"That's not your concern. Before the night is through, you'll both be dead."

She didn't get a sense of how large he was until he strode up to her. Dust and specks of insulation clung to his black beard. He wore gloves over his hands. She nodded at them.

"Burned yourself pretty good last night, didn't you? How did it feel having your plans blow up in your face? Literally."

"Shut your mouth."

"Or what? You already promised to kill me."

"Trust me," Knowles said. "I can make your death peaceful or wrought with agony. Which do you choose?"

"Why kill a fellow officer?"

He whirled to her.

"Because Barrett wanted to bring me down."

"You took money from the Royals," she said, "and Officer Barrett found out."

"I kept the streets safe, dammit. Yeah, I accepted the gang's money, but they agreed to confine operations to their territory. They kept that promise. I saved lives."

"You're a sellout."

"Shut up, Hopkins. What do you know about enforcing the law? You're just a small-town PI."

"You killed Christopher Fieldman too. Why?"

Knowles displayed his teeth when he grinned.

"Why not? He insulted me and said I'd never amount to anything in the business world. Told me to stick to playing cops and robbers. Now half his brain is splattered across the pavement beneath the Jefferson Building."

As Knowles ranted, she searched for a way out. To reason with a psycho wouldn't help matters; he was too far gone in his own delusions of power and revenge. Running her eyes through the dark, she spotted a pipe wrench on the ground, too far away to reach with her hands tied behind her back. Even if it lay within reach, she couldn't use her arms.

He stood eye to eye with her. When she didn't flinch, he slapped her across the face and made her ears ring. Refusing to cower, she stared daggers at Knowles, her face smudged with dirt and sweat. She wouldn't be intimidated by the man, despite the horrifying methods he used to kill his victims.

"You think you can come into my city and tell me how to do my job?" Knowles spat, his eyes blazing as he raised a fist. "You're out of your league. I run Harmon, and I'm not about to let some amateur get in my way. Look at you, so bold and strong. Nothing frightens you, does it, Hopkins?"

She held her chin high.

"You aren't fooling anyone. I know what scares you."

With a frenzied laugh, he stalked into the dark and returned carrying an armful of wood—dilapidated boards, a broken chair, part of a rotting table. He tossed the debris in a circle around Raven. Her eyes widened when he pulled a lighter from his pocket and lit the debris. Smoke billowed. The psychopath stood back to admire his work.

"What do you think? Burning alive doesn't get your blood pumping? You never should have pushed me. After the flames melt the flesh off your body, I'll take care of your friends and family. I'll especially enjoy setting fire to your druggie mother and gangster brother. LeVar and I go way back. He's had this coming for a long time."

Knowles turned and started up the stairs, leaving her to die. The flames grew higher, spreading across the dry kindling with terrifying quickness.

After the door slammed, she began to scream.

CHELSEY BOUNCED TO STAY WARM. She had to keep moving. If she slowed her thoughts, she'd lose her mind. Knowles had taken Raven, and she'd learned what happened to the madman's victims. Thomas arrived at the same time as Deputy Aguilar climbed out of her cruiser. Chelsey rushed to them and threw her arms around the sheriff's shoulders. He patted her on the back.

"She's been missing for less than an hour," he said. "We'll find her."

Would they? They hadn't found Officer Shawn Barrett until he lay dead and disfigured in a field. The police hadn't even known Christopher Fieldman was in danger before they scraped his remains off the sidewalk. She couldn't lose her best partner, her rock, her best friend.

"Show me where you found the phone," said Thomas.

She led them to the abandoned Rogue. The door stood open. A gust of wind rustled the old tissues.

"Under the seat. I wore leather gloves before I touched anything."

"No matter." He smiled, trying to keep her calm. "The odds that the kidnapper knew about the phone and touched it are steep."

He nodded at Aguilar, who eyed the phone on the driver's seat. The deputy pulled latex gloves from her pocket and snapped them on before lifting the device.

"We checked for improper security code entries when we searched the phone," Chelsey said.

"Were there any?"

"None."

"That confirms the kidnapper didn't know about it. Trix Barrett hid the phone well. Where's the recording?"

Aguilar scrolled through the applications and located the file. She played it back. Thomas leaned forward and shielded his ears from the wind. After the voice came through the speaker, he straightened his back.

"That sounds a lot like Officer Knowles," he said.

"Put out an alert. He took Raven."

"This is a police officer we're accusing. I need to be sure."

To Chelsey's consternation, Thomas dialed Chief Pauley. He shuffled his feet as the wind wrapped around his body. A whirl of snow took flight and made him turn his face.

"Yeah, Chief, it's Thomas." The sheriff paused as Pauley spoke. "You stopped the heroin shipment?" Thomas raised a thumb at them. "That's tremendous news. I'm glad Deputy Hopkins served you well. Listen, we found a recording on Trix Barrett's phone. I'm sending it to you now. If you recognize the man speaking, tell me who it is." It took a minute for Pauley to play the recording and respond. They didn't have time to wait. Chelsey didn't want to imagine what Knowles was doing to Raven. "It's Officer Knowles? Are you certain?"

After Pauley confirmed it was his officer, Thomas ended the call.

"Harmon PD is putting out a BOLO on Knowles," he said. "They think he stole a Harmon PD squad car this afternoon."

"Because he wanted Raven to trust him before she recognized his face."

"That might be the break we need. Harmon PD can locate its squad cars with GPS tracking devices. We'll trace Knowles's car and find Raven."

They split up, Thomas and Aguilar jumping into their cruisers, Chelsey climbing behind the wheel of her Civic. She followed them toward the department.

Were they too late to save Raven?

46

An eerie orange glow burned away the pitch-blackness of the basement. Time was almost up. Black smoke, carrying a putrid chemical scent, choked Raven's lungs and drew tears from her eyes. Now wasn't the time for false bravado.

The ropes held her tight to the beam. No amount of yanking or squirming budged the bindings. Officer Knowles knew how to tie a knot. Good for him. Maybe he'd receive a merit badge in the afterlife. Because once she got out of here, she would send the officer to his own private hell.

"Come on!" she screamed, her arms slick with sweat.

The flames grew to her chest and threatened to encase her. Unable to free her arms, she thought about the beam Knowles had tied her to. The wooden structure extended from the floor to the ceiling, but if it was anything like the rest of this basement, it was falling apart.

She could do this.

With a grunt, she threw her weight against the ropes, trying to shift the beam rather than break the bindings. Soon the fire would chew through the ropes, but she didn't intend to be here when it happened. Pulling with her front leg, she pressed the heel of her back leg against the beam. She strained, perspiration dripping into her eyes and soaking her hair.

The flames popped and snarled. They were neck-high and rising toward the ceiling. The heat was too much to bear.

Despite her effort, the beam refused to budge. Raven stopped to catch her breath and waited several hair-raising seconds for her strength reserves to recharge. She had one last chance to power her way free. Crying out, she threw her body against the ropes and tugged the beam forward. The wood made a splintering crack behind her. A lunatic's smile grew on her face as she lost herself in the struggle.

Just a little further.

A second before the fire touched her flesh, the beam snapped in half. She half-expected the ceiling to fall on her, yet it held. The ropes fell around her ankles. She was free.

She barreled through the fire and rolled across the dirt floor. If the flames had caught her skin or clothing, she didn't see any sign of them, though an acrid, smoky scent wafted off her shirt.

Behind her, the fire burst and caught the ceiling. She stumbled up the stairs in growing panic. The fire was gaining momentum and engulfing the walls with each breath she took. Out of the cellar, she felt heat on her back as she staggered towards the front door, praying for fresh air.

"Someone, help!"

Smoke obscured her vision. She'd lost sight of the entryway. For all she knew, she was walking into the heart of the fire. A sickening crack under her feet gave her no warning. The floor collapsed.

One leg plummeted through the boards. Jagged wood punctured her flesh and tore through her thigh. She could feel the flames along the basement ceiling crawling toward her trapped limb.

Struggling to escape, Raven pressed her hands against the floor and pushed, attempting to dislodge her leg. The wood clenched its incisors with greedy hunger.

CHELSEY COULDN'T SIT STILL. She paced the floor of the sheriff's department while Thomas monitored the Harmon PD tracking software. Chief Pauley was on speakerphone as they combined forces.

"Knowles is on the interstate," Pauley said. "We already sent two squad cars to his house in case that's where he's headed, but they haven't arrived."

"Where's Raven?" she asked.

Neither Thomas nor Pauley replied.

Her gaze shot to the clock. Raven had been missing for ninety minutes. She had to be alive. Chelsey couldn't live with the alternative.

"State police are closing in on his cruiser," Thomas said. "We need to know where he's been over the last few hours."

"Working on it, Sheriff," Pauley said. "Okay, I've got something. His GPS shows he stopped at 56 New Hope Road about an hour ago. He was there for twenty-five minutes."

"What's at 56 New Hope Road?"

She already had an answer. Typing at an open workstation, she pulled up the address.

"That's an abandoned house, Thomas."

Pauley must have heard because he directed a squad car and an ambulance to the address.

"We'll meet you there," Thomas said, grabbing his hat off the desk and setting it on his head.

Without a pause, Thomas and Chelsey raced to the cruiser. She leaped into the passenger's seat and buckled the belt as he turned the key in the ignition. The vehicle backed out of the parking space with swirling lights and a shrieking siren. In minutes, they were out of the village and thundering toward New Hope Road, yet the drive was taking too long.

"Hurry," she said through gritted teeth.

Though Thomas didn't reply, his grip tightened around the wheel. How long had Raven been held by the murderer? Would they find her on New Hope Road? A vacant home was the perfect place to stash a kidnapping victim.

Or a murder victim.

They were a mile from the destination when she noticed a red and yellow glow through the barren trees.

"Fire," she said with a hiss.

The sheriff stomped the gas pedal and raced faster, speaking into the radio as they drove. In a tone a small step away from frantic, he requested the fire department.

The blaze was out of control, consuming the abandoned house like a hungry beast. Red and orange flames reflected in Thomas's eyes as he stopped his cruiser across the road, frozen in shock that they were already too late. They couldn't make out anything through the flames. If Raven was trapped inside, she could be anywhere. How would they find her?

Thomas burst out of the cruiser and sprinted towards the burning house, shouting her name. Even as the heat of the fire scorched his skin, he pressed on, searching for a way in.

Chelsey touched the doorknob and shouted. It was hot enough to blister her hand. Black smoke rolled through the shattered windows and drew demonic horns against the night sky.

A honk made him turn his head. Darren Holt's truck braked behind the cruiser, and the ranger jumped out and rushed toward the doors. She didn't have time to find out how Darren had learned about Raven's whereabouts. Thomas wrapped his arms around the ranger, preventing him from rushing headlong to his death. Stronger than the sheriff, Darren pulled free of the grip and ran to each window, covering his mouth and coughing as he yelled to his girlfriend.

"Raven! Tell me where you are! Raven!"

"You'll kill yourself," Chelsey said, trying to force Darren away from the house with Thomas's help.

"We've got to get her out!" the ranger shouted above the roar.

A grim determination passed over Thomas's face.

"No," Chelsey said, understanding her fiancé's intentions.

The sheriff nodded at Darren and moved toward the front door. Instead of reaching for the knob, he raised the heel of his foot to kick the door in. Nobody wanted to save Raven more than she did, but losing three friends in one night wasn't an option.

"Wait!" she shouted. "We need to find a way in without the roof collapsing on us!"

They scanned the house for any potential entry point, their eyes squinting against the heat of the flames. Then she spotted a window on the side of the house.

"Over here!" she shouted. They ran to the window and kicked at it, the smoke stinging their cheeks. The window shattered. Fed by the night air, the fire exploded higher, sending shards of glass across the lawn.

Thomas covered his mouth and fought his way inside, with Chelsey and Darren right behind. Flames licked the walls and skittered higher, but the source of the inferno came from below. The basement. If Raven was in the basement . . .

Chelsey's gaze landed on her unconscious partner. The investigator lay face down on the floor, her shirt pulled over her head to shield her from the smoke and flames. The door and windows stood steps away, but she wasn't moving. Darren's eyes followed Chelsey's and landed on his girlfriend.

"No," he sobbed and slid down next to her.

With Thomas's help, the ranger lifted the unconscious woman's upper body, but she slumped forward and didn't reply to their words.

"Help me get her to her feet," Thomas said.

"Hold on a second," said Chelsey. "She's trapped. Her leg plunged through the floor."

Thoughts of the investigator's leg burning below sent a nauseous wave through Chelsey. A pop made her jump. The fire had spread across the floor and caught a stray board.

She pried her hands between the jagged board and the trapped limb. Intense heat sought her fingers from the basement. There was no way to snap the floorboard and free her friend.

A horrible thought shot through her head—severing the leg and saving the woman's life. Darren seemed to read the idea on her face. He shook his head and worked his fingers between the trapped leg and broken board from the other side. Thomas squeezed his hand into the remaining opening. Together they strained and lifted, eyes bulging, sweat rolling down their faces. The heat grew unbearable. If they didn't free Raven soon, the fire would consume them all.

With a deafening snap, the floorboard broke apart and Raven's leg came free. Before Chelsey or Thomas could move the unconscious woman, Darren lifted her into his arms. His girlfriend's body hung limp. A circlet of blood on Raven's pants marked where she'd caught her leg.

The flames rose higher, the heat oppressive, the smoke making it impossible to breathe. All around them, the fire crackled and roared, advancing across the room and cutting off their only escape route.

Heedless of the danger, Darren rushed to the front door and kicked it off its hinges. He stumbled out of the inferno and collapsed on the melting snow. He laid Raven down and looked back as the roof caved in. One more second inside, and they all would have perished.

"We need an ambulance," Darren said, turning to Thomas, who kneeled on the ground and hacked into his arm.

Thomas shook his head. "I can't get a signal out here. The fire department is on the way, and there should be an ambulance right behind."

"How long?"

Thomas raised his palms. He spoke into his radio and contacted dispatch.

"Raven," Darren said, patting her cheeks. "Wake up."

Darren kneeled next to Raven and felt for a heartbeat. Nothing.

Chelsey leaned over and listened for a breath. The fire drowned out all sounds. She searched for movement on Raven's chest and saw none.

Darren looked back at Thomas with tears in his eyes. "She's dying."

47

T he east end of Harmon carried a putrid stench, a blend of musty brick and dirt, exhaust fumes and garbage. There was a hint of something sweet and inviting, like overripe fruit left too long in the sun. Decay and neglect colored the air, along with the distant odor of motor oil.

LeVar sent another unanswered message to let his sister know he was safe and the mission had been a success. Raven had been the first to question his motives and suggest he could evolve without leaving his former home behind. As he stood perplexed, wondering why she hadn't replied, Officer Schott of the Harmon PD stepped out from an alleyway and approached. Schott was the man who'd helped LeVar take down the fleeing gang member.

The officer was tall and broad, his body a product of weightlifting and running. He wore a stern expression, his jaw set and unwavering. In a traditional navy-blue police uniform, unadorned except for the badge pinned to his chest, he assessed the junior deputy with eyes that were both vigilant and intimidating.

"You showed character tonight, deputy."

"Thank you, sir."

Schott looked him up and down. "You should apply. We have three open positions and need people like you."

LeVar nodded, his head spinning. This was all happening too fast. He had plans for the future, plans that didn't involve the police force, but now that Schott had planted the seed, he could imagine himself defending the city he loved.

"College is my priority," he said.

"Why go to school when there's already a job waiting for you? Doesn't that defeat the purpose?"

"Nah, bro. Until I figure out my destination, I don't want to start down any paths."

"Where are you going to school?"

He glanced behind him. The school lay a few miles outside the center of the city.

"The community college. That's where I met Officer Barrett."

"I'll bet he liked you."

"We got along okay. Would have liked to know him better."

"After you earn your two-year degree?" Schott asked.

"Kane Grove."

"Fine school. You have a good head on your shoulders, deputy. I hope we work together again."

"Me too."

Before LeVar turned away, Schott said, "Will CJ be a problem?"

He lowered his brow. "Why would you say that?"

"Now that the Royals are gone, it will be easy for the Kings to take their territory back."

"CJ won't put the gang together. He moved on like I did."

"I hope you're right."

"I am. Hundred percent."

His cruiser sat beside a mailbox outside the post office. LeVar opened the door when his phone rang. Dispatch. He hoped the man had good news about the hunt for Officer Knowles. Last he'd heard, Knowles had stolen a squad car and taken it on the interstate.

"LeVar, you okay?" the dispatcher asked.

"Yeah, why wouldn't I be?"

"You haven't heard about Raven?"

He sat forward. "What about Raven?"

THE NIGHT WAS dark and limitless, the air filled with an eerie stillness that only enhanced the chill in the air. Stars sparkled like icy diamonds in the sky while the pale crescent moon struggled to illuminate the landscape below. Across the field, a freezing blanket of fog crept out of the ground, brushing a hazardous sheen over the trees.

Thomas stood beside Darren and Chelsey, watching with helplessness as the paramedics worked on Raven's unmoving body. They had risked their lives to save hers, but was it all for naught? The investigator lay on the frozen snowpack, her beaded hair wild, lips blue, eyes closed. Thomas's heart ached at the sight, and he wanted nothing more than to turn back time and save her before the smoke had ravaged her lungs.

The paramedics kept radios on their hips. A medical bag lay between them at their feet, and stethoscopes hung around their necks. Their faces were calm and focused as they worked on Raven, monitoring her vitals, yet their placidity only made Thomas pace. How could they remain calm when his friend lay dying?

A paramedic held a mask over Raven's mouth and nose, while the other pumped her chest. They worked in perfect concert, but it seemed as if no matter what they did, the investigator's flame flickered and dwindled.

A siren broke the silence. The firetruck arrived, but there was little left to do but watch the abandoned house crumble.

"Come on, hon," Darren said, wiping a tear from his eye. "You and I have too many plans to quit now. I'm here for you."

The paramedic holding the mask looked back at them in regret.

Then Raven stirred.

Startled, the man with the mask drew his hand away in shock. Could nothing stop Raven Hopkins?

As they regained their composure, she coughed and pushed the paramedics away, weakly gesturing for Thomas to approach. Darren cradled her head in his arms.

"Knowles," she croaked, hacking and wheezing.

"He abducted you and set fire to the house?" Chelsey asked.

Unable to summon enough strength, Raven only nodded.

Thomas kissed her forehead. "I'll never doubt you, my friend."

She waved him away, a signal to catch Officer Knowles and end the madness. He didn't want to leave her side, but with Darren and Chelsey here, there was nothing left to contribute.

When he stood, Chelsey grabbed him by his jacket.

"Be careful, Thomas."

"I will."

"And when you catch him, give him a little payback from Raven."

"You can count on it."

He tipped his cap to Darren, but the ranger hadn't taken his eyes off the recovering investigator.

As he climbed into the cruiser, the radio placed Knowles five miles outside of Wolf Lake and speeding toward CR-26.

Thomas shifted into gear. It was time to stop a killer cop.

48

A chilling breeze crawled through Thomas's hair as he stood at the police roadblock, eyes scanning the horizon for the first sign of Officer Knowles's stolen squad car. It wouldn't be long before the headlights came into view. The blockade lay at a crossing between CR-26 and a farm to market road; news had spread over the radio that the fugitive had left the interstate and was trying to lose his pursuit in the country.

Trooper Fitzgerald organized the officers, a combination of state troopers, Harmon PD, and sheriff's deputies, all intent on stopping one of their own. If any officers had felt reluctant to shoot Knowles, that changed after learning the man had murdered Officer Shawn Barrett.

"Sheriff," Fitzgerald said. "Glad you joined the party. How's Raven Hopkins?"

"She's conscious, but it was touch and go for a long time."

"Was anyone else caught in the fire?"

"I don't believe so, but the flames consumed everything. Until the inspector makes his rounds, we can only hope there weren't casualties. Any update on Knowles's house? Last I heard, Harmon PD was laying siege."

Fitzgerald's face brightened.

"They found Trix Barrett in the basement. She's alive. Except for bumps and bruises, she survived the abduction unscathed."

"Terrific news. Now all we have to do is stop Knowles and put an end to this."

The state trooper lowered his voice. "Thomas, Harmon PD discovered four rattlesnakes in heated enclosures. They think Knowles meant to release them in the basement."

Thomas couldn't imagine being attacked by rattlesnakes. Wasps were bad enough.

Deputy Aguilar, who stood more than a foot shorter than Fitzgerald, worked by the trooper's side. That they were forging a relationship wasn't a secret, yet they maintained professionalism when on the job.

It seemed Thomas had been in this position on Halloween night when a roadblock stopped a kidnapper carrying two young girls in his van. The accident almost killed the girls, and officers might have lost their lives had the fugitive not wrecked before reaching the blockade. He hoped this night would end more peacefully, but he didn't believe that was possible.

He overheard the conversation between Trooper Fitzgerald and Deputy Aguilar. Fitzgerald would take the lead if the officers opened fire on Knowles.

"I can handle the situation," she said.

Thomas wondered whether that was true. Aguilar had shot a crooked officer in April and carried guilt on her shoulders for months.

There was no time to assess his deputy's state of mind. A bright speck on the horizon grew larger. Knowles was coming. Fitzgerald motioned to the officers, signaling them to take their positions, but most were already there and waiting for the inevitable. Thomas crouched below the hood of his cruiser, heart pounding as the squad car neared.

Tires screeched. Knowles spun to a halt. The stolen squad car stopped fifty yards away and parallel to the blockade. Was the killer about to turn and head in the opposite direction?

Knowles stepped out of the vehicle with a smirk on his face. Thomas felt his grip on the gun tighten.

"Beautiful night for a showdown, wouldn't you agree?"

The killer's laughter echoed down the pavement.

Fitzgerald stood up behind his SUV and pressed a bullhorn to his mouth. Knowles gave the trooper no opportunity to end the altercation without bloodshed.

The killer opened fire with a revolver in each hand. Certainly, he wasn't crazy enough to believe he could overcome the army of officers blocking his path, but a trooper three steps from Thomas fell to the blacktop, clutching his knee as blood pulsed between his fingers.

Thomas fired back. Knowles kept coming, closing the distance, taking another officer down as he advanced.

Aguilar shouted something he couldn't make out and raised her gun, firing three shots in rapid succession. One bullet struck Knowles in the thigh and took him down. Another blasted the killer in the forehead. Blood sprayed.

"No!" Aguilar screamed, horrified she'd killed another police officer. "I aimed low!"

Fitzgerald grabbed her arm. "That was my kill shot. You did nothing wrong."

Thomas led the charge to check on Knowles, but the officer lay unmoving, dead eyes inspecting the stars as blood trickled from the bullet wounds.

49

The hospital room featured beige walls and white bed linens tucked with military precision under the mattress. A small nightstand sat in the corner with a lamp perched on top. The machine monitoring Raven's vital signs blinked every few seconds. The quiet beep of the machine filled the air, punctuated by the occasional sound of Darren's and Chelsey's voices murmuring comforting words. There was a soft rustle as Scout settled into her spot at the foot of the bed beside LeVar. The intermittent hum of activity continued in the hallway as nurses and doctors went about their business.

LeVar fought back tears. His sister had survived the first hurdle, but smoke inhalation was serious business. The doctors had told them little. They seemed more cautious than optimistic.

Raven lay in the hospital bed, looking much smaller than he remembered. Her face was drawn and pale, her breathing labored, but her chin was set with determination. She relaxed when she opened her eyes and saw her friends gathered around, bringing a much-needed lightness to the somber setting. Darren and Chelsey took their places on either side of the bed, squeezing her hands.

"How are you feeling, sis?" LeVar asked, his voice gruff with emotion.

Raven smiled weakly. "I'm okay," she said. "I just need time."

"Well, you'll have plenty of it," Darren said. "Between the concussion and the fire, it's time you took a break from fieldwork."

She opened her mouth to argue and stopped.

"Take as much time as you need," Chelsey said. "When you're ready to return to the office, your workstation will be there for you. If you prefer to work from home, I can arrange that too, but no chasing bad guys until your doctor gives you clearance." Chelsey gave Raven a meaningful look. "And I'll want to see that letter."

"As will I," Darren said.

Raven rubbed the irritation out of her eyes. "How did you figure out it was Knowles who took me?"

"Thank goodness Scout found that recording," Chelsey said. "That was my mistake. I shouldn't have allowed you to drive to the sheriff's department alone."

"You couldn't have known he was waiting for me."

"Yeah, I could have. Anyway, we're fortunate you didn't have the phone on you when Knowles dragged you out of the Rogue."

Furrowing her brow, Raven stared at the ceiling. "I lost the phone and couldn't find it."

"It was under the car seat, you slob," LeVar said. "How many times have I told you to clean your SUV?"

"Leave me alone. I'm in a hospital bed and not strong enough to punch your lights out."

He snickered. This seemed more like the Raven he knew and loved. To his surprise, Scout took his hand in hers as a happy tear crawled out of her eye.

"I miss watching the two of you bicker." The girl laughed.

Darren and Chelsey watched, their eyes bright with love and admiration. No matter what happened, they were here for her.

Thomas strode past the room, stopped, and poked his head inside.

"I forgot which room you were in," the sheriff said, still in uniform. "How are you doing?"

"I'm surviving despite my brother," Raven said.

"He gets a free pass for the next week. Harmon PD said he did a fantastic job."

"As if anyone expected differently," LeVar said, grinning.

Scout released his hand. At first, he was relieved, but it didn't take long for him to miss her touch. No, he couldn't allow his thoughts to wander. She was his friend and like a little sister to him. Anything more was wrong. Terribly wrong.

"How's Trix Barrett?" Raven asked from the bed.

"Getting there," Thomas said. "She's dehydrated and shaken up, but now that she knows her husband's killer is dead, she's hopeful for the future." He turned to Chelsey. "By the way, she wanted me to thank you and your team for figuring out it was Knowles."

"Thanks to Trix's quick thinking," Chelsey said. "If she hadn't recorded the conversation, we might still be looking for her."

LeVar checked his watch and saw how late it was.

"Yo, I better get Scout home before the sun rises. She has school in the morning."

"As if I'm going in early," the girl said. "I think Mom will let me sleep in, given the circumstances. Besides, I'm only missing gym class."

Darren and Chelsey made room for them. Scout kissed Raven on the cheek, then LeVar had his turn. He gave her a hug and planted his lips on her forehead, which seemed colder than it should have been. As he thought of something snarky to say before leaving, she wrapped her arms around his shoulders and drew him close. Her chest hitched with sobs.

"I love you so much," she said. "You don't know how proud of you I am."

Before he knew it, tears streaked his face. He cleared his throat and stood, regaining his composure. Almost losing his big sister crushed him to the core.

"I love you too. And when I come back in the morning, you'd better be in that bed. If I catch you doing push-ups or squat thrusts, we'll have words."

Fighting not to burst into tears again, he kissed her one more time and took Scout home.

50

A mix of cool blues and grays stretched high above the village, with the sun a muted yellow-orange. Bare trees stood stark against the sky, some with a blanket of morning fog obscuring their branches. Frost tinged the back deck, and the air was thick with the smell of wood burning in fireplaces.

While Tigger watched from the porch and swished his tail back and forth, Thomas tossed the ball across the yard. Jack ran, barking and wearing a big doggy grin. This was when the sheriff felt most at peace—being outdoors and spending time with Jack. Perhaps it was the wonder nature provided, the mystery of its perfection. Or maybe he'd established a connection to the outside world during his youth, when he escaped from his parents. Either way, it was wonderful to release his worries and simply exist. No kidnappings, no murders, no county politicking. Here, on the shores of the greatest gem in the Finger Lakes, his stresses drifted away.

Jack ran, chasing after birds and retrieving the ball. Thomas watched, amused by the dog's enthusiasm and energy. Dogs didn't care about presidential elections or all the bad news on television. They were put on this planet to love and laugh.

After Jack brought him the ball, he wound up to throw it as far as his arm allowed. He stopped when Naomi Mourning left her house with a fuzzy robe wrapped over a sweatshirt and sweatpants. She wore boots to traverse the snow, which melted down to a crunchy rime. Naomi clutched the robes when the wind tossed her hair around.

"You're up early," she said, patting Jack on the head.

Now that she was here, the dog had forgotten about the ball and only wanted her attention.

"Chelsey and I are replacing the windows before the true cold hits. It's supposed to drop into the teens after Thanksgiving."

She shivered. "I heard the forecast. Sorry, but I'm not ready for that much cold."

"You and Chelsey both."

He glanced over her shoulder and spotted Scout in the kitchen, carrying breakfast plates to the sink. The girl had proven her worth more times than he could remember. She deserved to pay a penance for misbehaving on Halloween. Misbehaving? Heck, she'd broken into the abandoned house of a deceased serial killer. But everyone deserved a second chance.

"I wanted to talk to you about Scout," he said.

She swiped the hair off her forehead.

"I'm all ears."

"If it hadn't been for her, we wouldn't have caught Officer Knowles and saved Raven's life. She's as talented as anyone I've worked with, and that includes FBI agents."

Naomi cast a troubled look back at the house.

"Scout amazes me every day, but she's growing up so quickly, and I'm worried about the decisions she'll make in the future."

"If it matters, I'm willing to vouch for your daughter. You can trust her to make wise choices."

Naomi sighed. "Ever since Halloween night, I've second guessed myself. She deserved a grounding, but I'm walking a fine line. Without a father figure in the house, Scout likes to test her limits. I depend on her to act like an adult when I'm not watching."

"Working for Chelsey and volunteering at the soup kitchen are important. Just in the last two weeks, I've seen her mature. She's talking about college and planning her future. Which, by the way, is limitless."

She puffed out a breath. "You're right, of course. We all made mistakes at her age. Well, maybe not you."

He laughed. "That's because Mom and Dad never wanted me to leave the house. But I got away with a few transgressions they never learned about. What about you? I bet you have a few stories to share from your younger days."

"The truth is, I was a lot worse at Scout's age."

"Really? You?"

"Oh, yes." Naomi studied her boots. "I used to sneak out with my friend Noreen and drink. Mom figured it out when I came home after curfew. I thought I'd sobered up, but my speech was slurred. Besides, my jean jacket smelled like a brewery."

"What did she do?"

"First she laughed and pointed while I leaned over the toilet and puked three beers. Then she grounded me for two months. No school activities, no hanging out with friends, especially Noreen. And if you thought Noreen was trouble, you should have met her sister Vivian."

"Somehow, I can't picture you getting drunk and throwing up."

"Trust me, it happened." Naomi kneeled and kissed Jack on the head. "Now that you've reminded me of my glory days, it's time I had a talk with Scout and eased up. Thank you for lending your two cents. Though Glen isn't doing his job, having you and Chelsey next door helps. You're like a father to Scout." She turned her head toward the guest house. "And so is LeVar. Let me talk to Mrs. Yarwood."

"Liz's mother?"

"We've been chatting lately. The girls are thick as thieves . . . that might not be the wisest description . . . and I don't feel right keeping them apart. Thank you, Thomas."

As Naomi crossed the yard, Thomas saw Scout waving at the sliding glass door. He raised a hand.

She was the most incredible teenager he'd ever met, and it was time to let that bird soar.

51

The aroma of baked turkey and freshly cooked vegetables filled Thomas's A-frame, from mashed potatoes to carrots and squash. He placed a perfect golden-brown turkey at the center of the dining room table, while the counter held pies and holiday desserts. More guests than he'd ever invited before circled three tables, including two set up in the living room.

"Coming in hot," Chelsey said, warning the others to make room as she carried a tray of candied yams from the kitchen.

Raven, Darren, Serena, Thomas's mother, and Buck Benson gathered around the dining room table, while LeVar and Scout sat in the next room at the card table the investigators used. A third table held Deputies Lambert and Aguilar, along with Naomi and Sheriff Gray, who seemed to have dropped twenty pounds since retiring.

"Everything looks and smells incredible," said Darren, one arm wrapped around Raven's shoulder.

The ranger had been more protective of his girlfriend since the fire. Initially, she'd balked, but now she seemed to enjoy the added attention, as if she'd waited for him to show his soft side.

Serena set a bowl of grilled brussel sprouts beside the yams, while Buck placed the stuffing near the turkey.

"You really outdid yourself this year," Raven said to Chelsey.

"Don't give me all the credit," said Chelsey. "Thomas roasted the turkey, and your mother and Buck made several dishes. Naomi's desserts will knock you on your backside."

"So you cheated and tried them ahead of time?"

"Guilty as charged."

To Thomas's delight, Jack didn't beg for food. The dog was busy in the corner, gnawing on a turkey leg and smiling at everyone.

When they were all seated at their respective tables, Chelsey asked someone to say grace, and Thomas's mother did the honors. Before they dug in, Mom asked what everyone was thankful for this year.

LeVar began.

"For the support y'all showed me. If it wasn't for you, I wouldn't have gotten into Kane Grove."

"And I'm thankful for my friend not living on the other side of the country," said Scout, drawing nods from the others. "And for second chances. Right, Mom?"

"We'll see about that," Naomi said, drawing laughs.

After they stuffed themselves, the conversation turned to Raven, who finally had her breath back after the fire.

"You're keeping track of that one, I hope," Serena said to Darren as she pointed a fork at Raven.

"Oh, she doesn't leave my sight."

Darren gave Raven's shoulder a playful shake.

"Watch her like a hawk. Give her an inch, and she'll run off to chase criminals again."

"Ma, I'm listening to my doctor this time," Raven said, rolling her eyes.

"*This time.* At least you admit you never did before."

"Please, we just shared a wonderful dinner. It's not beat-up-on-Raven time."

"We all care about you," Darren said.

"And we need you at one hundred percent," added Chelsey. "That's why it's important you recover. I'm giving you the rest of the month off, then we'll reassess."

Raven's jaw dropped. "The entire month?"

"Don't worry. It's paid vacation time."

"I'm not concerned about my salary. What the heck am I going to do to stay busy?"

"Nothing," Darren said, "and like it."

"You're all making too much out of my hospital stay. I wasn't even there twenty-four hours."

"Hon, we intend to have you around for next Thanksgiving and many more after that."

LeVar wandered over. "Isn't it time for dessert?"

It seemed as if Raven wanted to comment on her brother's bottomless pit of a stomach. Instead, she gave him a grateful smile. The word *dessert* got Serena and Naomi moving, and soon they were setting pies and various goodies on the table while Thomas and the others carried their plates into the kitchen.

When they finished dessert, Thomas couldn't help but beam. He was thankful for his new family—the one he'd created with the people in this room. Even Sheriff Gray seemed like part of the family now, and seeing them all together made Thomas feel a peace he hadn't experienced during his growing years. It filled him with even greater joy that his mother, who'd acted so stern and proper during the Thanksgivings of yesteryear, laughed and joked with the others. In some ways, she didn't seem like Mom anymore; yet, in more important ways, she was the mom she was always meant to be.

Thomas whistled to grab everyone's attention.

"Before everybody collapses in the living room and turns on football, I want a group photo."

Good-natured moans followed, but everyone played along. He set down his glass of wine and grabbed a camera from the closet. When he returned, everyone posed beside the couch, their arms linked or their hands on each other's shoulders. As he snapped several photos, everyone recounted stories of how they'd met and their shared adventures.

It warmed his heart to hear Sheriff Gray talk about the old days and when he'd first hired Lambert and Aguilar. Scout recalled the first time she'd met LeVar after the sheriff brought him into the backyard and offered the gangster a place to live in the guest house. She was nervous at the beginning—the boy's reputation preceded him—but she thought he had trusting eyes. Next thing they knew, they were discussing hip-hop.

More than a few tears were shed as people remembered coming together. Raven and Buck had a laugh about their inauspicious start, including the Confederate flag he flew behind his house.

"I appreciate you for allowing me to grow," Buck said. "But I have to warn you: I still love Lynyrd Skynyrd."

Raven chuckled. "Buck, I love Skynyrd too."

"*You*?"

"Just because I can't deal with hearing *Sweet Home Alabama* every hour on the classic rock station doesn't mean I don't appreciate their music."

"Well, I'll be damned. You know what? The four of us should catch them in concert next time they come around."

"I'm game, but unless the warm-up act is Earth, Wind, and Fire, you'll have to do a lot of convincing to get Ma to go."

The men washed the dishes and put the plates away. In an ironic turn, the women were the first to collapse on the couch. Raven tossed up her hands and shouted when the Buffalo Bills quarterback threw an interception. Sheriff Gray wandered out to see what the commotion was about.

A little after six o'clock, the doorbell rang, and everyone wondered who was stopping by. It seemed the entire gang was gathered. Naomi gave Thomas a knowing glance, and the sheriff opened the door.

Gwenn Yarwood waited beside her daughter Liz, both trembling from the cold. Gwenn stood several inches taller than Liz and wore her blond hair in curls. Otherwise, they were spitting images of each other.

Scout sat up, stunned to see her friend. The girls weren't allowed to speak outside of school until their groundings ended.

"Mrs. Yarwood," Scout said, raising a questioning brow.

"It's okay," the mother said. "The two of you can say hello."

Liz and Scout approached each other with timidity. Like magnets, their attraction grew the closer they came. They hugged, and a few people clapped.

Gwenn cleared her throat. "Liz, isn't there something you want to say?"

The girl lowered her head and crossed the room until she stood before Thomas. LeVar muted the sound on the television.

"Sheriff Shepherd?"

"Yes, Liz?"

She scuffed at the floor with the tip of her shoe. "I'm . . . I'm terribly sorry for breaking into the Samson house, and I swear I'll never do anything crazy like that again."

Thomas folded his arms and gave her a reproving look.

"You could have hurt yourself. Or worse."

"I understand that now."

"Do you know what breaking and entering is?"

"Yes," Liz said. "My parents made it quite clear."

He nodded. "I accept your apology, Liz."

"Thank you."

To Thomas's shock, she threw her arms around him and sobbed. After she finished, he held her gaze.

"But you know what your biggest crime was?"

Liz glanced around uncertainly. "No, sir."

"You didn't catch Alec Samson's ghost so I could put him in jail."

The girl gave him a perplexed look. Thomas couldn't hide his grin any longer. They both broke into laughter.

Gwenn agreed Liz would join Scout in the soup kitchen and serve the needy. Otherwise, their groundings were over, and they could be friends outside of school again. Plenty of desserts remained. Liz and her mother joined the others over cookies, pie, football, and good times.

Thomas draped an arm over Chelsey's shoulder and kissed her on the head.

"Best Thanksgiving ever?" she asked.

"Oh, yes. Not even close. And you know what the best part is?"

"What?"

He planted his lips on hers.

"We'll still be together when it's over."

Thank you for reading!

The Thomas Shepherd series continues in book four.

GET A FREE BOOK!

I'm a pretty nice guy once you look past the grisly images in my head. Most of all, I love connecting with awesome readers like you.

Join my VIP Reader Group and get a FREE serial killer thriller for your Kindle.

Get My Free Book

www.danpadavona.com/thriller-readers-vip-group/

SUPPORT YOUR FAVORITE AUTHORS

Did you enjoy this book? If so, please let other thriller fans know by leaving a short review. Positive reviews help spread the word about independent authors and their novels. Thank you.

ACKNOWLEDGMENTS

No writer journeys alone. Special thanks are in order to my editor, C.B. Moore, for providing invaluable feedback, catching errors, and making my story shine. I also wish to thank my brilliant cover designer, Caroline Teagle Johnson. Your artwork never ceases to amaze me. I owe so much of my success to your hard work. Shout outs to my advance readers Ted Browne, Donna Puschek, and JJ Voyageur for catching those final pesky typos and plot holes. Most of all, thank you to my readers for your loyalty and support. You changed my life, and I am forever grateful.

ABOUT THE AUTHOR

Dan Padavona is the author of The Wolf Lake series, The Thomas Shepherd series, The Logan and Scarlett series, The Darkwater Cove series, The Scarlett Bell thriller series, *Her Shallow Grave*, and The Dark Vanishings series. He lives in upstate New York with his beautiful wife, Terri, and their children, Joe, and Julia. Dan is a meteorologist with NOAA's National Weather Service. Besides writing, he enjoys visiting amusement parks, beach vacations, Renaissance fairs, gardening, playing with the family dogs, and eating too much ice cream.

Visit Dan at: www.danpadavona.com

Made in the USA
Las Vegas, NV
17 April 2023

70714267R00163